Iago's Fool

A Novel

By

Shawn Kerivan

Auberge Books

Stowe, Vermont

Auberge Books
An imprint of The Vermont Press
Stowe, Vermont 05672
www.TheVermontPress.com
AubergeBooks@gmail.com
info@TheVermontPress.com

This is a work of fiction. Any resemblance by any character in this book to any person, living, dead, or drunk, represents a fatuous leap of imagination and a Narcissus complex in need of therapy.

ISBN: 978-0692269244

Library of Congress Control Number: 2014914283

The text of this book is composed in Garamond 3 font.

Printed in the United States of America

For Seamus and Brendan

Then must you speak
Of one that loved not wisely but too well,
Of one not easily jealous but, being wrought,
Perplexed in the extreme; of one whose hand,
Like the base Indian, threw a pearl away.
  -Othello, *Othello*, William Shakespeare

I am not what I am.
  -Iago, *Othello*, William Shakespeare

Part I

Green Harbor

The stern of the fishing boat exploded in a shower of splinters. As the blacked-out Apache attack chopper roared overhead, its M230 Chain Gun belched out flame and lead, turning the ice-smooth surface of the ocean into a boiling foam.

Large-caliber slugs slammed into the boat with enough force to lift the limp and unconscious body of Rance Vaughn into the air, then slam him back down on the engine hatch. Black diesel smoke billowed up from below, and Rance gagged back to life.

High above the water the helicopter screamed into a vertical turn, banking at the last second and whipping around to renew the attack on the bright red fishing boat. Inside the sleek aircraft, the pilot waited for the chopper's nose to return to the boat's water line before nailing the red trigger.

Back aboard his bullet-shredded boat, Rance stood, shaking, hanging on to the wheel, coughing smoke. His blazer was torn from sleeve to breast, and around him the world blurred into a ripped canvas of smoldering wood, shattered glass and the menacing thump of the returning chopper.

He lifted his burning eyes just in time to see the attacking helicopter, black guns dangling grotesquely from its underbelly, erupt a fresh volley of fiery death.

Gritting his teeth, he dove into the forward cabin, bracing himself for a violent landing. Instead of crashing onto the deck, the soft form of a woman cushioned his fall.

The spot where he had been standing vaporized amid the chopper's wrath. His boat lurched wildly to port, tossing him and the woman against the hull. When it snapped back to center, they were dumped onto the cabin floor. Combining in a deadly cacophony, the chopper's thundering blades and booming cannon invaded the forward space, pounding painfully into his head. Louder than all that were the woman's screams.

Rance's world was suddenly a putrid miasma. Acrid black smoke choked the cabin and the boat began to list fatally to starboard. As he struggled to his feet and reached under a bench, the woman's shrieks became louder. He turned to her.

"Here!"

She didn't respond.

"Here! Take this!" he yelled, jamming a floatation cushion into her chest. Abruptly she stopped sobbing and opened her eyes. Seeing the cushion, her face registered an understanding, and Rance dragged her to her feet. Grabbing his own cushion, he kicked open the forward hatch and they tumbled into the water.

As the chopper completed its second pass, the man in the passenger's seat-a red-headed bear of a man-strained to get a look at the boat as they screamed past it. He turned just in time to see someone dive out the forward hatch.

"They're out!" screamed the big redhead to the pilot. "Go back and finish them off!"

The pilot hesitated, then pointed to the 11 o'clock position. With its bow three feet out of the water, a Coast Guard cutter was charging out of the harbor toward them.

"We're breaking it off," said the pilot. "They've got enough firepower to blast us-"

His sentence was cut short by the end of a pistol, which was shoved in his mouth by his passenger.

"You're breaking nothing off, lad." The big redhead's eyes glowed an iridescent blue that sent a shiver through the pilot. "Now turn her around and go back and get them or I'll blow your fucking head off and take my chances in the drink."

With a violent tug on the chopper's control stick the pilot threw them into a severe turn. The aircraft's nose came back around to the fishing boat, but only a huge plume of thick, black smoke remained where the boat had been.

"I don't see-"

"Shut up and shoot your fucking guns! Just open her up!"

The pilot did as he was told, and the chopper lurched anew as the cannons erupted destruction. On the surface of the water, two hundred yards ahead of the chopper, fountains of water shot up, tracing the line of fire right up to, then disappearing into the fiery end of the boat.

From six feet under murky water Rance could hear it all:

the growing reverberation of the approaching chopper, the muted ack-ack-ack of the cannons, and the bubbly swish of the rounds as they harmlessly spent themselves in the dense salt water.

In the murk and cold of the water, Rance heard it passing away, and his aching lungs sent him shooting back to the surface.

Inside the helicopter the big redhead turned again just in time to see Rance and the woman break the surface of the water. He pounded his pistol off the inside of the aircraft.

"Sweet Jesus! They're still there! Go back!"

The pilot was about to bank the chopper again when the helicopter lurched crazily sideways. An explosion followed, and only the pilot's quick reflexes saved them from smashing into the ocean. The pilot turned in time to see the Coast Guard cutter's deck gun licking out a steady flame at them. The chopper took another hit, and one of its guns was blasted away.

The hulking passenger dropped a rubber band that he had been fidgeting in his left hand. His face mottled with anger.

"Fuck all! All right–get us out of here!"

The pilot tried to bank the chopper west toward land and escape the cutter's fire, but nothing happened.

"The stick's jammed! We'll have to try and outrun them to that peninsula!" He pointed to a spit of land jutting into the ocean a mile in front of them, then pushed the stick forward and opened up the engine to full throttle.

Hanging onto the flotation cushion and swimming away from the sinking remains of his boat, Rance saw the Coast Guard cutter take off after the wounded chopper.

"Where's the Coast Guard going?" cried the woman. As she tried to stay afloat, she clawed and grasped at him. "Don't they see us?"

"Doesn't look like it." With his belly sick from salt water, he started kicking toward shore.

"Rance!" the woman called. "I can't swim!"

Rance took her cushion and repositioned it under her chest.

"You can kick, can't you?"

Fear, frustration and anger balled themselves up in his voice. Splashed across her face was utter terror, plain fear. He didn't want to see it because he didn't want to think about it. The chaos that had just played itself out was way beyond him, and looking at her, seeing her petrified look, brought it all home.

But boy, was she was beautiful, he thought. Even clinging onto a floatation cushion with her hair matted down and her makeup smeared garishly across her cheeks he could see that she was a real beauty. Only you, Rance, he thought. Only you could have a near death experience and in the same breath be looking a woman up and down.

"Just hug the cushion and kick," he said, calmer this time. "Come on."

A minute later they were kicking up a reasonable foam wake, riding the incoming tide to the beach. The Coast Guard cutter had briefly pursued the retreating chopper, then returned to the remains of the boat. By that time Rance and the woman had nearly reached the breakwater of Green Harbor beach.

"Rance?"

He was trying not to think about anything. The pain of fear and bad bourbon pounded his head.

"Rance, what happened?"

As she struggled in the water he thought she looked like a little girl, somebody's daughter. A child. Seeing her that way made his stomach knot into a hot ball because he had a vague memory of the sex being very, very good.

"I don't know." He ventured a look back and saw the smoldering remains of his boat. "I really don't know." A swell lifted them up and began pushing them the last few yards to the beach. "I...I..."

"Gina," she said reflexively.

He started to feel less guilty about her.

"I'm sorry, Gina."

The sound of crashing surf greeted them as they stood and slogged the last few yards to shore.

Having witnessed the helicopter attack and ensuing explosion, a small crowd gathered on the beach. A murmur washed through them as Rance, still clad in his blazer and slacks, and Gina, wearing the remains of her skimpy cocktail dress and one red, high-heeled pump, exited the ocean.

Parting silently as Rance and Gina passed through, the crowd remained hushed, except for a boy who ran up to them.

"Hey, mister, are you James Bond?"

He shook his head. "Not me."

The boy took a look at Gina, struggling to walk and keep the better parts of herself covered.

"Well then, who are you?"

He stopped and looked back at the boy.

"I'm just a guy in the wrong place at the wrong time."

§

When they reached the parking lot, Gina ripped her lone pump off and began briskly walking away from him.

"Gina-hey, wait. Where are you going?"

"Don't get me wrong, Rance," she said without turning around or breaking her stride. "You're a nice guy and everything, but I don't think it's a good idea for me to hang around you right now. You know what I mean?"

He stopped. "At least let me call you a cab."

Her reply was a wave as she disappeared into the bathhouse. Rance stood in the parking lot full of asphalt and hot metal cars and was all alone. Move, a voice screamed inside him. Move!

So he did just that, moving without thinking, trying not to remember that he had just been attacked by a helicopter gunship, how insane that sounded. He moved, going under the Beach Street bridge, cutting through the parking lot of the Green Harbor Lobster Pound and going into the marsh, choked with reeds and cat tails that whipped him until he emerged on the other side: The parking lot of the Harbor Club.

By the time he reached the edge of the lot, Rance's shivering fears had been replaced by sticky sweat. As hot as it had been out on the boat earlier, it was at least ten degrees hotter on land, and the sweat of his body mixed with his salt water soaked clothes. Squatting behind a shrub, he quickly scanned the dirt parking lot of he Harbor Club. Seeing only cars and trucks belonging to the Club's regulars, he stood and headed for the door.

Working behind the bar was a bosomy, curvy redhead named Becky, and when Becky tended bar, Rance rarely paid for his drinks.

The place was cloaked in a pall of cigarette smoke, the usual blue haze that Rance found bizarrely inviting.

Seeing Rance emerge from the shadows, Becky brightened into a huge, toothy smile.

"Hi, honey-what happened to you? You look worse than usual."

Without waiting to be asked, she filled a rocks glass with ice and inundated it with Jameson. Rance looked down at his formerly expensive clothes, the only dressy threads he owned.

"I went to a wake."

"Looks like it was your own, honey."

Becky cocked her head and leaned forward on the bar with her arms crossed beneath her breasts.

"Must have been the same wake they went to," she added, nodding in the direction of the laughter, but her eyes followed Rance's as they dropped down to her cleavage.

"I'll have to go see." Rance tore his eyes from Becky's breasts and headed toward Father O'Brien.

"Whenever you want, Rance," Becky called after him. "All you have to do is ask."

As Rance approached, Larry Flemming's back was to him and Father O'Brien was rubbing tears of laughter out of his eyes.

"What's the joke?" Rance asked.

Larry, in the middle of a long pull off his beer bottle, turned as he heard the question. As their eyes met, Rance saw

Larry's bulge in surprise. Larry gagged and aspirated his beer, blowing a stream of thick froth through his nose. The bottle of beer slipped from his hands, shattering on the floor.

"Hey, big guy, take it easy," Rance said, slapping Larry roughly on the back as he bent over and coughed the beer from his lungs. "You okay?"

Larry snorted and looked at Rance through watery eyes.

"Yeah," he said, his voice hoarse and strained. "Thanks."

"Do I look that bad?"

Larry coughed one final time. "I just didn't expect to see you here."

Rance frowned. "I practically live here, Larry."

"I mean, ah, you're still wearing a jacket and tie, that's all. What happened?"

"What do you mean, what happened?"

"Well, ah, you know, you're just all wet, that's all. What, did you fall in the drink?"

Rance drained his glass. "Buy the next round and I'll tell you all about it."

"Sure." Larry got up from his barstool and looked around expectantly. "Give me a minute, will ya? I gotta hit the head."

Rance followed him with his eyes as he walked to the back of the big room. But instead of taking the stairs up to the bathroom, Larry turned toward the kitchen where the pay phone was.

"Father?" Rance said, still watching where Larry had disappeared. "Have they moved the crapper?"

"Lord, I hope not." Father O'Brien raised his thin eyebrows and looked at the harbor. "If they have, I've been peeing in a closet for the last three hours. That ought to be worth at least ten Hail Marys."

Rance turned back to the priest and smiled.

"Don't tell me you've been going strong since the wake last night, Father."

"Mea culpa." He sipped his drink, a large gin and tonic. "But in all fairness, it was a heckuva wake."

"Pops McGill knows how to throw a party-even when he's dead."

"Not to intrude, but did that young lady in the tight dress you brought to the wake have anything to do with your soaking condition?" Father O'Brien turned his hanging face to Rance and mustered a smile amidst the lines. After all these years, Rance thought, those milky eyes and thick, tinted glasses still gave him the look of a blind man.

Becky had refilled Rance's glass and Rance took a sip, a little slower, a little calmer.

"She said she was some niece of Pops', but I never saw her before."

"Well, she certainly saw you. Tell me Rance, do you carry copies of your books just in case you need to melt a young lady?"

Rance was about to josh his parish priest for asking such a secular question when a knot formed in his stomach. Now that he thought about it, Gina had been the aggressive one last night.

"Rance?"

"Huh?"

Father O'Brien was smiling at him.

"Was it that good? Maybe I should give more thought to leaving the priesthood."

"Don't do that. If you left, who would we have to blame? To answer your first question, she was a fan. I guess. I don't remember too much. Tommy had the blender going, cranking out-I forget."

"Frozen Mudslides."

"Right. Anyway, I don't know. When I told her I didn't write much anymore, that I fished lobsters for a living, she said she wanted to see my boat."

"Really? I would've thought an autographed copy of *Jungle Water* would've have done it. Shows you what I know. Maybe I'll stay in after all."

Rance had a thought that was mired somewhere in the mush of his brain. Something Father O'Brien had said, something about Gina and his book...

"Whew! I had to go! How about that drink, Ranny boy?"

Larry was back and strangely happy, given his odd behavior a few minutes ago. Rance shook it off. I'm hungover, he thought. Correction, you were hungover. Now you're getting drunk again. So what? So a helicopter blew your boat out of the water, that's what. "I don't even want to think about it."

"What do you mean, you don't want to think about it?" Larry asked. "You're quitting drinking right now? At least let me have the pleasure of buying you your last drink."

"I was talking to myself. Must have missed you at the wake last night, Lar."

As Larry was counting out some money onto the bar his hands began to shake badly enough for him to drop several notes onto the floor. Larry clenched his fists and regained control, but Rance saw it. *What the hell's the matter with this guy today?* he wondered.

"Yeah, well, I popped in early and didn't stick around. Wasn't feeling well." He kept looking at the money on the bar, a stack of ones, as if he didn't know what he was doing.

"You missed a helluva bash. Little Pops sent the old man out in style."

"I heard you got lucky, Rance."

"Did you? Where'd you hear that?"

"I-you know, around. Eddie told me, I guess." Larry was grabbing the money off the bar fast and stuffing it into his pockets. Change spilled onto the floor, but Larry ignored it. Rance searched for Larry's eyes, but they avoided his. Rance could see one thing, however: Larry Flemming's face was death white.

"Listen, uh, I gotta go, I'll see ya around."

The side door flung open with a bang, and a second later Larry could be seen running through the marina next door. Becky looked at Rance and shrugged.

"Jesus H. Christ-excuse me, Father-but what the heck was wrong with him?"

"Who knows? The usual, probably-can't stand not being a cop anymore. That will be five and five, by the way."

"Five and five?"

"Five Our Fathers and five Hail Marys, for taking the name of the Lord in vain." The priest smiled contentedly and sipped his drink.

Rance laughed. "Without a confessional? Attendance must be really bad, Father."

"Desperate times call for desperate measures."

Rance laughed again but cut himself short when he saw two men entering the Harbor Club. His heart flopped hard once and his throat went dry. They walked up to him.

"Rance Vaughn?"

The one who spoke was a small, thin man wearing a gray suit. Behind him was a redheaded giant of a man. Besides his size, Rance noticed the man twirled a rubber band in his left hand. The small man continued.

"I'm Special Agent Muller, this is Special Agent Mannix, we're with the FBI and we'd like to speak to you about what happened earlier today." They flashed their IDs.

Beside Rance Father O'Brien's eyebrows raised.

"You've been holding back on me, Rance. Make it ten and ten."

Rance's heart was pounding too hard to hear the priest's quip.

"Sure," said Rance. "Take care of my tab, will you Father?" He winked at the priest and Father O'Brien knocked on the wood of the bar twice. Rance followed the men.

Once outside, Agent Muller continued speaking. "You probably can guess what this is all about." The little man smiled badly, revealing brown stained teeth. The big redhead stood a few feet away, twirling the rubber band and scanning the area. "Did you get a good look at the helicopter that attacked and sunk your boat?"

Rance rubbed his chin. How did they know it was my boat?–it sunk before the Coast Guard had returned. Okay, he thought, something stinks here. But I don't have much of a choice right now.

"Too good a look, I'm afraid."

"A short time after the attack on you, a helicopter crashed into Duxbury Bay. We'd like to take you over there to see if you recognize it as the chopper that fired on you earlier today."

"You get a lot of Apache helicopters crashing into Duxbury bay?" he asked, but the sarcasm bounced off these guys.

Rance sat in the back seat as they drove through Green Harbor and into Duxbury Beach. His mind raced with confusing thoughts. What was the FBI doing on a case like this? Isn't this the Coast Guard's domain? And how the hell did they know where to find me? Almost as if they were waiting...

Rance leaned forward.

"I'm sorry, did you say you were out of the Boston office of the FBI? I have a friend there, maybe you know him–"

"No, we didn't," said Muller, cutting him short.

"Could you show me your IDs again, please."

"We'll be there in just a few minutes, Mr. Vaughn," was the answer.

The car turned onto the Gurnett Road, a long wisp of asphalt that bordered the marsh of Duxbury Bay on one side, and the cottaged strand of Duxbury Beach on the other. A lump grew in Rance's throat. With the exception of his friend Michael O'Meara, it had been a long time since he had been around these types, but the feeling never dies.

In Rance's mind something clicked, and his heart began to thud audibly. There was no helicopter crash in the marsh because these guys weren't FBI. They probably weren't even CIA. That left one option, one he didn't want to consider. But why? Why is someone trying...to kill me?

He didn't linger for an answer. Ahead he could see the Gurnett Inn, its barroom perched next to the road. It was a place full of people who knew him, and if he could get there...

18

As the car passed the inn it entered a series of snaking turns. Rance made his move, reaching for the door handle, pulling it hard and preparing for the spill out onto the broiling pavement.

But nothing happened. The door would not open. Rance turned back just in time to see the big redhead, the so-called Agent Mannix, lean over the back seat and clout him with the butt of his pistol. He crumbled to the floor of the car unconscious.

§

He felt wet.

A door slammed behind him, and Rance was suddenly lifted up. Tiny stabbing sensations peppered his legs as the blood rushed back into them.

"There, there, that's a boy." Agent Mannix finally spoke, and Rance knew he was in big trouble. Agent Mannix spoke with a brogue that could only come from a native of an emerald isle on the other side of the Atlantic.

They were standing in the middle of the marsh that surrounds Duxbury Bay, the huge inlet of water that leads to Plymouth Harbor. Having grown up on the other side of the bay, the Green Harbor side, Rance was familiar with every creek, tussock and island in the area. As far as he could tell, he had been driven to the end of the road called Miller's Landing, a narrow spit of land that was exposed only during low tide.

Though he was now standing on his own, his legs were still wobbly, and he nearly fell over as he turned to see where

Mannix had gone. The wetness Rance had felt earlier was blood flowing from a gash that Mannix had opened up on his head. He touched his fingers to it as he stared at the two men. Muller was leaning against the car, smoking, looking bored. Mannix stopped, turned and drew his pistol in one motion. Rance's eyes widened in terror.

"Good-bye, Mr. Vaughn."

A blast of white-yellow flame erupted from the barrel of the gun, but Rance was already diving. He felt something hot and burning enter him as he broke the surface of the water and sunk into its muddy depths.

§

Funny, Rance thought, how your brain kicks into overdrive when there's a good chance of dying.

For the second time that day he found himself underwater with the knowledge that to return to the surface was to die.

And as he tried to blink the muddy, salty water out of his stinging eyes, as his lungs burned with a mortal pressure, as his side throbbed with a foreign pain that tried to gush the life from him, he remembered the tunnels.

Like some giant circulatory system, the marsh was a collection of drainage canals and deep mud pools. An arterial network of tunnels interconnected them all, a fact that Rance and his friends had discovered during the hot summers of his youth. He had to make a decision and make it fast.

If he rose up to the surface for a breath, Big Red would empty his clip into his gaping mouth. But if he could find a tunnel...

Reaching out, Rance began feeling along the slimy surface of the walls that served as banks for the marsh creek. Once again he felt his lungs ache for oxygen, their surface shrinking smaller and smaller, the walls of his chest painfully constricting. As he groped and bled and held his breath, he had the distinct feeling that he was forgetting something, something his boyhood friend Eddie Dodge had told him never to forget when he was looking for a tunnel.

His hand closed around something rigid. It jerked away from his grip, then teeth sunk into the flesh of his hand.

Water rats!

Rance screamed the words underwater and loosed the last few bubbles of rancid breath from his lungs as the giant rat swam out to greet him. He batted it away and then felt the opening to a tunnel. The rat swam to the surface for a breath of air and was immediately blasted to oblivion by gunfire.

Flailing his way through the short tunnel, Rance broke free suddenly and found himself in a quiet pool. It took every last bit of his remaining strength not to rocket up through the surface and noisily gasp the precious air. Instead he rose up gently, broke the surface and breathed as silently as someone who has been under water for two minutes could breathe. When he felt his lungs unclench and tingle back into his limbs, he lifted his head for a look.

He was behind them. He could see the big redhead and his friend leaning over the spot he went under. After a quick look around, he slid back down to the surface of the pool. He put his hand over the wound in his side and tried to listen.

§

"It was a fucking rat, Jackie," said the man who called himself Agent Muller. "Way to go."

"Shut your fuckin' trap," said the big red-head, a.k.a. Jackie, a.k.a. Agent Mannix. He reloaded his weapon and continued looking over the edge into the creek. Three more minutes that seemed like three hours to Rance passed.

"I guess he's dead, Jackie. I guess you got him all right. I didn't think so at first. The way he spun around when you shot him, I thought you only winged him at best. But I guess you got him all right, Jackie."

Jackie turned and stalked past Muller. "Shut the fuck up. And stop calling me Jackie."

When he heard the sound of approaching footsteps, Rance took a deep breath and sunk down under water. Two muffled thunks, car doors closing, brought him back to the surface. The crunch of tires on the dirt road of Miller's Landing was his cue to climb up out of the pool. A cloud of dust billowed into the hot air as the two phony FBI agents took off down the road. Rance felt the blood flowing from his wounds and wondered what in the hell was going on.

§

The sun was setting behind Green Harbor. As was his custom each summer evening, Larry Flemming rowed the dingy out to his fishing boat. Despite the amount of alcohol he had ingested during the day, Larry's strokes were still compact and powerful. His breath, however, came in short gasps.

As he boarded the boat, his mouth watered, but not for

food, and as soon as he found the bottle of vodka and drank a glass he began to feel better.

A chill ran down Larry's spine. He poured another glass of vodka and walked around the deck in the thin twilight. All his gear was there, not that he spent so much time lobstering these days. Plenty of fuel in the tank. Nothing amiss. But Larry felt something wrong, they way only a fisherman can feel a storm coming on a clear day.

"Not enough booze," Larry mumbled to himself. He popped open a lawn chair in the middle of his deck and sat facing out over his stern. Another glass of vodka dispelled his feelings of anxiety. And it dulled his senses enough so that he did not detect the man coming up behind him.

The man was clad in a dark blue wet suit that matched perfectly the amount of light penetrating the atmosphere. He took two silent steps and wrapped his left arm around Larry's face and mouth. His right hand darted up, the knife blade plunging deep into Larry's brain. The man twisted the blade twice, then let Larry's dead body fall to the deck.

Backing off, the diver washed the blade off over the starboard side, then replaced the knife on the rack where he found it, hanging to the right of the wheel.

The water of Green Harbor made no sound as the man with the wet suit slipped back into it and sunk beneath the surface.

§

Inside the Oval Office, the President lined up his shot with the Washington Monument and took a full swing with his 5-

iron. Outside, the day was perfect. The lawn of the White House, so vividly green, was but a portend to what awaited him at the Potomac Country Club in just an hour. He took a few more swings.

There was a quick knock on the door and the National Security Advisor entered. Richard Armstrong was a short, balding man with a grim visage that was accentuated by his marching gait. He stopped in front of the desk and waited for the President to finish his swing.

"I can feel it, Dick," said the President. "I'm going to break 80 today for sure."

Armstrong took a deep breath and pursed his lips.

"Sir, I have a progress report for you on the SDS issue regarding the Chinese."

The President straightened up. "Did you find out who's been leaking that stuff?"

Richard Armstrong grimaced.

"This is serious, Dick," the President continued. "We let their people into the country to attend fine universities like MIT, and what do they do? Take their knowledge and connections and use it to evil ends. Software piracy. It's bad stuff, Dick, bad stuff."

The President shook his head and looked down at his 5-iron.

"What are they so worried about China for anyway? I'm serious, Dick, I need to have something to hit Premier Cheng over the head with when I go there this fall. These people have to realize that they can't push the United States of America around."

The President was gesticulating at the window behind his

desk. Armstrong bit his lip, something he did dozens of times a day in the presence of his boss.

"Sir, if I could speak frankly..."

The President looked up. "Sure, Dick, go on."

"Sir, the Chinese and their video game piracy are really not what this issue is about." Armstrong braced himself. "It's about SHAKESPEARE."

"SHAKESPEARE? Who told you about that–?" The President caught himself. "Nevermind. Tell me how the Chinese are involved in...that."

Now Armstrong had his attention, a little too much, in fact, for the President was circling now, probing.

"They're not. In fact, we really have little to worry about with them. We know exactly where they stand. It's the...other elements, the fringe elements, that we need to be concerned about."

"Terrorists? What are you saying, Dick? You're talking about SHAKESPEARE and, and—al-Qaeda?"

"Not exactly. I–"

"I thought we were still in the developmental and testing stage with that anyway."

"We're completed. But there's been...a breach."

"A breach?" The President bent his lanky frame to get close to the NSA director's pinched face.

"A leak, if you will. But that should all be taken care of by now."

The President spun around. "Don't tell me, Dick. I don't want to know. That's dangerous information and I'll deny it to your grave." He walked over to a shelf containing dozens of framed pictures.

"I said nothing, sir."

The President picked up a picture of himself with two Green Berets. He smiled.

"Just take care of all this crap, Dick. The midterms are coming up this fall, and I want to get a little momentum going into November, you know what I mean?"

Richard Armstrong was biting his lip again.

§

As Jenny Ryan walked into her beachfront house, the remnants of the summer sunset, a pink magenta swirl cut by the dark horizon, flooded her kitchen with a surreal sepia feeling, turning everything into a faded photograph. It was well after 9 p.m.

She stopped suddenly in the front hallway. A tingle raced unpleasantly between her shoulder blades as the fuzzy darkness closed in on her. Did I leave the front door unlocked?

Some sense that she didn't recognize was registering...something. Like a change in the barometric pressure of the house's interior, signifying—what?

A gentle breeze wafted in from the ocean, lifting a paper on the hall table and delicately drifting it down to her feet. Jenny let out a long sigh of relief. She went into the kitchen and made herself a cup of tea. It's these long hours, she lamented. Stress and fatigue are going to give me a heart attack.

Padding softly across the hardwood floors, she moved to the darkened front of the house that faced the ocean. Late hours were the price she paid for her huge, magnificent—and empty-beachfront house. Through the open jalousie the sound of the waves lapping the sand rolled in like a healing tonic.

Even at home she couldn't escape the pull of her career, and she put her mug down atop a sheaf of papers all bearing the letterhead of the law firm of Javitz & McGillicuddy. Slipping off her shoes, she rested her feet on a pillow emblazoned with the J&M logo. The toil of ten long years manifested itself everywhere.

Eighty-hour weeks melted away along with her school loan payments and her social life. Her one bedroom apartment in the city had been motivation enough for her to spend endless hours pouring over tax law cases at the office. But last year, when she finally made junior partner, she ran from the city, ran all the way back home, all the way back to Green Harbor and the beach.

The commute was killer-an hour and a half on the Southeast Expressway in the morning-so Jenny stayed late each night to avoid the evening commute, buzzing home in half an hour at nine in the evening. Just another ten years, she promised herself. Then I'll have enough squirreled away to hang out my own shingle down here and practice a more benign form of law.

Another ten years.

The words rung in her ears. Under her severe suit she felt a firm, fit body that looked much younger than its 35 years. Would it be that way in another ten years? And that would probably rule out children completely. On that thought her heart skipped a painful beat, but she closed her eyes against it.

When she opened them a man was standing in front of her.

Loosing a piercing scream, Jenny flung her mug of hot tea into the intruder's face, causing him to scream in return. Simultaneously her right foot shot up and found the man's crotch, dropping him to his knees.

She leapt to her feet and danced to her right, pummeling the prone man with vicious left hooks. When he tried to cover up, she delivered a terrifying right that dropped the intruder flat.

"Jenny! Jenny! What are you doing? Stop! It's me!"

She was poised over him, a chair raised high.

"Rance?" Slowly she lowered the chair. "What are you doing here?"

"I didn't come over here to rob you, if that's what you think." He groaned. "When I taught you how to defend yourself, I didn't mean for you to use it on me."

His voice was thin and weak, and though she had dealt him some good chops, it was nothing devastating. But Rance remained on the floor.

"Are you okay?" She took a tentative step toward him. He didn't respond, but she could hear his breath coming in short gasps. Reaching up, she clicked on the light-and saw a dark pool of blood growing around his battered body.

"Oh my God," she said.

§

When Jenny was finished, she stepped back.

"You're lucky. Damn lucky."

Rance smiled. "I'm always lucky."

Just above his belt a white bandage was taped securely in

place.

"Bullets aren't a very good way to get rid of love handles," she said.

"And left hooks aren't a good way to get rid of your friends." He laughed, but his smile faded quickly under the pounding assault of his head. "Right now I'd be grateful for some aspirin."

Jenny left and returned with a bottle of Tylenol 3. As he swallowed a couple of tablets, Rance looked down at the bandages on his hand and side. "Fine job you've done there, Nurse Ryan. Your talents never cease to amaze me. I've decided to let you marry me."

"I'm so honored, Mr. Vaughn, but you've had your chance with me. I'm over you and on to bigger and better things now."

"That explains the Lexus in the driveway. Single seater, no doubt."

She ignored his remark. "Am I supposed to believe that story about the attack helicopter and the bad guys with the guns? Don't tell me they missed you and got your date."

"Do I detect a note of jealousy?"

"Pity, actually." She took his blood soaked shirt and tattered blazer and stuffed them in a plastic bag, then handed him an old sweatshirt.

"Really, Rance, bringing your peroxide floozies to a wake."

"Hey, she wasn't my date. I met her there–she was some niece of Pops'. Didn't you know her?"

"She wasn't Pops' niece. Little Pops said he had never seen her before."

That's bizarre, he thought. Why would someone go to a

wake and say she was related to the dead guy? Maybe she was hungry and wanted to go to the party afterward.

Turning his attention to the sweatshirt, he tried to pull it on, but his side was too stiff. Jenny lifted his arm for him and slid it on.

"Hey, this is one of my old sweatshirts. I've been looking for this."

She sat back and sighed, looking at Rance in the small light of the table lamp, his face half-shadow, half-yellowy warm. "You left it over here a long time ago."

"Too long," he said, softer.

"Please, Rance."

He sat up and winced. "Hey, if you think I got myself shot just so I could sneak over here in the dark, get my ass kicked by ninja shyster, then have you fix me up, and, and...well, don't flatter yourself." The outburst drained him and he sat back with a groan. But already he could feel the pain killer beginning its magic. Looking at Jenny, he tried to frown.

"Well, the thought has crossed my mind-"

"Can't you ever be serious? About anything? Look at yourself, lying there with a chunk taken out of your side, a rat bite on your hand, and you're still cracking wise, still the life of the party. Maybe if you had taken yourself more seriously, maybe..."

"Maybe what?" He sat up and leaned toward her. "Maybe what? Maybe things would have worked out between us? Maybe you wouldn't be hiding out for 90 hours a week at Mickey & Jacob's ambulance chasing service?"

"It's Javitz & McGillicuddy, and it's corporate law."

"Oh, you mean you find ways for billion dollar thieves to

wring the last buck out, right?"

"It's better than staying drunk all day," Jenny said softly. Rance reached for her cheek but she turned away.

"I'll quit drinking if you quit being a lawyer," he said. "And then–"

"And then what?"

"I'll finish that novel I've been working on."

"Oh, Rance, give it up. You sound like one of your own characters now–except you haven't written any novels lately, have you? You're not even working on one."

"I've written enough so that I don't have to write any more if I choose."

"Are you referring to *Jungle Water*, the runaway bestseller that established you as the premier one-hit wonder of the second half of the 20th century? Or are you speaking of *Snake Ranch*, that misogynistic action thriller, the book that everybody, including you, hated, the book that died a quick and painless death?"

Rance shrugged. "My bank account speaks for itself."

"So does your ravaged liver."

"Touché, Counselor."

The three minutes of silence that followed were thunderous, deafening. Finally Jenny rose. "Come on, I'll take you home."

Before they had covered the half-mile to Rance's house, he told her to let him off.

"Rance, promise me you'll call the police in the morning."

"I'd promise you anything." He leaned over and gave her a quick buss on the lips, then got out. Watching her disappear around the corner, Rance wondered how right she had got it.

Tonight she was the quick mouse to his stumbling cat, escaping mutual complicity. But it wasn't always like this. Sometimes they called off the game. Sometimes...

Cutting through the quiet and darkened back yards of his neighbors, Rance made his way to his house. The painkiller Jenny gave him was strong, and he felt a second wind arise. His big, white shack stood at the edge of the seawall, and on this moonless night it looked forlorn and lost. After sneaking around the dark perimeter, Rance entered through the basement. He methodically picked his way inside the house, doffing his shoes and letting his night vision take over.

Satisfied that no Irish phony FBI killers were going to jump out at him, Rance double checked the doors and made for the kitchen. From the fridge he pulled out a bottle of Sam Adams Lager and popped the top.

"I could drink a beer," said the voice from behind him.

§

"And don't turn on the lights," finished Michael O'Meara.

Rance handed O'Meara a beer and sat on a stool facing him in the dark kitchen.

"I can't say that I'm happy to see you, Michael."

O'Meara tipped the bottle back and the sound of glugging filled the dead air between them. "Don't tell me, you're having a bad day."

"Especially with FBI Agents. A couple tried to murder me earlier today, so the Bureau isn't exactly high on my list of favorite people."

"Then again," said O'Meara, "it never was. That's why you

let the CIA recruit you, right?"

"Why, Michael, I have absolutely no idea what you are talking about."

"Now that just breaks my heart. You won't tell your boyhood chum about the two years you spent under the influence of Langley, but you will write it all down in a book and make gazillions off it."

"That was fiction."

"That was bullshit. You should have joined the Bureau. Then you wouldn't have spooks in helicopters gunning for you."

"What do you know about that?"

"I'm sitting here in the dark, ain't I?"

Something about Michael's voice bothered him. It was shallow and tinny, hesitant.

"All right, Michael, I've been shot at, my boat was bombed and sunk and two clowns claiming to be FBI Special Agents tried to kill me. I've had enough of the cloak and dagger shit for one day. What's it all about?"

In the black atmosphere of the kitchen, Rance thought he could see Michael's eyes brighten for a moment. Then, utter silence.

"Your ex-wife," O'Meara said. "Katarina Favergé."

And then he tumbled to the floor unconscious.

§

The name of his ex-wife was a vicious blow to Rance's midsection, doubling him over with painful memories–ten year old memories.

"What profane wretch art thou?" she whispered to him. Trapping his earlobe with her incisors, she would run her tongue over his ear, her breath coming in shorter and shorter gasps.

He didn't answer. Instead his hands swept over her body, kneading the muscles in her shoulders, sliding down her back to the curve of her bottom, then tracing around to her flat belly, and lower, until her felt her thin tangle of hair.

"What profane wretch art thou?" she repeated, her voice barely audible above the clamor of their bodies on the sweat soaked bed.

Beneath her, Rance was fused into a single muscle, and he felt her body answer his thrusts with a grinding retort. Involuntarily his eyes closed. She sat up and whipped her long hair into a frenzy, tearing at his chest, her voice climbing steps of ecstasy until they both met with a resounding shudder.

Later, a warm breeze carried the sounds of London in the summer up to them. She nestled in the crook of his arm and smoked while he enjoyed the last of the champagne.

"You still haven't answered my question," she said softly.

"What question?"

Everything in the bedroom tingled, struck by their lightning, leaving the atmosphere supercharged. Rance's hot skin beat with its own pulse.

"What profane wretch art thou?"

He remembered her saying the words earlier, but now her tone was different, mocking, sardonic, giving her French-accented English-the accent he found so fixing, so alluring-a queer, wavering tone.

"I am one, sir, that comes to tell you that your daughter

and the moor are now making the beast with two backs."

"Very good." She sighed deeply and nuzzled his chest. "There is hope for you yet."

"Who's next?"

"*Macbeth*."

"All the tragedies. Don't you find all that treason and treachery and darkness so much ado about nothing?"

Katarina looked up quickly, and he was treated to her huge dark eyes, erotic black holes sucking the light of the world into them. When she did that he found himself swallowing against a dry throat, and it reminded him that there was a lot about her he didn't yet know.

"You told me you didn't study Shakespeare."

"I didn't. But like most former English majors, I have read his works. And you still haven't told me how a Frenchwoman came to be such a scholar of the greatest English author."

She sat up and snuffed out her cigarette, treating him to a silhouetted view of her body against the lights of London.

"When your father is a diplomat and your mother an actress, well, they tend to import a certain...lifestyle on you. The curriculum at Swiss boarding schools for young ladies was especially heavy with Shakespeare."

He mused on her careful choice of words, feeling his pupils dilate in the dark. "Maybe that's why the CIA wanted you. You have tremendous possibilities." He reached up and pulled her back down atop him.

"Possibilities," she said. "I am little more than a secretary, one who gets things-"

"A computer programmer is hardly a secretary."

"Whatever. But you, however, have a chance at-"

"Going nowhere. The CIA has had me proofreading fine print for ages, and I'm just about sick of it. I told you I'm nearly finished with my manuscript. I've met a few people here who think I might have a chance."

"A writer."

The words came out on a breath, fragile and soft, gently shooed from within. Though she didn't move, Katarina shrank in his arms, becoming a little smaller, a little cooler, a little withdrawn. She fell asleep without saying another word.

That summer ten years ago, Rance and Katarina spent themselves arm in arm around London, shopping on Regent and Oxford streets, taking long drives through the splendid countryside and seeing every production of Shakespeare they could.

"Don't you think that Iago is the most painfully misunderstood character in the history of Western literature?"

An empty magnum of Moet & Chandon stood guard by the bed next to a half filled basket of fresh strawberries. It was their way of putting the accent on a night of theater, and that night had been *Othello*, the third time that summer they had seen the play.

Her dark beauty flooded out every other thing in his mind. He could spend hours tracing her slender shape with his fingertips, caressing her endless legs, fondling her straight, black hair, drinking her mysterious, brown eyes.

"Iago was a cruel shell of a man, the incarnate of all that is evil in men, a man who wanted nothing more of life than to see his own inner misery shared with everyone around him," he replied groggily. "What is it about Iago? You seem totally fascinated by his character."

"But don't forget, Iago was an honest man, by his own admission," she said, ignoring the last part of his question. In the darkness of the bedroom, Katarina faded in and out of his consciousness. He reached for her, but she was gone. Then he felt her touch, and he rolled over to envelope her with his ardor.

It was the end of July and he wanted to marry her.

§

Michael O'Meara was bleeding badly.

Rance helped him up from the kitchen floor and half carried, half dragged him into the living room where he laid him gently on the couch. Lacking any other resources, he pulled a bottle of bourbon from his liquor cabinet and poured a trickle down Michael's throat. O'Meara came coughing back to life.

"God!" O'Meara gasped. "What the hell was that crap?"

"That crap was Woodford Reserve. Twelve years old."

"Bourbon?" With Rance's help he sat up. "Have you gone soft? Don't you have any Jameson?"

Rance frowned and clicked on the small lamp beside the couch, but he wasn't prepared for what he saw.

"Michael, what–"

"I told you to keep the lights off." He winced in the glare. "Probably the same two that did it to you, buddy. Let me guess: A big red-headed guy with a brogue and a thin guy that didn't say boo, right?"

Rance sat dumbfounded. "Jesus, Michael, what the hell's going on?"

"Fix me a real drink and I'll try and tell you what I know."

Rance went to the liquor cabinet again and this time returned with a bottle of Jameson Irish Whiskey and a glass. O'Meara looked at the glass and laughed.

"Can't use a glass when you don't have a lip."

Michael's face looked like a package of raw hamburger, ground up and bloody. His right eye was completely swollen and his bottom lip was split down the middle. And under his jacket Rance could see a large red stain overspreading his white dress shirt.

"Christ, Michael, you've been shot."

O'Meara waved him off. "Just a flesh wound. Nothing serious."

"The hell with that. You need to get to a hospital." He reached for the phone and was about to dial when he heard the distinctive click of a pistol being cocked.

"Put the phone down."

Rance replaced the headset of the phone. "You know, I'm getting tired of looking down gun barrels."

O'Meara faded and slumped back onto the couch.

"I know how you feel, buddy. But I've already tried the hospital-saw our two friends there. I'm not sure who they are, but they've got resources, and they've probably got every hospital in the state staked out. If I don't miss my guess, there's a story about how I went nuts and shot up a convenience store on the 11 o'clock news."

The soliloquy wasted O'Meara, and he closed his eyes and tilted the bottle to his mouth, his throat pumping rhythmically. Sweat matted his thinning hair and his unshaven face-where it wasn't scabbed or bleeding-was craggy and beaten. He took a deep breath and continued.

"That's why I came here. From the way you were sneaking around, I'd say they probably think you're dead by now."

"Six feet under, so to speak. Now level with me–what the hell is this all about? And what does Katarina have to do with it?"

"Do you remember when you met her? She was supposedly some low-level computer programmer? Well she learned fast, hacked into some CIA databases after you left, and took off. The info was some stuff the CIA was helping the British army with in Northern Ireland. Katarina sold the info to the highest bidder–in that case, the PIRA, the firepower arm of the IRA."

"You mean–"

"Yeah. Our big red-headed friend. He doesn't seem to have a name–I was running a check on him when all this happened."

"So what are Katarina and this guy after me for?" O'Meara reached a hand inside his blood soaked jacket and pulled out a self-seal plastic bag covered in his still warm blood. Inside was a thumb drive. He tossed it to Rance.

"SHAKESPEARE," he said.

§

It was Paris in October, and it was raining. Rance could see it as if it were yesterday.

"Here is my uncle's pharmacy," Katarina said. Despite the rain, she and Rance strolled along the Avenue Paul Doumer in Paris's chic 16th arrondisment without hurry. Ahead of them, at the end of the avenue, the Place du Trocadero was swept from view by a veil of rain. "And across the street, do you see that building with the courtyard entrance? That used to belong to my grandfather."

"You didn't tell me I was marrying into money."

She looked up at him, her long hair matted with rain, and smiled. They stopped and kissed, causing the flustered pedestrian traffic to part and flow around them.

"Will you still marry me if I tell you I am poor?"

"It's not true," he insisted. "Because money has nothing to do with it."

They were married by the prefect of the arrondisment an hour later. Two of the secretaries there provided their services as witnesses.

"It is not Niagara Falls, but the food is better."

As she spoke, Katarina pulled Rance into a small restaurant near the Gare de l'Est.

"Why would you say Niagara Falls."

"Isn't that where all Americans spend their honeymoons?"

Rance let his head roll back and he laughed. "Are all French people rude? Of course not. And this is far better than any normal honeymoon. This is us–you and me forever."

"Forever? Really forever?"

For the first time since he had met her, Rance saw a look of vulnerability creep into the features of her face. Her eyes, normally brown and piercing, flattened and lost their shine, and her mouth, usually mocking, pushed itself thin. It sent a shudder through him, and he quickly took her hands across in his own.

"Isn't that what we promised each other an hour ago? Forever?"

She squeezed his hand and looked away, and for a moment he thought she might cry.

"Of course, darling, I-it's just an emotional thing. Can you forgive me?"

"That's part of the love I feel for you. You could never do anything that would have to be forgiven."

§

"Let me ask you something, Rance. Do you know who Katarina is?"

Rance couldn't tell if the question was real or rhetorical, so he didn't answer.

"She's a very bad girl, Rance," said O'Meara. "She was pretty bad when you knew her, but she's very bad now." The pain of speaking was clearly evident on O'Meara's bruised face, and Rance winced along with Michael as he spoke. He steeled himself with another swig of whiskey and continued.

"Couple of weeks ago we were investigating a routine bank heist in Boston. We narrowed it down to a couple of punks in Charlestown, so we set up an ambush. Got these two chowder heads clean. But cash wasn't the only stuff they had piled in their apartment. They had a bunch of software that nobody in our office could decipher."

His voice was growing wispy and he closed his eyes as if speaking from a memorized script. Then he nodded to the thumb drive.

"So the D.A. put the fear of Jesus in these two punks, and they spilled their guts. Seems they were also doing B & E's over at MIT for some Indian gentleman. Not woo-woo Indian. Curry powder Indian. Funny thing is, the place they were ransacking was some high-level government project that officially didn't exist. You can bet we were surprised when we got a visit from a couple of your CIA buddies."

"CIA?" asked Rance. "What did they want? They don't have any domestic jurisdiction."

O'Meara opened his eyes and tried to focus them on the bottle.

"They wanted the software and they wanted this professor chump we arrested from MIT. Of course, being the fine disciples of Bobby Kennedy that we are, we told them to go fuck themselves. An agent was sent to D.C. with a copy of that thumb drive to be analyzed at headquarters, but he still hasn't show up down there. That was a week ago."

"I still don't see the connection with Katarina. Or me, for that matter."

"While we were holding this professor-a Mr. Gengi-we had a chance to talk to him, if you know what I mean." He winked at Rance with his good eye. "He was scared. Real scared. Said they were going to get him. Who? we asked. And that's when he came up with Katarina's name-in exchange for protection. He also told us that the software was national security stuff-some kind of weapons system technology, something do with the Star Wars crap that Reagan was pushing a few years back. We called the NSA-National Security Agency-and they were supposed to come down and take custody of this guy. Yesterday I was in the van that was transferring Mr. Gengi to maximum over at Walpole when we were ambushed by your big red-headed friend. I managed to getaway, but they saw me. I've been hiding out since then, making my way down here."

O'Meara closed his eyes again and his chest began heaving. Rance came to him but O'Meara held up a hand.

"It's not easy getting a lift when you're all shot up."

"I don't understand, Michael. Why didn't you just go back to Boston, to your office?"

"Couldn't. They jumped us at a stop light in Dedham, right next to a 7-11. After all the shooting was done some asshole was running around telling everyone I was the one doing all the shooting. He was probably a plant. Anyway, I didn't want to wait around for the local cops. Besides, cops would've taken me to a hospital, and they would've got me there. I needed to see you first, Rance."

Michael grimaced, gripped by a deep and abiding pain. Not much time, he told himself.

"We think that thumb drive contains the password codes for this defense software that this Gengi guy—and possibly Katarina—are trying to peddle. I need you to find out, and I need you to tell the world about it."

"Wait a minute. You're talking about the IRA—didn't they just turn in their arms? Isn't Northern Ireland over?"

O'Meara managed a smile. "Sure it is. But the players still need a hobby, if you know what I mean."

"Al-Qaeda? The Taliban?"

"Yeah, whatever. There's something about terrorism you gotta understand, buddy. It's just another business, another industry. It's like baseball. The uniform isn't as important as the salary."

O'Meara groaned and bucked as another shot of pain ripped through his body, rolling his eyeballs back. Now Rance rushed to him.

"Michael, you're nuts. You need to get to a doctor. Let me at least call Jenny. She knows every lawyer in Boston. We can bring you somewhere-"

O'Meara was waving him off. "Rance, you're the only one that can find Katarina. She's gone big time now, and she's bad. She's working for the highest bidder. This stuff is sensitive. We think she's some kind of double or triple agent. She was working for the SDECE-the French equivalent of the CIA. But she was getting hot and she took off. She's selling secrets, Rance."

"I still don't see-"

Michael sat up and grabbed Rance. His face was a white sheet of pain and his breath...his breath was dead, and Rance realized right there that Michael was gone.

"You have to write the story, Rance," he said through gritted teeth. "All these people, they think it's some kind of game. If the damn North Koreans or the fucking Russians gets a hold of this stuff, they could hold the world hostage. Everyone is just going to try and sweep it under the rug. But remember, you can't trust anyone, anyone, Rance. They'll come at you from every angle. Here."

Michael stuffed a business card into Rance's hand.

"This is a guy I work with. He's the only one you can trust. You have to stop her, Rance. You have to do it for me. And you have to find your daughter."

O'Meara passed out in Rance's arms.

§

"Katarina?"

Rance was excited, but as he searched through the small flat for her, a tightness in his stomach mitigated his joy. She should be home, he thought, it's Sunday. The apartment door opened.

"Katarina."

She bolted upright, dropping the keys loudly on the tile floor. For an instant Rance saw a mute aggression wash over her, and her hand darted into her purse. Just as fast it passed, replaced by a look of surprise.

"Rance, darling." Katarina withdrew her hand from her purse and dramatically placed it on her chest. "I thought you said you had a meeting with you boss, Mr. Greene, this morning."

"I did. But I don't remember telling you."

Katarina knelt quickly to pick up the keys.

"Oh, look, darling, I've torn my stockings." She stood and walked quickly to the bedroom, avoiding his eyes.

"What did you need to speak to Mr. Greene about on a Sunday, darling?" she called back once she had reached the bedroom. "I'm surprised they let you in the building."

"How did you know that security is tight on Sundays?"

Silence. Rance could hear the hiss of her stockings as they slid off her legs, but for the first time, he was not filled with sexual excitement. Something else was muddled within him. She emerged from the bedroom clad only in her typically arousing lingerie, smiling in a teasing manner as she headed for the bathroom.

"Isn't it like that everywhere in London? We never know when your cousins will bomb a shopping plaza, do we?"

The bathroom door closed softly, but resolutely.

"I quit."

Rance looked out the window at the cold rain beating down. Christmas was a month away, and the summer felt like a fossilized display in a museum. He closed his eyes and tried to recall its hot passion, but succeeded only in invoking the memory of something he felt might be gone forever. The bathroom door opened a crack.

"Really?"

He walked up to the door, but he could only see a thin slice of Katarina, bathed in the yellowy bathroom light, but still she looked dark to him.

"Yeah, really."

"So you really are serious about being a writer."

"Isn't it what I always talked about?"

Their voices were barely whispers in the flat. An assortment of dripping and splashing noises echoed in from the rain outside, creating a soft, natural disharmony.

"Yes, it is."

The door swung open slowly. The warm light spilled out, carrying her with it. She came to him fast, taking him by surprise, and they made love where they fell, on the bathroom's threshold. When they finished, Katarina said nothing, going back to the bathroom and showering.

"I have to go away, she told him later that night as she crawled into bed

"Away? Where?"

"For work."

"For work? To do what?"

She was silent for a moment. "We have a formation is Zurich. I might be getting a promotion."

"To what?"

"Rance, you work-worked-for the Agency. You know I'm not allowed to talk of it. And now that you are no longer-"

"How long will you be gone?"

"They haven't told us."

Rance frowned. "Us? Who else is going?"

"Rance, please."

She turned her back to him in the dark. In the morning when he awoke she was gone. Rance rushed down to his office, but since he had quit, he was not allowed access. Instead he had to wait for his old boss to be contacted. Finally he was shown to Mr. Greene's office.

"That would be highly irregular," Mr. Greene said to Rance's request to check on Katarina. Greene was a small, ordered man, probably an accountant by training, and he looked nervous.

"Please, Mr. Greene, I'm worried about her."

"Oh, all right," he said, picking up the phone. After a few minutes of being transferred, he inquired about Katarina from the head of computers.

"I see," he said, replacing the phone. "It seems your girl-friend-"

"Wife."

"Oh, really. Well then, it seems your wife has left the Agency on not so amicable terms. She, too, quit-last Friday-but there are some sensitive programs missing that she was working on. You don't mind if I ask you to stick around and answer a few questions, old boy, do you?"

It took Rance a month to get out of England, during

which time he was essentially under house arrest until he was cleared of any complicity in Katarina's crime.

What that crime was, Rance never found out.

It was Christmas and Rance had only an unfinished manuscript and enough money for a plane ticket back to the States.

§

O'Meara slept for two hours.

Rance spent the time sitting out on his porch, looking at the black Atlantic, wondering what events were transpiring on the other side that could reach across and touch his life so profoundly. O'Meara groaned and Rance went back to him, giving him some more whiskey.

"You don't believe me, do you," O'Meara said. He squinted his purple and swollen eyes against the light until Rance switched it off, leaving them as silhouettes against the starlight. "I mean about you having a daughter."

Michael's voice was rasping now, almost gurgling. Rance knew that if he didn't get him to a hospital soon the internal bleeding would kill him.

"Remember when we won the state hockey championship, Rance? It was overtime and you were tied up in the corner with that big thug from Catholic Memorial. Then-"

"Then I heard you yell my name, and I threw the puck out to you in front of the net, and you stuffed it in the 5-hole. We won."

"Yeah." O'Meara closed his eyes. "Wasn't that sweet." He smiled, and for a moment Rance thought he was gone. But

Michael continued speaking.

"This Gengi guy told us we could get to Katarina through her daughter. Said the little girl was living with Katarina's sister in Paris."

"Jesus, Michael, she could be anybody's daughter."

"She's ten years old, Rance. Born nine months after the last time you were with Katarina. Remember, you told me all about it when you got back to the States? And her name–her name is Michelle Vaughn Favergé. Find her, Rance. Do it for yourself or do it for your country, whatever. Just promise me you'll try. Promise me you'll try and write the story. Promise me you'll do it for me, buddy."

The well of confused emotion that flooded Rance's head was a bad LSD trip. Things came in and out of focus. Katarina. Some spy story. The red-head with the gun shooting Rance. Michael bleeding to death. A daughter.

"Rance?" Michael's voice was a whisper, but his grip was suddenly iron-strong on Rance's arm. "Rance, promise me."

Rance was crying, holding O'Meara's head in his hands. "I promise, Michael. I promise."

The body in his arms convulsed a final, and Rance re-opened his burning eyes. Michael O'Meara had finally found his peace.

§

The second day of the rest of Rance Vaughn's life was another scorcher.

The patio of the Beachcomber, a crowded beach bar in Wellfleet on Cape Cod, was jammed with drunk college aged kids. Boyish-faced Rance blended right into their midst. Except he wasn't partying. He was drinking–hard. Bloody Marys and Screwdrivers first thing this morning, then more fruit and vodka drinks: Seabreezes and Greyhounds and Madrases. Beers with lunch, then some daiquiris the way Hemingway drank them: doubled up, no sugar. A few Rum and Cokes to kick off the afternoon and now he was in whiskey country: Jameson, in memory of Michael.

But right now memories were what Rance was trying to avoid.

Wellfleet was far enough away–for now. Only an hour and a half drive from Green Harbor, Wellfleet was a mix of artists and tourists during the summer, and he sought to lose himself in crowds. Time was what he needed, time to think without having to look over his shoulder every five minutes. The booze was doing its job, rendering his thoughts into a mush of muted pain and fear.

"You look so sad," the girl said. Rance blinked slowly and looked at her. She had long, black hair and a lean body clad in only a bikini top and cut-off shorts.   He smiled...

...and saw Katarina.

In all her sexual vigor Katarina came flooding back into him. Her soft lips, naturally brick-red and turned down at the corners, her thick hair piled haphazardly perfect, her silky saunter. Closing his eyes tightly, he fought her image off.

"Sad?"

When again he opened his eyes, the girl had ceased being Katarina, at least for the moment. Though Rance had a blood alcohol level that would get him declared clinically dead by any doctor, he was a pro, a seasoned drinker with the ability to function despite his inebriation. This girl, however, the beautiful girl smiling at him, was no pro. He figured she probably wasn't even twenty, so whatever she had drunk was coursing through her veins with morphine speed, having its way with her. Which didn't sound like a bad idea.

"I mean, you're Rance Vaughn, aren't you?"

Terror widened his eyes for a brief second. Then he remembered he was a relatively well-known author, even if he hadn't written anything prolific as of late. He smiled and shrugged. "I'm he."

"I've read both your books, and I think you're a great writer. By the way, my name is Julie."

"Why, thank you, Julie. If you don't mind me asking, how did you happen to read my books? I mean, they were written almost ten years ago, and you don't look..."

"Old enough? I'm a sophomore at U-Mass, and one of my English lit teachers uses *Jungle Water* as part of the class. I just love your writing, and I've read all the short stories you've published, too."

"Short stories seem to be about the only thing I can get out these days."

"Have you thought about collecting them in a book?" Julie looked excited, her bosom heaving, and Rance didn't mind. "I've even thought of a title for the book: *Songs of Pain, Cries of Joy*, by Rance Vaughn. What do you think?"

"I think I've found my biggest fan."

Julie took a sip of Rance's whiskey as if it were water. "I liked the movies, too. The second one, *Snake Ranch*, was good, but I actually liked the book better."

"You were the only one."

"I hate Tom Cruise and Madonna."

"I didn't pick them." Rance refilled the glass with whiskey. "Now, Harrison Ford and Kathleen Turner, they really torched a rendition of Jack and Alice in *Jungle Water*."

"You're so right," oozed Julie. Her eyes rolled and Rance thought that if she smiled any wider her lips would tear. "God, I just can't believe this. I can't believe that I'm sitting here talking to my favorite writer."

"Tell me about your professor–the one drunk enough to refer to my books in class."

Julie giggled. "Professor Waters is real cool–except for the sexual advances."

"A wise man. You must remind me to shake his hand."

Julie giggled again, something that Rance found simultaneously annoying and arousing. "Professor Waters is a she."

Rance finished his drink without missing a beat. "Then you must remind me to sleep with her." More giggles, and Rance realized that he would not be able to stand up without embarrassing himself.

"Well, Professor Waters isn't here, and I don't expect her." Julie's smile was replaced by a look of pure carnal aggression. "So why don't you sleep with me?"

§

The thick, tinny smell of sex hung in the humid air.

Thin, gray light began to seep through the blinds and touch Rance's left eyelid. His mouth was cemented open and filled with dirt–at least it felt that way. Swallowing was not an option. From head to toe his body ached as if he had been beaten. And at his crotch he felt a rawness that explained the pungent aroma of dried body fluids.

His face was turned toward the door, away from...

Trying to remember her name hurt his head, but for some reason his body began to respond to the move command. Still drunk, he thought. I'm still drunk.

Julie!

Rance let out a sigh of relief that set his heart racing. With his right elbow he nudged to see if she was still there. Something soft enveloped his forearm–a breast?–and that was followed by a soft, muted groan.

The thumping in his head became more acute, a machine gunner concentrating his fire. And he had to pee. Pee and aspirin became the two motivating forces in his life.

Outside the motel door a floor board creaked.

Where are we, anyway? Rance thought. The image of a cheap motor court, the kind with rotting porches out front, came to his mind. Focusing on it, however, was impossible.

The next sound he heard was more than a creak; it was a step, an aggressive, deliberate step, and it stopped outside the door. His left hand dropped to the floor, feeling for his pants. He found a cuff and slid the pants to him, feeling up the leg to the pockets, where his hand closed around the shape of the thumb drive Michael had given him last night.

In his chest Rance's heart began to pound frantically, loudly, almost loud enough to drown out the sound of a lock being jimmied. Amidst the pain and dizziness he heard the distinctive click of a sprung mechanism, and the door swung slowly open. Rance withdrew his left hand and closed his eyes.

Okay, okay, think! he screamed to himself. Think!

Given the events of the last twenty-four hours, the chances that this was a random B&E were remote. Then what was it? That big Irish goon? But how could he have found out I'm still alive? Only three people knew that: one was Jenny, whom he trusted with his life; one was beside him sleeping; and one was dead.

Julie, he thought. She came on fast and hard, waiting until I was smashed enough not to notice anything suspicious. Dammit! Nobody in their right mind would ever teach anything you wrote!

Rance didn't need to hear the footsteps approaching. He could feel the barometric pressure of the room change as another body moved through it. The intruder was walking right up to him.

And that's when he realized he had a chance. If they weren't going to shoot him at a distance, they either didn't have a gun, or they preferred a high percentage shot—meaning they weren't good with a gun. Trying not to move, Rance sucked in a final breath to steady himself and cracked open his left eye.

He saw sneakers, small, white women's sneakers, and faded jeans. The sneakers stopped at his pants. There was a silence, a prolonged quiet during which he held his breath and thought he might go mad. Then he heard the click of the gun's hammer being cocked.

He didn't think. He did.

With one explosive movement he threw himself off the bed, shoulder rolling into the knees of the faded jeans. As he struck the woman's legs he heard a cry of surprise and the muffled thwack of a silenced revolver being fired.

Rance and his assailant tumbled to the floor, and he kept rolling, feeling his shoulder blades dig into her chest, then his right shoulder slide down into her neck. Something skidded across the floor, and when Rance completed his roll off her head, he saw the gun with its gross muffler lying by the bathroom door.

His left hand found a clump of hair, and he pulled the woman up, cocking his right fist in preparation for–

"Gina?"

With her loose fitting jeans and dark sweatshirt, Rance almost didn't recognize her. That critical hesitation was all she needed, and her knee came up fast and hard, narrowly missing his crotch but catching him full in the stomach.

The sudden vacuum of expelled air doubled him over and she tore free from his grip. He saw her dive for the gun, and he tried to follow, but he stumbled on his pants, looking up just in time to see her level the gun at him. But the shot never came.

Instead Gina was smothered by a pillow-wielding Julie. The two women crashed into the bathroom door. Rance saw the ungainly barrel of the gun appear, then disappear as they wrestled on the cold tile floor. Finally his wind returned with a rush, and he lunged toward them.

But before he could hit them, a foot caught him in the crotch, deflecting his charge. Bouncing back into the wall, he saw Julie fall away and Gina come up with the gun. This time, Julie was the target. As Gina brought the gun up, Rance swung his leg out, catching her shin and sending her down. He quickly tried to smother her, but the barrel of the gun was suddenly jammed under his chin.

Rolling off, he grabbed Gina's wrist and twisted it back as far as he could, just as he heard the thwack of the gun being fired again. The recoil bucked the gun into the air and Gina's body went limp, landing on the ground with a heavy thud. A pool of blood began spreading out from under her head.

Rance rose and retrieved the gun. He cocked it and went over to Julie, calmly putting the barrel under her nose.

"Would you like to tell me how she got here?"

"I don't know, I don't know." Julie began to sob. "I swear to you, I met her yesterday, right before I met you. She pointed you out to me. When I told her how much I liked your writing, she encouraged me to introduce myself to you. I never saw her after that, I swear."

He pulled the gun away from her and let out a deep breath. He believed her. He had to. She had saved his life a minute ago, something she wouldn't have done if she were working with Gina. He looked once more at the body on the floor. Death was suddenly a maggot infesting his decaying reality, and he felt the burning bile rise to the back of his throat. He began pulling on his clothes.

Julie looked up from her crying. "Where are you going?"

"To keep a promise I made." For a final time he looked at the dead body, but he didn't see Gina. He saw Michael O'Meara, and his eyes filled with tears. He blinked twice. "And to write the story."

Part II

Paris

A large mirror rose up from behind the legions of liquor bottles lining the back of the bar. An image reflected in it caught Rance's eye. The back of someone's head, someone sitting alone at a table, someone with dark red curly hair, reading the paper. So familiar was the image that Rance was about to get up and walk over to the man, to tap him on the shoulder and say, "Excuse me, but I thought you looked familiar..."

Then he saw the man's left hand.

As the man turned the pages of the newspaper not ten feet away, he twirled a rubber band over and over in his hand. With a heart-stopping shock Rance suddenly recognized the big red-head–the man who had tried to execute him two days ago.

Stinging sweat instantly soaked his upper lip, clenching his mouth into a tight line. His jaw began grinding his teeth together with increasing pressure that pulled his scalp tight.

After a turbulent flight and an unnerving go round with French customs, the last thing he thought he had to worry about was this. But there sat the man who had tried to kill him two days ago.

He knew he wasn't seeing a reflection of booze sitting there. Though he had quickly quaffed two beers as soon as the customs dogs released him, there was no mistaking the man sitting a few tables away. The rubber band in those giant hands gave him away.

This is what you deserve, you clown, he chided himself. What did you think–that you're some kind of agent? You were a bookworm for Langley, nothing more. And what if you do find her? Can Michael's ex-partner help you? Unless he shows up right now, I'm afraid not.

The rattle of debate within him only delayed the inevitable. But maybe, he thinks, maybe if I just sit here and stare at my suds, maybe he'll get up and walk away.

And then I'll get on the first fucking plane back to Boston and stay drunk until I die.

Sitting there, sweating cold bullets, he tried to focus on getting out of there alive. The nausea left him instantly. Gone too was the warm, liquid emotion of the beer. He was left with only a cold, empty feeling in his gut, a flimsy tether to reality. Beneath his feet the floor of the bar began to rock back and forth, gently at first, but with an increasing cadence that threatened to topple him.

Rance no longer felt like finishing his beer. Fear was back, and he causally turned and tried to sneak a peek at the big man. He seemed engrossed in his paper. Maybe I can slip by him. Maybe...

Rance stood and nonchalantly walked past the man. He was almost to the busy concourse and anonymity when the big red head looked up from his paper. As if guided by some manifestation of destiny–shit luck was Rance's appraisal–the big red head's small, cool eyes locked on his. The big man didn't even blink before exploding out of his chair and lunging at him.

Like a tailback dancing through the line, Rance spun wildly, staggering out into the busy concourse. There was a whoosh of air as the big red head's mitts swiped the air where he had been standing a second earlier. A few people screamed, and there was a general parting of the seas.

As the big man crashed hard onto the floor, Rance's own momentum carried him into a baggage rack. What felt like a ton of suitcases smothered him. Panic welled in his belly, and he began kicking frantically, trying to flail his way out. He made it to his knees before he felt an iron grip on his ankle.

Some beastly grunt was issued and he was flipped onto his back. A cold steel gun barrel was shoved in his throat; beyond the weapon's cocked hammer were the vicious metal eyes of the big red head.

"Arretez-vous! Arretez-vous!"

Somebody was yelling at the big red head, but his eyes never left Rance's. He wanted to swallow, but with a lethal tongue depressor occupying most of his mouth, all he could manage was a gag. Then, the big red head smiled.

A hand fell harshly on the big man's shoulder, pulling it back. When his captor twisted his head to see who had accosted him, Rance saw his chance. He brought his knee up violnetly into Big Red's crotch. The ensuing scream cracked Rance's ear drums, but it also got the gun barrel extracted from his mouth. With a wild thrust he kneed him again, then shoved him off.

Without looking he exploded to his feet, stopping long enough only to grab his bag. He sprinted as hard as he could through the airport, tripping on a carpet and crashing through an exit, precipitating a hail of oaths in his wake.

Finding himself on a sidewalk lined with buses, he dove into the first one he saw. Its opposite terminus was the Gare de l'Est, the train station that served all of France's eastern train lines. There were no seats, and his rushed, frantic behavior attracted no more than the pitiful glances reserved for dopey travelers. He gasped hard, finally regaining his breath.

As the bus pulled out into traffic it joined a half dozen others. Rance peeked through the jam-packed bodies just in time to see the big red head explode out the doors and onto the sidewalk. A gust of wind blew open the man's jacket, revealing for an instant the large black handle of a gun.

Though he had caught his breath, his pulse was still slamming through his veins, aping his racing brain. Who the hell is this guy that he gets to travel with his sidearm into other countries? he wondered. If he remembered correctly, the bus ride into Paris would be about 25 minutes. Time enough to begin considering his options.

So how about it? he thought to himself. Coincidence that this big red head arrives in France at the same time as me? Or not? A third option manifested itself suddenly, clenching his bowels with a cold fist.

Michael said that Katarina and this guy were somehow mixed up together-maybe even partners. Maybe he's coming back to France to tell her how he killed me-maybe he can lead me to her.

But he was long gone, left at the airport. And the thought of sneaking around someone that reckless and instantly violent-he tried to kill me in the middle of a crowded airport!-held little appeal. Maybe Paris itself would hold the answer. Maybe something from his past would show him the future.

And when he stepped out into the stifling French heat, the memories began. Directly across the street from the Gare de l'Est was a restaurant called Au Gare des Alsacians.

§

"You must have the *flammenkeuche-tarte à flambé*, as we French say it," Katarina had said. "Me, I will have the *choucroute*." And together we will have the biggest, coldest bottle of Alsatian Riesling we can order."

Rance remembered the difference in the weather: compared to the sunny, warm summer of London that year, Paris was a tinder box, an oven of stifling perspiration. Rance also remembered that little restaurant across the street from the Gare de l'Est, where Katarina had taken him one sultry night.

"Why is it the Gare de l'Est?" Rance had asked as he sipped his wine.

"Because it serves the east of France, silly," was Katarina's reply. She had not looked up at Rance during her reply, and Rance was amazed at her transformation. It was the food. Katarina looked down at the portion of choucroute-a pile of cabbage boiled in wine and topped with an assortment of sausage and other pork products-in pregnant savor. She arranged the items in a specific order on her plate, so that the result was a symmetrical presentation that gratified her before she ate.

"And how many train stations are there in Paris?"

"Oh, many. There is the Gare du Nord, just around the corner from us here, the Gare St. Lazare, the Gare Montparnasse, the Gare d'Austerlitz, and the Gare de Lyon."

"All as big as Gare de l'Est?"

"Of course. Some bigger and busier." She daintily tore into her food, looking off into the distance as she chewed, as if in preparation for some culinary question. Rance crawled into that look, deep into it.

§

It was the wail of a horn and the screeching of tires that ripped him back. A cabby leaned out of his window and was about to curse him when he saw the travel bag.

"*M'sieu?*" he said, his demeanor changing as quickly as Rance had nearly lost his life.

Rance climbed in and said, "*Place de la Republique,*" before he realized it.

"*Vous êtès touriste, bien sûr,*" said the cab driver, looking at Rance in his rear view mirror. "*Anglais?*"

"*Americain,*" he answered in a sugar coated French accent, pleased with how easy the motions of forming the French language returned to him.

"I can always tell, *m'sieu*," the cabby said in heavily accented but otherwise fine English. "You I guessed English because of your pale skin."

"*Et mes vètements*?" And my clothes?

"*Ah, oui.* You dress like a foreigner. We French are very observant, you know."

The cab stopped, and Rance paid his fare and got out. He was standing across the street from the Holiday Inn, in the square known as the Place de la Republique.

§

"All you Americans are so funny," Katarina said.

Their huge Alsatian meal had warranted a long stroll, and they had come down Boulevard de Magenta from the Gare de l'Est to the Place de la Republique.

"What?" was Rance's snappy reply.

Katarina laughed the laugh that so maddened Rance. Head thrown back, hair tumbling behind her, eyes half closed, teeth bared and hand gently resting at the top of her chest, Katarina laughed ha-ha arrogantly.

"You Americans come to France and stay at your big American hotel, eat hamburgers at McDonalds, then go home and complain how arrogant we French are. It is all so amusing."

Though Rance's nationalistic pride had been wounded, he knew she was right. Living abroad gave him a perspective on his own people that surprised him. His belief that America and Americans were the greatest show on earth had shifted slightly to the belief that America was a vast country with a lot of natural resources and hard working people, and we'll leave it at that.

"And you French come to America, eat at McDonald's, buy Levi's and Elvis records, return home and decry the shallowness of American culture."

Katarina stopped and whirled to face him. Her eyes were dark, glowing coals and her lips heaved and quivered.

"*Touché*," she said. "Well, said. So very well said."

She slid a hand up around his neck and pulled him to her, kissing him long and hard in the middle of the crowded summer street. When they parted she said nothing more, pinning herself to him as they walked their dinner off.

§

Rance turned away from the Place de la Republique, biting back the unforgiving tide of memories that was following him around Paris. He was suddenly glad he was not in London, for he began to realize that the booze and the escapism had only turned his focus away from the object; the object itself still remained.

Now he followed Boulevard de Temple until it turned into Boulevard Beaumarchais. Before him was the Place de la Bastille, an angry hurricane of vehicles swirling around a phallic monument. Some brave tourists tried to make the dash to the center, and were rewarded by curses and shouts. Above the monument the sky had become a darker shade of haze, and a hot breeze began to convect the city. Thunderstorms, he thought. Rance looked to his left and saw the Hotel Lyon-Mulhouse.

There had been thunderstorms that night with Katarina, too, he remembered. A dash for a Café, a couple of bottles of wine, and a room at the Hotel Lyon-Mulhouse, where they had spent the night making love, their wet bodies illuminated by the electric blue of the storm. Now he entered the hotel again, to search the memories, to use them instead of the other way around.

"*Vous avez un chambre, monsieur?*" he asked the man at the desk.

"*Mais oui, mais oui,*" the man replied. As he flipped through his schedule of rooms the man glanced at Rance several times.

"*Un problem?*" asked Rance.

"*Non, non. Mais, avez-vous déjà rester avec nous?*" Have you ever stayed with us?

"*Oui,*" Rance answered cautiously "*Il y a longtemps.*" A long time ago.

The man broke into a huge smile, revealing stained, irregular teeth. "I knew it! I never forget a customer! For you, our best room: private shower, television, mini-bar!"

"Thank you" Rance signed the register as Samuel Adams. "Can I still get breakfast?"

"Of course, Monsieur...Adams."

After showering and shaving in his room, Rance returned downstairs where he gratefully sipped a bowl of Café au lait and watched the guests file in and out of the small breakfast room. Next to him was a loud American family causing him to cringe with embarrassment.

"Waitress! Waitress!" the father called. From his accent and his girth Rance guessed he was from the farm belt. Beside him sat his equally huge wife. They both wore shorts that let their flabby white legs ooze out like some chemistry experiment gone awry. Two children, a boy and a girl, both well on their way to their parent's blubbery fate, amused themselves by throwing bits of baguette at each other.

Madame Bertrand, the wife of the man at the front desk and a sad eyed wisp of a woman, hurried over to them, her heels clicking on the tile floor.

"I asked for a coffee with cream in it, not this, this kiddy crap," the fat father said, gesturing at his bowl of Café au lait. One of Madame's eyebrows crinkled down and Rance detected the faint glow of red on the back of her neck.

"Oui, mais, m'sieu, café au lait est le boisson traditional, sûrtout pour les touristes, alors, si vous voulez autre chose, il faut le dire-"

The fat man was waving her off. "My Gawd, can't you people speak the King's English?" He turned to Rance. "How about you, buddy? Do you speak English?"

Rance gave his best Gallic shrug. "Desolé." He stood and made a show of dropping his napkin on the floor next to the fat man's fat wife. As he bent down to retrieve it, Rance slipped his hand into the woman's purse and snatched her cell phone. He stood and smiled.

The fat man threw down his napkin. "Damn frogs. I knew I shouldn't've listened to Wilbur. Come one, we're going."

As they waddled out the door arguing about Wilbur's advice, Madame Bertrand looked at Rance. "But aren't you also American?"

Rance shrugged Gallicly again. His shame about the comportment of his fellow Americans brought a grin to Madame's face.

"You will get along fine with my husband," Madame said in charmingly accented English. "He enjoys eccentric visitors."

"You speak English?"

Madame smiled again. "Never around Americans."

He sipped the huge bowl of coffee again, feeling it infuse him as the beer had done earlier. But instead of dulling his senses, the potent coffee sharpened them, restoring a vigor to his lethargic limbs. The creamy aroma drifted up and bathed his sense of smell, threatening to unleash a new tide of memories. He took a deep breath and fought it off.

Finishing the coffee, he looked around for a quiet spot. There was a phone booth in the lobby of the hotel, a leftover from the pre-cell phone days. He crammed himself into it, ever aware of the size differences between the average Frenchman and the average American. Though not the equal of his obese countryman, he was well over six feet in height and broad shouldered, a character trait the French were not known for. After a few false starts figuring out the configuration of the American woman's cell phone, he got the connection he wanted.

"Agent Donovan, FBI," the voice on the other end of the line said with remarkable clarity.

"My name is Rance Vaughn."

There was a brief silence.

"Hold on a minute," Agent Donovan said, "I gotta switch phones." A few seconds later, Donovan was back on the line. "Rance Vaughn. Jesus H. Christ, did you know that every agent in the world is looking for you?"

"Look, I didn't kill Michael–"

"Yeah, I know."

A lack of enthusiasm in his voice startled Rance. But maybe that was his style, or maybe it was the smallness of his voice over the long distance line.

"Michael called me," Donovan continued. "Told me what happened. Told me he was going to find you. Don't worry, I'm working on straightening it out. Where the hell are you?"

"Far away."

"Let me guess: Paris, France."

Rance swore under his breath and kicked the phone booth door in frustration. Mr. Bertrand, his nose buried in that morning's Figaro, looked up.

"Listen," Rance said, "I need some help and Michael said you were the only one in the world that I could trust."

"Well, God bless you for the compliment, Michael. Yeah, I can help you. And don't worry about the rap on you over here. The theory is falling apart rapidly. They found Mr. Gengi's body this morning."

"Mr. Gengi?"

"The MIT spook that Michael was escorting over to Walpole MCI when he got jumped. Apparently, that's why they swiped him-they were afraid he was going to talk. Anyway, Gengi's body was found hanging from the flagpole in City Hall Plaza this morning."

Donovan lowered his voice.

"Look, Vaughn, I know you probably don't trust your own image in the mirror these days, but Michael and I were close. Real close. He told me a little about what was going on, and what connection you have to all this. So I know you have your own reasons. But we both have the same goal, so I'm gonna help you any way I can.

"You can ignore that crack about Paris. I don't know where the hell you are, and I don't give a shit. But if you do get to Paris, there's somebody there who can help you. An agent of the SDECE-that's the French equivalent of the CIA-named Francoise Chaumont. Don't try contacting these people. Leave it to me. I'll arrange it and get back to you-better yet, I don't want to know where you are. Call me back in three hours."

Rance took a deep breath. "Thanks, Agent Donovan."

"Don't mention it. And call me Marty. Oh, Vaughn?"

"Yes?"

"How are you set for dough? You got enough to keep moving?"

"Don't worry about that. I have little stashes squirreled away all over the place."

"Yeah, that's right. They made a couple of movies from your books. Listen, Hollywood writer, buy me a steak dinner when this is all over."

"You're on." If he got out of this with his skin intact he'd buy Donovan a whole restaurant. His next phone call was to Jenny.

"Rance, where are you?"

"Out of the country."

"That's probably a good idea. The police think you're somehow involved in Michael's death. They're even trying to link you to some prisoner escape and murder. What are you into?"

"I can't explain it, but there's somebody who can. His name is Marty Donovan, and he's an FBI Special Agent in Boston. He was Michael's friend. Go see him, do what he says. But until then, I need some help. I need you to search some court records-anything to do with Katarina Favergé. Do you have access to some kind of national database concerning federal court cases?"

"Sure, that's no problem, Rance. But what-"

"I have to go, Jenny. Take care of yourself."

Rance carefully wiped the phone of his fingerprints, then dropped it in a trash can.

§

The Latin Quarter was Paris' eternal Bohemian enclave.

Revived and invigorated by three bowls of Café au lait, Rance took advantage of the beautiful morning to stroll from the Place de la Bastille down to the Seine, the famous river that bisects the city. He crossed over to the Île St. Louis and promised himself that if he ever made it out of this mess, he'd write the book he promised Michael, then he'd by a flat right here on the chic island in the middle of the Seine.

Crossing to the Rive Gauche, he strolled along the banks of the river, past the myriad artists and booksellers hawking their wares out of the stalls that lined the side of the street. Across the river rose Notre Dame, magnificently imposing, byzantine in detail, poetic in its dominance of the city. Putting his back to the cathedral, Rance entered the Latin Quarter.

The Sorbonne, one of the world's most prestigious universities, dominates the Latin Quarter. A place of cobbled alleys and narrow, twisting streets, the Quarter is crammed with pouting women and artist's storefronts. The women were, he thought, unlike any others in the world.

Katarina.

French women were everywhere, and every one of them seemed to posses some quality that reminded him of Katarina–the reason he was here. The whole thing came crashing back. Katarina, long-legged and clad in black tights, black mini skirt, black top, the style that never went out in Paris.

He turned a corner and saw it. When he called Marty Donovan back the FBI agent gave him the name of a Café here in the Latin Quarter. After dawdling inconspicuously for a few minutes while he checked out the surrounding area, Rance made his way to the Café d'Esprit.

A conflagration of red metal tables and chairs spilled forth from the door of Café d'Esprit and out onto the sidewalk. All the chairs were arranged with their backs to the Café, so that the patrons could view the world flowing by as they sipped their pastis. He found a seat and ordered a coffee. A minute later the waiter returned with what in America would be called an espresso.

Rance sat back to watch the people, tourists, students, businessmen, workers, the living Paris, pass him by. "Don't worry, they'll find you," Marty told him this morning regarding the SDECE agent he was supposed to meet. It was a reassurance that chilled his spine. But soon the coffee and the view worked its magic, and he felt almost Parisian.

She came from a moped, seizing his attention. Improbably beautiful, the woman shook the helmet from her head and ran her fingers through short, unkempt hair. When she finished mussing, her hair held a style that women would pay hundreds for in one of the many salons located within the city. Her miniskirt didn't begin to approach mid-thigh, and the skin of her legs, smooth and olive tinted, needed no stockings. In his libidinous mind Rance begged God to bless the women of France.

Katarina had called them "French thin." Meaning long, shapely but thin legs, no discernible bottoms, slender but active hips, pears for breasts (never encumbered by bras), and necks. It was the necks, Katarina had said, that separated French women from other women in the world. French women had the most remarkable necks. The woman who walked from her moped and sat next to him was French thin, and he suddenly found himself very badly wanting a drink to share with her.

"Me, I am not French-thin," Katarina had said. "It's the damned Slavic bones my mother gave me. They require more meat to hold them upright."

The French-thin woman sitting beside him had a face to match her exquisite body. Large, dark eyes and full lips, lips that probably never smiled. She pulled a long, thin, brown cigarette from a case and kissed it between her lips. Then, she turned her head slightly, letting her eyes engage his.

For a moment he sat stupefied, engrossed in her eyes. Then he reached over to her table and picked up the lighter laying there. He lit the cigarette and returned the lighter. She never took her eyes from his. After a deep, satisfying drag, she finally broke her gaze.

"*Merci, m'sieu.*"

"*Je vous en prie,*" he answered, trying to return his gaze to the street before him. Her legs were the problem. Unabashedly she had crossed them. Long and flawless, they jutted into his field of vision, drawing his eyes up their length, caressing them back down, intoxicating his thoughts.

"You see something you like, *m'sieu?*" the woman asked.

Rance gagged on his Adam's apple. By now he was beyond wondering how he could constantly be fingered as an English speaker. My accent, he thought. But I only said four words. My appearance? True, he was taller and fairer than the average Frenchman, but Paris was a big city with dozens of different races coexisting on a daily basis. And he had gone that very morning to a clothing shop to find something a bit more Continental to wear, something less English.

"It's a beautiful city," he answered in English. "There is a lot to like."

She smiled, but not at him, and dragged on her cigarette. "I'm sure you don't have women like this in your Green Harbor, do you?"

He froze as a wave of hysteria-induced sweat simultaneously broke out of every pour on his body. When he turned to her he saw that her smile had become a pleasant look of determination, a look that conveyed many things, but above all, a look that he could not doubt.

"I am Francoise Chaumont, Mr. Vaughn," she said.

§

"Don't look so surprised, Mr. Vaughn. And please don't look at me."

"Both very difficult tasks."

"Ah, Marty told me that you would charming. He didn't say how handsome you were, though. Though I would prefer it otherwise, please continue to watch the street."

73

"Am I supposed to be looking for something specific?"

"I thought that was why you came to France, Mr. Vaughn."

"Rance."

"*Pardon?*" Francoise turned her head and fixed him with a frown.

"What's this? You get to ogle me but I have to sit here like a good boy with my hands folded on my lap? Sounds rather sexist to me."

Out of the corner of his eye Rance caught her smile as she turned quickly away.

"You can call me Rance," he said. "Mr. Vaughn was my father."

Her reply was the slightest turning up of her mouth's corners. "Did you have a pleasant trip?"

"Until I got to Paris. The guy who tried to kill me-the one who killed my friend Michael O'Meara-showed up at Charles de Gaulle just as I did. Then he tried to kill me again, which I find a bit too serendipitous."

Francoise showed no emotion as she stared straight ahead and smoked her cigarette. "I know."

"Excuse me?"

"There was someone...watching for you at the airport-to make sure you entered the country without any problem. You did a fair job of losing them. We are presently running the gentleman's photograph through our databases."

"This guys bops around the world heavily armed and you need to run his picture through a computer? Did you try Googling him?"

"I assure you we're doing everything we can. You'll be safe now."

"I'm touched, but not entirely convinced."

"Come now, Mr. Vaughn-Rance-let us work together."

He smiled. "Together would be nice."

For several moments there was silence.

"Well, Francoise, shall we sit here enjoying the electricity between us, or shall we do something about it."

A grin. "Forgive me. I was just thinking of a place where we can go to talk. Someplace...quiet and secure. There is a bistro called Chez Olivier in the *Seizieme*-you know the arrondissments of Paris?" He nodded. "Very good. Chez Olivier is on the Rue Boissiere, close to the Place de Victor Hugo. I will be there in an hour."

Watching her speed away on the moped, he thought she looked ridiculously out of place with her miniskirt and dazzling legs squeezing the moped's seat. But Paris was filled with gorgeous young women speeding about on their basic means of transportation. He just happened to be prejudiced toward the one who just left him.

Paris, he also knew, was filled with every type of terrorist possible. Diplomats were assassinated with frightening regularity. For a country that boasted such a tiny rate of homicide involving firearms, it was certainly a dangerous place to be an international target.

Just as he was fishing about in his pocket for a few coins to pay his tab, a wedge shaped Citroen pulled up opposite the Café with a squeal of its tires. Looking at the car, Rance halted, half in his chair and half out of it. Nobody was getting out of the car, and its windows were tinted black. The bottom fell out of his gut, and he swallowed hard once, twice.

Then the driver's side door opened. A man with black

curly hair stepped from the car. Before Rance had a chance to see his face, the man had turned back to the car, flipping the front seat forward and bending over into the back seat. Rance moved quickly to the entrance of the Café.

The man at the car wheeled suddenly, an automatic weapon pressed to his hip. The staccato burst of small caliber gunfire smashed the sounds of the city to pieces. Rance saw the window directly behind his chair shatter inward under a hail of bullets. Everywhere people fell to the ground, and the bullets began walking their way toward him.

Without thinking he turned and sprinted into the Café, diving over the long wooden bar just as the bullets caught up to him. Glass rained everywhere, and as he fell hard to the floor he covered himself with his arms.

Just as suddenly as the gunfire began, it ceased. From outside the Café came a stream of curses. Chancing a peek over the bar, he saw the gunman trying to insert a fresh banana clip into the weapon. Rance seized his chance and ran into the back of the Café. A new burst of gunfire told him that the shooter had succeeded in reloading the gun.

In the back of the kitchen, past terrified waitstaff, he found a door. As he crashed through it he heard the short bursts of gunfire coming from within the Café now. Realizing that he was the intended target, Rance stumbled out into an alley. When he saw the huge dumpster blocking the alley's entrance, his heart sank. The alley ended in a brick wall opposite its impassable entrance, and the only way out was back through the kitchen. But the screams of the staff, punctuated by short bursts of gunfire from the approaching shooter, nixed that option.

So he looked up.

Directly above the door was the bottom stage of a wrought iron fire escape. Rance leaped up and caught it. Then, he lifted his legs and chinned himself. His feet barely cleared the door before it flew open.

Peaking down, he saw the man with the machine gun stumble burst into the alley below him. The man snapped his head back and forth. Rance felt his arms quiver under the strain of his own body weight. Leave, he thought. Go away. But the man didn't leave. Instead, he looked up.

Fine, Rance thought, locking eyes with the man as he hung upside down. If that's the way you want it, that's the way you're gonna get it. He let go.

Gravity dropped his 190 pounds fast and hard, directly on the shooter's head, and as the man folded beneath him, he heard the sickening crunch of bone. He rolled off the man and exploded to his feet. In a second he was back on top of the man, clutching his head in a half nelson and running it hard into the brick wall. The man collapsed upon himself, and Rance didn't hang around to take his pulse. He climbed over the dumpster and lost himself in the gathering crowd outside the Café d'Esprit.

§

"I was beginning to think that you had stood me up."

Rance found Francoise installed at a table tucked back in the extreme corner of Chez Olivier. In the deep shadows of the bistro, Francoise took on another persona. Earlier, in the bright light of day, she was two dimensional, a model from the pages of some magazine. But here, in the low, dusty light, she breathed in and out of focus, her texture becoming palpable.

"It almost wasn't my choice," he said, sliding into the seat next to her.

She caught the look on his face and frowned. "You look upset. Has something happened?"

"You might say that. Somebody tried to cut me in half with a machine gun ten seconds after you left. Of course, my first thought is that you had something to do with it-sorry, but your departure was just too convenient."

Her frown deepened, but she held his eyes with her gaze.

"That thought is a mistake, Rance." Her voice came low and breathy, the words with a physical presence. "Many years ago Martin Donovan and Michael O'Meara saved my life. I owe them an enormous debt. And it so happens that my agency-the SDECE-also wants to find your Katarina."

With an unblinking stare he looked at her. He wanted to believe her when a confining thought struck him: he had to, he had no choice.

"To execute her?"

"To try her for crimes against her country. Why must you find her?"

A waiter appeared at the table just then. He presented Rance with a bottle of champagne, which he had produced from a silver bucket filled with ice and mounted on an iron post. Rance looked to Francoise in confusion.

"Well, do you like it?" she asked, a smile breaking her lips for the first time. "Is it satisfactory?"

He saw it was a bottle of Tattinger. "Um, yes, it's fine."

"*Tres bien, m'sieu,*" she said to the waiter. He poured two flutes and left them with the bottle. Francoise raised her glass.

"To your success," she proposed. They clinked glasses and sipped.

Rance put his glass down. "Francoise, why all this?" He vaguely gestured at the bistro. "Why the champagne, the Café?"

"Because, Rance, it is what people in Paris do. A man and a woman sharing a bottle of champagne over lunch in a bistro does not attract attention in Paris. But, if you prefer, we can put on trench coats and exchange notes in dark alleys..."

He held up his hands, smiling. "*Touché.*"

"Tell me what happened after I left you," she said, changing the mood suddenly.

Recounting as best he could, Rance told her about the car, the man's description and his subsequent escape. Francoise stopped him frequently, asking detailed questions that he thought aimless.

"Was the man wearing a double breasted or single breasted blazer?"

"How was his hair combed?"

"Did he shoot the weapon well?"

"Did he say anything that you could hear?"

"How did the people around react?"

"Was he able to fight you back at all?"

"He was much smaller than I was," Rance answered the last question. "And I had the element of surprise."

"From your description of the fight, it doesn't sound like he will survive. Not bad for someone who has spent the last several years drunk on his boat."

Rance's eyebrows rose in surprise. "But how did you–"

"I would not agree to meet you unless I knew a little about your background. I only regret that I have not had the opportunity to read either of your books, although from the spiciness of the reviews, I shall have to make it a point to do so."

The waiter arrived with lunch's first course, a slice of rich pate de fois gras encased in a border of gelatin.

"The man who tried to kill you," Francoise said between delicate bites of her pate, "he was not a professional. He was hired off the street, probably an illegal Algerian, a subversive, someone difficult to trace. He possessed no skill whatsoever." She cut herself short when she saw his face go pale. "Don't be upset, Rance, but you were an easy target sitting there. Someone who had wanted you dead would have had no trouble at all. This man, he drove a distinctive car, he fumbled for his gun, he shot badly, and then he allowed you to surprise him at the end. He would not even be allowed in the Belgian military."

He looked at her blankly.

"It is a joke, Rance. To be so bumbling and not even have the Belgians, a far inferior breed, take you in is the utmost insult."

"Oh, I didn't know that France and Belgium..."

"And everybody else. It is a European thing. To be serious again for a moment, let it be a lesson for you. It sounds as if you sensed something amiss from the start, but do not ever let your guard down. We still don't know what we are dealing with."

"We don't?" He leaned forward to continue, but she motioned behind him.

The waiter had returned, and he now held a bottle of red

wine, which he positioned under Rance's nose for inspection. A Chateau Margaux, from Bordeaux. He nodded and the waiter uncorked the bottle and half filled Rance's glass before stepping back.

It was coming back to him now. Katarina had reveled in his uncouth American behavior the first time she had taken him to France, and now he was experiencing a form of deja-vu. Beautiful women, it seemed, loved seeing him out of his element. But his memory served him, and he had a surprise for Francoise.

Holding the stem just below the cup, Rance lifted it to the light, gently swirling the contents.

"*Trés bon jambs*," he said just loud enough for Francoise and the waiter to hear him. "*Couleur sanguin, mais pas trop.*" His nose was stuck almost rudely into the glass. "*Un néz delicate mais pas inferior.*" He sipped a mouthful, aerating the wind, rolling in over his tongue until finally he swallowed. "*Un peu fûmé, mais je sais que 87 n'était pas l'anneé prefreé pour Chateau Margaux. Il est bon.*"

The waiter nodded politely and filled Francoise's glass, then refilled Rance's and left them.

"*Bravo, Monsieur Vaughn. Vous connaissez bien le vin et la langue francaise.*"

You know well the wines and the language of France.

"*Écoute, Francoise, avec moi il faut tutoyer, d'accord?*"

Don't be so polite with me. Please use the familiar conjugation, okay?

She smiled, for real this time. "*D'accord.*"

The plat du jour was escalope de veaux, followed by a salad of lettuce leafs doused in olive oil, then a wheel of cheeses, all of it washed down with the bottle of Bordeaux. The conversation during lunch was intentionally superficial. Francoise seemed highly interested in Rance's life as a writer and why he essentially abandoned it, a question to which Rance had no answer.

"You still haven't answered my question, Rance," she said when they finished their meal.

"Which one was that?"

Studying her closely, he felt his heart race loudly as she returned his gaze with her eyes, luscious black gems. He tried to ignore the welter within and concentrate on the question, but her presence muddled his brain.

"Why must you find Katarina Favergé?"

That question sufficed in snapping Rance from his wine-induced swooning.

"Because I promised somebody I would."

"Oh, really? You mean to tell me that you are not doing it for yourself? You are some kind of patriot trying to avenge injustice?"

Rance felt the back of his neck flush with blood, and he ceased swirling the wine in his glass. "A dear friend of mine is dead. I've almost been killed three times now. It seems to me that I don't have much of a choice. Either I find the source of who or what is trying to kill me, or I die."

"And Katarina Favergé is that source?"

"All roads seem to be leading to Rome."

"But you haven't mentioned to me anything about your daughter."

He froze, his eyes growing. Francoise's face did not change. "How did you-"

82

Francoise reached across the table and took his hands in hers. Her fingers were long and slender, genetic matches to her legs, and he noticed that even though the nails were short, they still projected an air of femininity, as if to say, "Here is a woman; a professional, yes, but still a woman." Her grip was strong and her thumbs stroked the knuckles of his hands.

"Rance, I told you I did a background check of you before you arrived. You were CIA, though a very low level. Almost an outside contractor, yes? You did some file sorting in London for a while, that is where you met Katarina Favergé."

He felt the surprise grip his face, but he let her continue. "It is well known that Katarina has a daughter whose name is Michelle Vaughn Favergé. One does not need an active imagination to make the connection. Your daughter lives here in Paris with her aunt."

"Isabelle."

"Yes, Isabelle. I will take you there tomorrow."

For a moment, he felt the earth stop moving.

§

"You must remember that we are working together, Rance."

Francoise was dressed a lot less seductively today. The slacks and jacket gave her the air of somebody professional. She had picked Rance up in front of his hotel in a Mercedes, and she wore eyeglasses to complete the look. Rance didn't ask if the glasses were real or not. This woman, he realized, was a puzzle he might never solve.

After the long, wine-laced lunch, he returned to his hotel where he collapsed on the bed before he could undress. His sleep had been long but fitful, filled with alternating images of Francoise and Katarina.

"I don't really think that you are going to run away from me, but I still don't know you that well," Francoise said as she negotiated the car through the impossible traffic of Paris. "You will be tempted, but remember that I have vast resources at my disposal, resources that can help us in ways that not even you, the dreamer and writer of fiction, could imagine."

She smiled and looked at him kindly.

"Oh, I'm sure that I could imagine a few things if given the opportunity," he said. "But before we go any further, I'd like you to tell me something-if you could. Why are you-I mean the SDECE-so hot for Katarina? And spare me-if you can-the treason rhetoric."

The car came to a stop at a traffic light, and there were several moments of silence.

"I met Katarina at the Sorbonne," she said when the car began to move again. "We shared a tiny apartment and just about everything else for a few years. We were very close friends."

"She never told me."

"She wouldn't. But that shouldn't surprise you now. In any event, we were both recruited by the Agency. We went through our training together, and we were teamed together on our first assignment."

"Which was?"

"London. The CIA was cultivating an Iranian diplomat for information against the Ayatollah. This man also had compromising knowledge of some very sensitive information regarding the dealings of the French and Iranian governments.

It was a testy time between my country and yours. So we were dispatched to London to try and intercept the data that he was feeding the CIA."

"Me."

His heart suddenly felt punctured and deflated. In one short moment his memories went from that fuzzy, warm region of the brain to a black, void scar. One paragraph of thought had reduced two years of his life to utter failure. And suddenly, a thousand tiny things became clear. Too clear.

§

"I just have to stop by my office for a moment."

"Oh, Rance, darling, must we?" Katarina pouted in a way that would bring Hollywood to its knees.

"It's on our way out, sweetheart. I've just got to drop off some paperwork."

It was her innocence that he could see from the perspective of history. They were in his office.

"Darling, is there a lady's room I could use?"

Rance gestured around the corner and went back to sorting a few folders for the morning. She could have been gone for a minute, could have been ten. But she was so happy when she returned.

"I'm hurrying, sweetheart," he said without looking up.

"Take your time," was her reply.

§

"I'm sorry, Rance," said Francoise.

"Don't be. It's part of the business, right?"

Her reply was a weak smile and the squeeze of his hand.

"I'm not burned by the spook stuff–I'm even surprised that the CIA accepted me in the first place. The part that really hurts is..."

"You mustn't," she said. "You mustn't waste precious energy on things of the past. Please, Rance, it's not worth the trouble."

"I'm about to risk my life on a thing of the past. Somehow, I think that finding out about who she was might help me discover who she really is."

The car came to a stop before a large black wrought iron gate. Behind the bars he saw a courtyard with a circular driveway.

"Sometimes it is better not to know too well who you are falling in love with," said Francoise. She removed her glasses and looked plainly at Rance.

"So what's the lesson here? Never fall in love with the agent of another country?"

Her eyes darted quickly away and she pretended to check the rearview mirror.

"Go now," she said. "You are here."

He looked around again. "Where?"

"Isabelle's residence. It is number 51-D."

"How am I supposed to get in to see her?"

Now she smiled. "That is your problem to solve, *mon cher*."

Rance got out of the car, then turned back and spoke to Francoise through the open window. "You still haven't told me why you want Katarina as much as I do."

"I'll call you later. *Ciao*." And she sped off, expertly lost in the maniacal Parisian traffic a second later. Before he could move, another car pulled up where Francoise's had been a second earlier. It was the plain blue car of the Gendarmerie, France's state police.

§

Jenny Ryan's eyes were burning.

Around her, the offices of Javitz & McGillicuddy were darkened and quiet. She looked out her 28th floor window. Below was State Street, leading due east to the waterfront. Perched at the edge of State Street was the Customs Tower, its brightly colored clock face an anachronous Christmas ornament in the hot July night. It read 11:30.

The building engineers had long since shut down the air conditioning system, and now the skyscraper was radiating inward the heat stored up from the 90 degree day. She removed her glasses and rubbed her tired eyes. Then she turned back to the computer screen.

It's in here somewhere. She had been searching WESTLAW, the on-line electronic legal library that gave her access to every federal criminal case in America, for hours without result. I'm just not searching in the right place, she told herself. At the "Define Search" prompt she typed "Northeast" again. And again she came up empty. She sat back and sighed.

There was little solace for her in the city lights of Boston. She stood and stretched in front of the window, looking out into the light dazzled darkness. The view was as magnificent at night as it was during the day, she thought, trying to take her mind off the case search of Katarina Favergé. From her office she could see jets, winking red constellations, taking off and landing at Boston's Logan Airport. Of course, if she had one of the corner offices, she could watch the traffic from the North Shore move at a snail's pace all morning and afternoon. A corner office would be a nice change of venue...

Change of venue, she thought.

She rushed back to her computer and tapped in several more commands.

"Bingo!" She sat back and savored the display on her computer screen.

The United States of American v. Katarina Favergé.

There had been a motion for a change of venue which was granted–which is why I couldn't find it. It had been transferred to a circuit court in Minneapolis, Minnesota. From the menu she clicked on "View."

And came up with a blank screen. Case sealed. There was a number code at the bottom of the screen, and she copied it down. Then she returned to the title screen. *The United States of America v. Katarina Favergé.* Under "Counsel" was listed the name of her attorney: Melvin H. Schwartz.

"Oh, no. Not Schwartz."

The phone rang.

"Marty Donovan," said the voice at the other end. "Attorney Ryan, I presume?"

"Unfortunately."

"Well, it's nice to see that not all you shysters are lackeys."

"Good evening to you, too, Agent Donovan."

"Be nice now, Miss Ryan. I have something for you. You free?"

"Sure. When?"

"Right now. Meet me for a drink. The Purple Shamrock."

§

The folk-rock band Mulligan Stew was winding up its second set of the evening.

The Purple Shamrock had a good crowd for a Tuesday night, the patrons merrily swilling pints of Guinness and singing along with the Irish balladeers on-stage. In the Irish pubs of Boston, St. Patrick's Day was a year round event.

Though she was still dressed in her blue pinstriped Brooks Brothers dress suit, Jenny did not stand out at all in the pub. The place was an eclectic mix of town drunks, drooling college kids and professional men and women. And the occasional FBI agent. Donovan stood alone at the end of the bar. He tipped his hat to Jenny when she arrived.

"Seamus," Marty Donovan called to the bartender as Jenny joined him. "Pull my date here a Black and Tan, would ya?" Seamus the bartender, a hulking red-head, smiled and began drafting the order.

"And what if I don't like Black and Tans?" asked Jenny as she squeezed into the corner beneath the television.

"Then you're a disgrace to your race."

"And what if I don't like being referred to as your 'date'?"

"Then you're queer as a three dollar bill. Any other questions, Counsel?"

"Just one. Why the Purple Shamrock?"

"Because there ain't a mole in the world could get by Seamus' brother Brendan at the front door. And because Seamus himself pulls the best pint in the city. Ain't that right, Seamus?"

Seamus thumped down two pints before them. "Been told, Da, been told."

"Listen," she said, rummaging through her purse, "I think I found-"

"Not until we've had a proper toast," Marty interrupted. He handed Jenny her pint and raised his own. "To the success of Rance Vaughn. May he defeat the great black powers of the world and come home to nest with the prettiest girl at the Purple Shamrock. *Sláinte.*"

Jenny blushed and sipped her pint.

"Agent Donovan," she said, "are you drunk?"

"Could be. That make you nervous?"

"It makes me excited." She smirked and now it was Donovan's turn to blush.

Mulligan Stew was back on stage, and the conversation was suspended long enough to let the band wind its way through a tearful ballad about sons lost to the Crown.

"What have you turned up, Miss Ryan?"

"A dead end. Have you ever heard of an attorney named Melvin Schwartz?"

"What are you, a comedian? The most famous Harvard law professor in the world? Christ, the man is a walking billboard who would defend the Devil against his own mother. If I see the bastard on television one more time I'm going to commit a felony."

"Well, get ready. He was the lawyer for Katarina Favergé in a federal case seven years ago."

"What'd she do?" asked Donovan.

Jenny shrugged. "File sealed. I was hoping you could help me on that one." She took out a notepad and gave him the file number.

"I'll see what I can do. I've been doing a little snooping myself. The guy O'Meara was transporting to Walpole when they were jumped–that Mr. Gengi–well, the software he was peddling was sensitive stuff. So sensitive that the NSA grabbed O'Meara's partner on his way to D.C. I mean they kidnapped him, held him for three days, then dropped him off in front of the Hoover building like nothing ever happened. The Director and the A.G.–that's the director of the Federal Bureau of Investigation and his boss, the Attorney General of the United States of America–are pissed. And guess who's caught in the middle?"

Jenny frowned and shook her head.

"The President. Of the United States. Yup."

"The President?"

"Seems he forgot to tell the right hand what the left hand was doing. So now he's spending a lot of time putting out internecine fires."

"What about the software?" she asked. "What was it?"

Donovan shrugged. "'Sensitive,' as they say in the spook business. The word that I've been able to pick up is that it something akin to the operating system for a nuclear defense system. And that it was supposed to be ultra secret. Not something we want Kim Jong-un or any other nut job to get a hold of."

Jenny still looked perplexed.

"Something bothering you, Counselor?"

"Katarina Favergé," she said. "Just what did she have to do

with all this?"

Donovan rubbed the stubble on his chin and looked around the pub. "At this point, I could only guess."

"And as a veteran of the FBI, what would you guess?"

"Well, nuclear weapons technology is very chic for third world terrorist nations these days. This software that was being developed before it was stolen–what if it were to fall into one of these countries' hands? Could they use it to develop a nuclear weapons program?"

"Wait a second." Jenny had seized on to something. "Think a step beyond for a minute. Our government wouldn't be developing nuclear weapons technology unless it was a step beyond what we have already. So maybe that software represents the next step in the arms race. Maybe that's what makes it so sexy."

"The next step?" asked Donovan.

"Think about it: No country can match the United States for nuclear superiority. So what would you do? Find a way to undermine the whole thing. Invent a way to compromise the high technology of the weapons, right?"

Comprehension spread like bad news in an airport across Donovan's ruddy face. "And," he said, "hold America hostage."

"Katarina Favergé was peddling it to the highest bidder."

§

"*Vos papiers.*"

Rance swallowed hard. Papers. My passport. He reached into his jacket pocket and handed them over to the Gendarmes.

"Is something wrong?" he asked in English.

The officer looked up from the passport.

"May I ask, *m'sieu*, what you are doing here in Paris?"

In an instant he knew he was in the clear. If they wanted you, the French police didn't beat around the bush and read you your rights like American law enforcement officials. In France they grabbed you, threw you in prison and let you think about it for a while. Rance told the truth. Somewhat.

"Business. And pleasure. I'm researching a book and visiting a friend."

The Gendarme handed him back his passport. "Thank you, *m'sieu*. And enjoy your visit."

Taking a deep breath, he watched the police car speed off into traffic. How much of that was chance? Was it a routine stop due to the string of terrorist bombings in Paris this summer? Or were the police watching Francoise? And if so, was she who she said she was? Or was she in the process of going to the other side? Questions for another time. But for the second time, directly after he had left Francoise's company, something had happened. He turned toward the building before him.

To the left of the large wrought iron gate was a door with the number 51 painted above it. He was about to push the buzzer when the door opened.

Ten years could be a long time. Or it could be a short time. To Rance, it felt like an eternity had been spanned in the space of an instant. He knew he wasn't looking at Katarina, but his reaction still surprised him. Though he had met Isabelle only briefly, and then she had only been a budding teenager, her resemblance to her older sister was marked, and it took his breath away.

Isabelle, too, was surprised, but if she recognized him she didn't show it.

"*Oh! Pardonnez-moi, monsiuer,*" she said, nearly stumbling into Rance as she hurriedly left her apartment. Then she locked the door and began walking away.

She was almost around the corner before he called after her.

"Isabelle! Isabelle!" He sprinted to catch up to her, and while he did, studied her face. The confusion on it now looked genuine. It was at that moment that Rance realized that he didn't have the first notion of what to do or say to Isabelle now that he was face to face with her.

"Isabelle, how are you?" he asked in French. She frowned more deeply, probably at his accent.

"I'm sorry, do I know you?"

"Yes you do," he said, this time in English. "I'm Rance Vaughn."

For a second, her eyes widened and she seemed to go pale. Then she turned away.

"I'm sorry, I don't speak English," she replied in French. She began to move away when he grabbed her arm.

"Don't play this game with me. I need your help."

She looked down at her arm and said, in English, "Please, let me go."

She began walking again, but he cut her off.

"I need to find Katarina."

"What is it you want with her?" she asked in French. "Haven't you hurt her enough?"

"What? What are you talking about?"

She stopped to face him. Her face had gone from the pale of surprise to the red of rage. "She always said you would come back, and that when you did, you would try to find her. Well I'm sorry, Mr. Vaughn, I don't know where she is, and if I did I wouldn't tell you. Good-bye."

Isabelle wheeled away from him and began walking. Once again Rance caught up to her.

"Then tell me where I can find my daughter."

Her step stuttered and she gave herself away.

"I'm sorry, I don't know what you are talking about."

"My daughter," he insisted. "Michelle Vaughn Favergé."

Isabelle refused to look at him as she continued marching. She turned into a small park and began cutting across it.

"You flatter yourself, Mr. Vaughn. To think that my sister had a child by you is utterly ridiculous."

They were almost to the edge of the park. Beyond them was the laughter of children at play. Rance didn't hear. All his effort was focused on Isabelle.

"Isabelle!" Once more he grabbed her by the arm. "Isabelle, this is important. I need to find Katarina."

"Why?" she shot back. "So you can once again abandon her for your life of debauchery as a playboy writer? So you can once more break her heart?"

"I don't know what–"

"Good-bye, Mr. Vaughn."

The sidewalk on the opposite side of the street was crowded. He turned reluctantly away as she melted into the tangle of parents and children. Had he stayed where he was, Rance would have seen a young girl about ten years old run into the arms of Isabelle.

"Hello Tante Isabelle," she cried, giving her aunt a hug.

"Hello Michelle. How was school today?"

§

The elevator had stopped.

Not only that, but the power was out, too. Jenny found herself alone in a dead and darkened elevator car somewhere between the 28th floor and the lobby.

"Shit," she said.

Nervously she felt for the handrail. Jenny Ryan, self-made woman, tomboy turned lawyer, was intimidated by almost nothing in this life. Except elevators. Her forehead was instantly transformed into a sweat-soaked arena for alternating hot and cold flashes, and her throat dried up as if she swallowed the sun. She blinked several times, trying to help her pupils dilate, but the elevator car remained pitch black and motionless.

Sometimes, she knew, elevators broke. And when they broke, just like planes, they fell.

She had been fifteen when it happened. Her father, a mechanic for Omega Elevator, the biggest elevator maintenance firm in the nation, had been working in a supposedly secured shaft. But thirty floors above him the safety cable of an elevator car snapped, its emergency brakes failed, and Denis Ryan was crushed beyond recognition.

And in Jenny's nightmares, she was always in the elevator car as it plummeted down to smote the life from her father.

Until she had been recruited out of law school by the firm

of Javitz & McGillicuddy, Jenny had done a fair job of avoiding elevators. In the shocking aftermath of her father's death, her avoidance had been vivid and deliberate, sometimes producing tears. But as she grew older, her fear became latent and repressed, and her constant use of the stairs whenever possible became just another personality quirk.

Javitz & McGillicuddy took up three floors of One Boston Place, a 45-story skyscraper in downtown Boston, and if she wanted to pursue the logical end to her law school toils, she would have to occupy an office on the 27th floor in a building whose stairwell doors were kept locked for safety reasons. In other words, you could use the stairs to escape the building, but not to access it. So, justifying her eclectic behavior by convincing herself and her co-workers that the walking was good exercise, Jenny walked down 27 (28 since she made junior partner) floors each evening.

Except tonight.

Tax season was ages away, yet her biggest client-one of the firm's top accounts-had decided to go into a new business venture, namely business systems. Actually, Albert Derry, founder, president, CEO and chief tyrant of Derry Industries, was simply buying up Delta Information Technologies, a rapidly growing purveyor of communications networks. Derry was in a dither because of the tax law ramifications the buyout could create for him and his company.

In other words, Albert Derry didn't want to pay a lot of taxes next year, so Jenny was on the job from now until next April 15th-longer if she had to file an extension. Her head fairly pounded with the prospect of months of squinting at fine print and contracts. Why tax law? she asked herself. The money. It was always the same answer. Just enough for me to leave it all behind, she assured herself in a conscience-clearing way.

So tonight she had stayed later than usual. It was almost midnight when she walked out of the office. She was exhausted. As she walked through the elevator lobby on her way to the fire escape door, something caught her eye.

The down button illuminated all by itself, as if pushed by a specter. She stopped and the doors to one of the six elevator cars that served the 28th floor opened. A deep sigh escaped her, and with one final look toward the fire escape door she stepped into the car, pushed the button for the lobby and closed her eyes.

Behind her eyelids tears burned into her head. Something else bothered her tonight, something that had bothered her off and on since she was in high school. His name was Rance Vaughn.

But tonight her fickle love for Rance was not what worried her. He hadn't called in over a day, and the last time she had spoken to him he sounded enigmatic. The conversation had been brief, raising more questions than it answered. Court records concerning Katarina Favergé. An FBI agent named Donovan and the set up of another. A sealed court case that looked like a dead end. And he was wanted for questioning in a kidnapping/double murder–after someone had tried twice to kill him.

Death was becoming mundane in its appearances lately. Larry Flemming, a fisherman that lived just down the street from Jenny, was found in his boat with his brains scrambled. And it all had to do with–what? The situation overwhelmed her.

And so she had stepped onto the elevator.

The emergency button. Jenny groped in the dark for the doors to the elevator. To their right, just above the bank of button denoting the floors the car stopped on, was a big red button marked "For Emergency Use Only." Push the button and building security would come to her rescue.

With one hand clamped onto the rail at the back of the car, she reached out into the pitch darkness and felt for the door. It seemed to her that she had to stretch too far out- shouldn't the door be right here? She needed the feel of the door to get her bearings. Where's the door? Her head swooned and she felt her heart pounding. Just when she thought she would scream with fright and frustration, her fingertips grazed the stainless steel smooth of the inside of the elevator door. Taking a deep breath, she let go of the handrail and leaned her weight forward against the door.

And fell.

By her own reckoning, she probably screamed for a solid minute. All of the mute, pent up horror that had followed her for twenty years spilled forth, and she sobbed uncontrollably. Then something happened. She was still alive, and not plum- meting to meet the same fate as her father. Slowly she realized that she was laying face down, her legs still in the elevator car, her upper body stretched out into a dark and empty lobby. She looked around.

Somewhere, far from that lobby, there was a light. It pro- vided just enough illumination so that she could make out shapes. To her left was a desk. To her right were double doors leading to another dark hallway. She tried to get up.

"Please don't. Remain where you are."

Jenny froze. The voice was behind her. In the elevator.

"What-who are you? Are you building security."

"No," said the voice. A man's voice, but it was muffled, almost garbled, as if the speaker were holding a pillow over his mouth. There were several moments of silence, then she tried to get up again. A foot between her shoulder blades forced her back down harshly.

"Hey, who the hell do you-"

"Don't talk," the man said. "Listen."

"What do you want?" Anger began to replace her fear. She wasn't going to die in an elevator accident like her father. She was going to live, and she had a lot of work to do. But this person was stopping her-hurting her. "Did you stop this elevator?"

"There's something you need to know."

"I need to get up. Now let me up-"

"About Katarina Favergé."

Jenny stopped. "What? What did you say?"

"It's not Schwartz's case. Don't look for Schwartz."

"How did you know-"

"Forget the defense, Counselor," the man said. There was something about his voice. Even though it was muffled, it struck something familiar within her. She couldn't place it. "Look to the offense. Turn it upside down. And don't trust them-anyone."

"And who are you? What are you talking about?"

Jenny didn't get the answers to her questions, for she was shoved the rest of the way out of the elevator. The doors closed and she heard the hum of the cables, the hum that had for the last twenty years nauseated her, she heard their humming as they delivered the car down and away from her.

She stood on wobbly legs. Without glancing back she walked directly to the fire escape door and practically ran down the stairs.

§

Instead of following Isabelle, Rance decided to stake out her apartment.

Isabelle's residence on the Boulevard St. Michel in Paris's 6th Arrondissment faced the splendor of the Jardin du Luxembourg. He found a small Café near the traffic snarl of the Place Edmond Rostand and ordered a Heineken. It was afternoon now and the sun was opaque and hot in the white French sky. The beer wasn't as cold as he would have liked it, but he drank it down quickly and ordered another.

He was halfway through his second beer before he realized what he was doing. Six days had elapsed since the helicopter had emerged from the summer haze and tried to cut him in half. And now that daily feeling was reappearing, that feeling of purpose, the thing that ignited a raging thirst within him. It was there the morning after Michael O'Meara died when he ended up in Chatham. And it was back now. It was the knowledge that he was going to drink a lot.

Rance had spent little time analyzing the evolution of his drinking. What mattered only was that he drank daily and always with the goal of becoming drunk. Somewhere in the recesses of his mind he was vaguely aware that the drinking coincided with the money and the relative fame. In his more lucid moments he blamed it on the absurdity of life. In his dark moments he blamed it on himself. It was the chief reason that he and Jenny were still...friends after so long.

As an artist Rance knew there was a place he could get to with his drinking. The place had many different names and different measurements. In the beginning it took only six beers. Then four mixed drinks. Then a pint of bourbon. Then a pitcher of double daiquiris. It depended on the season. In the summer, when he was out on his boat fishing, it was seventeen beers. Eighteen was one too many, qualifying him for shitfaced. Sixteen was one too few. But with seventeen Rance's muse was set free. Trouble was that he could never read the gibberish he scratched down after the seventeenth beer.

This is what he told himself.

Closer to the truth were the tireless clichés of a dysfunctional family, the death of his mother at an impressionable age and his own father's relentless pursuit of inebriation. Added to the formula were the loss of the love of his life, Katarina, and the sudden adulation of the literary and banking worlds.

And as he sat in the Café Somethingorother drinking his third Heineken, he felt it all coming back to him. The possibility that he had a daughter was too much. But this time he wasn't drinking to reach his muse. This time Rance was drinking for the truth, and if he couldn't get that, he'd settle for drunk.

"Vous voulez un menu, monsiuer?"

The Café was really a bistro and they were beginning to serve dinner. The waiter asked him if he wanted a menu and Rance nodded yes. What the hell, he thought. In Paris one should at least eat like the Parisians. When the waiter returned he ordered a double Scotch and checked his watch. He was supposed to meet Francoise back at his hotel later tonight.

There was a loud thud in the center of his chest. Along his hairline a fine stencil of sweat appeared. And his back shivered despite the flush of alcohol upon it. Francoise Chaumont had made an extraordinary impression on him. Her image stirred him sexually, but not in the delicate, compassionate way he was used to. When he thought of Francoise he felt a savage tightening of his sexual appetite. Especially now, with the aid of beer and Scotch.

The waiter returned to take his order. Another double Scotch right away. Then fixed 200 franc menu. An assorted smoked meat plate for an entree. Something vaguely Italian for the main course–a red meat and vegetable sauce over pasta. Salad, then a selection of cheeses. And a good red to go along with it. A Chateauneuf du Pape. No dessert. We'll talk cognac.

Things were getting complicated, but then again, that's what things did. You can't go backwards in time. Only forward. So that's what I'll do. Damn the torpedoes. The waiter brought his Scotch. I'm doing this for Michael, Rance thought. I promised him. I promised me.

The anxious moment passed and he settled down to dinner. The food was only okay, but that was because he was well buzzed by then. The wine, on the other hand, was outstanding. His last glass, the one he had with the cheese, was the best, and Rance gave his compliments to the waiter. The man neither smiled or frowned. Nor did he react when Rance ordered a large snifter of cognac. The waiter simply asked him if he would enjoy a cigar along with his cognac, and Rance said yes, he would.

Amazing. Not only was he never question about the amount of alcohol he was ingesting, but he was offered a cigar after his meal. He renewed his promise to himself about buying a flat on the Île St. Louis and retiring to Paris.

It was now after ten p.m. Rance paid his tab and left with his cigar. There had been no signs of activity at the entrance to Isabelle's apartment for the last four hours. He weaved across the Boulevard St. Michel and was nearly killed when he tripped over a crack in the pavement. The driver admonished him and Rance staggered to the sidewalk. Closer to your muse than you think, he thought to himself.

After ringing the bell three times and receiving no response, he moved away from the apartment. For a second he had the notion of walking back to his hotel, and though the cool night air felt fine, he didn't know his way around Paris that well. Besides, he had no idea how long it would take, and he didn't want to miss Francoise. His heart was racing as he hailed the cab.

"Hotel Lyon-Mulhouse," he told the cabby.

Rance wanted to doubt the existence of a daughter. It was just too impossible. But two different and disparate sources had confirmed the existence of a daughter to him, and it would be difficult to disbelieve them both. He would have liked to have devoted more time to the thought, but the flash of blue lights caught his eye.

Sitting forward in the backseat, he craned his neck as the cab driver entered the rotary of the Place de la Bastille. Outside the Hotel Lyon-Mulhouse were swarms of police cars, their blue lights plying the humid night air. His hotel. No coincidence. Rance spoke to the cabby quickly.

"I'm sorry, I've made a mistake. Could you please take me to the Place de la Republique?"

"*Pas de problem*." No problem, grunted the cabby.

To his horror, the cabby took the Boulevard Marchais spoke, driving right past the entire scene. Rance sunk down, permitting only his eyes to peek out the window.

Gendarmes were everywhere. He saw the hotel's proprietor, Mr. Bertrand, gesticulating to one of the policemen. And then he saw something beyond belief, something so shocking that he had to cover his mouth to keep from crying out.

Francoise was standing out in front of the hotel. Rance might have been able to rationalize, to justify her presence there; they were supposed to meet there. Maybe something else happened and she had to assume her professional role. But the presence of the big red-head obliterated all that. The man that had tried twice to kill him was standing next to Francoise, talking to her with an animation that could only denote familiarity.

"Jesus H. Christ," Rance said to himself.

§

He tried not to think about it.

At the Place de la Republique Rance took another cab back to Isabelle's. He wasn't surprised when there was no answer to his ring of her buzzer. A quick glance into the building's lobby revealed its layout. There were three floors, six apartments in all, denoted A through F. A, C and E were on the building's left side; B, D and F on the right. Isabelle was in apartment D.

Outside Rance quickly determined that the second balcony would-should-belong to Isabelle. A cursory look around and he was satisfied that the building had no security. A second later he was scaling the high fence that enclosed a small parking area and courtyard behind the building. From the top of the tall fence he was able to reach the bottom of Isabelle's balcony. Only with a monumental effort did he chin himself enough to swing his foot up. A second later he was entering the apartment.

This was it, he thought. They said I had a daughter, and they said she lived with Isabelle. Though the room was dark, there was enough ambient light to see that there were no children's toys laying about. He found the hall that led to the bedrooms. At the end there were two doors-the bedrooms.

Without having realized it before, Rance knew now that there had been more to this undertaking than his promise to Michael O'Meara. The implications of national security had not really stirred any deeply intense patriotic feelings within him. What had moved him was his committed sense of right and wrong. More than an allegiance to a nation, he was moved by the need to do the right thing. And now, to find out the truth about his daughter.

Turning, he took a tentative step down the hallway. Someone slipped a key into the lock on the front door, and Rance had only a second to turn around as Isabelle entered the living room and turned on the light.

"*Oh! Mon dieu!*" she cried, and would have continued had Rance not covered the distance between them in an instant and clamped his hand over her mouth. Her eyes went white with fear but she didn't try and struggle.

"Isabelle, I'm not here to harm you, do you understand that?"

She nodded.

"I'm going to take my hand away now. Please don't scream, all right?"

She nodded again, never taking her eyes away from his as he slipped his hand from her mouth.

"What are you doing here?" she said in a voice barely above a whisper.

It was a good question. "I need your help."

"I told you everything I know about my sister," she said. Realizing that he was not going to hurt her, Isabelle moved away from him and took off the light sweater she was wearing. There was a mirror hanging next to the door, and she stood before it, fixing her hair.

"What about my daughter?"

Isabelle froze. Her hands fell to her sides and she turned to face him. Her eyes, however, went past him, out to the open doors of the balcony and beyond.

"Yes," she said.

"Yes?"

"Yes, you do have a daughter. Is that what you wanted to hear? Yes, Rance, you have a daughter by my sister, a beautiful little girl, an angel who apparently inherited none of her parents' faults." Her eyes drifted up to his. "But she is gone now."

"Gone?"

She turned back to the mirror. "For the summer vacations. She has gone to be with some cousins far from Paris–in the country. Far from all this, this madness."

"Has someone else tried to find out about Katarina?"

Her answer was a smirk as she walked into the living room. From a case on an end table she produced a cigarette and lit it. One drag seemed to settle her. She had the floor now. She was in control. She was not the one looking over her shoulder, at least for the moment. It was a feeling she liked.

"Who has not tried? Today I spend half the day with the police. I tell them all the same thing–the truth. That I have not heard from my sister in over a year. That she has abandoned her daughter, and that even now I am in the process of legally adopting her."

Rance jumped at the words.

"That surprises you? Yes, it is true. Please don't try to stop me, Rance. It would only make things terribly messy. Besides, there are no documents stating that you are Michelle's father."

"But her name–it's Michelle Vaughn Favergé, right? And there's DNA and blood tests, and–"

She grabbed his forearm with force. "And what? And then you will take her from her home, the only family she has ever known? To go to America, and sit on a fishing boat with you while you get drunk all day?"

"How did you–"

She turned away, speaking now to the warm breeze that floated in from the still city. "Before I began the adoption process I hired an investigator. It was quite costly to track you down, but that was only because you were in America. Finding you was easy. I needed to know what I may be up against if somehow it was discovered that you were Michelle's father."

Rance was speechless. His life had just been neatly surmised for him by a someone he had only met once ten years ago. The shock of it physically hurt him. That and the fact that everybody seemed to know everything about him.

"Isabelle?"

She turned to him.

"I don't see any reason why you shouldn't adopt her. Up until a week ago, I didn't know I even had a daughter. That's part of what all this is about, and I thank you for being honest with me. But I would like to make one request. Some day, when this is all over, I'd like the chance to get to know her–if you don't think it would be too disruptive."

She visibly softened.

"No, I don't think that it would be disruptive. It might even be helpful as she grows older."

For a few seconds they stood there, out of words. Then the rest of reality reappeared before Rance. He was about to speak when she did.

"I'm sorry, how rude of me. Please sit down. Won't you have a drink?"

He decided that he had drunk enough for one night. "Coffee, if it's not too much trouble."

Isabelle raised an eyebrow. "Not at all."

She joined him on the couch with the coffee.

"Is there anything at all you can tell me about Katarina?"

"Maybe. But you must tell me what this is all about. I don't like being picked up by the police."

He shrugged and spoke cautiously. "I'm not sure I know everything myself." As of right now he trusted no one. "As far as I can tell Katarina is involved in some kind of theft of government material."

"But what could you possible do?"

The image of Michael O'Meara was evoked in his mind. "A friend-someone in law enforcement connected with the case-thought that since I had connections to her I might be able to find Katarina."

"Are you working again for your government?"

"No."

Isabelle looked down, as if she were studying the pile of her carpet.

"What is it?"

She took a deep breath and spoke.

"I have not heard from my sister for over a year. I fear that she might even be dead. Before that, she only checked in infrequently. She hasn't seen Michelle in over two years. The last I heard from her was when she was married-sometime last year to a Swiss lawyer or banker. She signed the adoption papers and that was it. I don't know where she is."

"Why did you say that you fear she might be dead?"

"The man she married, soon after he was involved in some kind of scandal in Zurich. There was a trial-embezzlement, I believe, but with the money of some very nasty people-and he was aquitted. I tried calling several times, but he told me that Katarina had left him and he doesn't know where she is."

"This man-what was his name?"

"Hurlimann. Franz Hurlimann."

§

Rance knew that sleep would be difficult.

Isabelle had offered him the couch when he had explained-in the vaguest terms-his predicament. He lay there in the dark, his mind awash with activity. After an hour of attempted sleep, he got up and went out onto the balcony.

Looking down, he could see that it was higher up than he had thought, and he was thankful that he had not taken the time to look back down when he was climbing. By virtue of a slope in the back, the balcony offered a decent view of some of the lights of Paris, and he gazed out upon them.

He was trying to decide whether or not he should contact Francoise. He wanted to believe that her presence with the big red-head was somehow coincidental. She even told him that her agency was running his photograph against the ones in their computer banks. As far as he could see, there were two possible explanations.

First, Francoise was not who she said she was. Though Rance was reluctant to admit it, bad things did seem to happen to him when they parted company. And the fact that she had been with the man that had tried twice to kill him did not bode well. But there was something about her that he had seized upon when he met her. A part of him said that it was sexual and that he should beware-he's already been down that road. But there was a quality to her, however, that made him doubt she was aligned with whomever was trying to kill him. A quality of honesty.

That brought him to the second explanation. And that was that the big red-head was a part of something else, something bigger, something that gave him access to countries in an official capacity. And that he was using this official capacity to try and get to Rance. Then something else occurred to him.

What if he-like Francoise-was also trying to find Katarina. Would he try and use Rance to find her? That didn't make sense. I can't find Katarina if I'm dead.

Though he didn't believe Francoise to be two-timing him, Rance decided not to reestablish contact with her. He would pursue the Hurlimann lead on his own in the morning. Zurich.

Rance had sat down in one of the chairs on the balcony. The warm evening air soothed him, and he closed his eyes for just a moment.

§

When he opened them again, it was morning.

Stiff from sleeping in the awkward position, Rance got up and went in. There were no sounds; Isabelle must have been sleeping. He didn't want to wake her, but he needed to leave right away and he was hoping that she might be able to help him leave France by means other than public transportation. If there were that many police at his hotel last night, the airports, train stations and car rental agencies were sure to be watched today.

He knocked on her door. There was no answer.

"Isabelle?"

He knocked harder. The door, already ajar, creaked open. She was still in bed.

"Isabelle?"

Something fluttered in his belly. For no reason he felt a little dizzy.

"Isabelle?"

As he walked to her bed his fingertips began to tingle. The pressure in the room became painful on his legs, and his feet dragged sluggishly. With a liquid detachment he felt his spirit ooze up and away from his body, a feeling that was becoming all to familiar lately. He saw his hand drift out on a stagnant current of air, his fingers reaching for her...

The moment he touched her shoulder his hand recoiled as a thousand volts raced up his arm. Her back was turned to him and the sheet looked hard, as if it had frozen in place over her body. A thick, fruity odor began to tickle his nose, and though he knew without looking, Rance slid the sheet away from Isabelle. Her skin was hard and ice cold. Slowly he rolled her over.

Her eyes, round and dark like Katarina's, were open and opaque, fixed on a point ins space somewhere beyond his shoulder. In the center of her forehead there was a small bullet hole.

§

The 18th at the Potomac Country Club was one of the finest finishing holes in the country.

Forget Doral and Pebble Beach. The members of the Potomac Country Club, one of whom was the President of the United States, had dedicated themselves to improving their course in hopes of attracting a PGA tournament stop.

The course was in its mid-summer splendor. It started tough with a dog-leg par 4 over a twisting tributary of the Potomac and finished brutally with the challenging par 5 18th. In between were sixteen twisting, undulating holes that commanded a course rating of 73.9. That meant that it took an average of 73.9 strokes for players holding a PGA card to make through eighteen holes.

The President reveled in its challenge. He had been playing hard all year long in hopes of breaking 80. Breaking 80 here, he knew, would be like shooting 74 or 75 anywhere else. And today his goal was within his sights.

His drive off the 18th tee had drifted to the right, settling in the rough 250 yards away. Taking a 1-iron from his bag and invoking the image of Jack Nicklaus, the President smashed the ball 220 yards onto the skirt of the green, carrying a nasty water hazard along the way. He had three shots left to make par, which would give him a 79 for the day. His heart was pounding in his chest as he drove his cart up to the ball.

"That was quite a golf shot, Mr. President."

Jerry Abel, the club pro and former U.S. Open champion, was the President's playing partner today. He was the President's playing partner most days, along with two Secret Service agents in another cart. Abel hated playing with the President. He knew it meant four hours of free lessons, trying to help the Commander in Chief break 80. But what really disturbed him was the team of Secret Service agents constantly lurking along the edge of the course, traipsing through the woods, examining every green before allowing them to hit up. It unnerved Abel, and he usually played poorly.

"Oh, Jerry, I can feel it. I'm close."

The President got out and examined his shot. The green at 18 was two-tiered, with the upper portion at the rear. Today the pin was up in the back, leaving the President with 75 feet of fringe and nauseatingly undulating real estate to work with.

"Jerry, I think I'm going to run it up with a 7-iron. What do you think?"

Jerry thought that he was going to switch party affiliations before the next election. The previous night had been spent drinking bourbon and screwing one of the member's wives out on the 6th green. He hadn't slept at all when the President's secretary phoned him to tell him he'd be up early playing with "The Chief," as she called him.

Abel examined the President's lie. "You've got a lot of green in front of you, and none of it's good. You've got a great lie. I'd use a wedge and drop it up there gently, knock it in with two putts and you've got your 79." And I'll have some peace and quiet to sleep this thing off.

"Pitching wedge, huh?" The President had a pathological fear of pitching wedges. It was the worst part of his game. His putting wasn't much better, but his pitching–good God! The whining approach of a golf cart broke their attention.

A Secret Service agent was driving. His passenger was the National Security Advisor to the President, Richard Armstrong. Armstrong was all work, habitually putting in sixteen- and seventeen-hour days. It was how he had built himself up into a multi-millionaire at the age of forty as a zealous lawyer representing some of the biggest names in the computer world, and how he stayed there until the age of 55, when the then candidate for president called him to be his campaign manager. Armstrong's reward had been the appointment as the President's NSA and twenty-hour days. His boss's work ethic irritated him.

"Good afternoon, Mr. President," Armstrong said tersely. "Jerry."

Armstrong continued to gaze at Abel for a moment, then the President caught on.

"Jerry, why don't you go hit a few out of the bunker," the President suggested, flashing Abel a disarming smile. The President watched Abel walk to the other side of the green and light a cigarette, then he turned to Armstrong.

"This better be good, Dick. I'm close. I'm really close."

"We have a problem, sir." It was all Armstrong could do to control his annoyance with his boss. If he had to listen to the banter about breaking 80 one more time he was going to scream. Instead, he bit his lip.

"Sir, I met with the DPI this morning and he said there's still an problem controlling the SHAKESPEARE leak."

"SHAKESPEARE? Again?"

Picked by Armstrong himself, SHAKESPEARE was the code name assigned to the operation initiated several months ago. The President was not supposed to be involved with operations on such an intimate level, but his own bumbling had led him to discover it. So now he had become a player.

"Our loose pistol showed up in France one step ahead of our own operative. He sufficiently screwed things up so that we're essentially back to square one."

The color drained from the President's face. "What are you telling me this for, Dick? I told you, I don't want to know." He turned and looked back at his shot.

Armstrong was biting his lip again. "You might get a call from the French ambassador asking what is going on. They have been helping out over there, so they are going to want to know what the story is."

"I'll deny everything. Tell 'em it's their problem."

"Yes, sir. Well, I just wanted to keep you up to speed, in case the press gets to you before you get back."

Armstrong turned and walked back to the golf cart. He was almost there when the President called out to him.

"Dick! Get somebody on that, will ya?"

"He's on his way, sir."

The President skulled his chip shot badly, sending the ball careening into the thick underbrush. His next shot sailed over the green and buried itself in a bunker.

"Pick up my ball, Jerry," the President said with preternatural calm as he got back into the golf cart. "We're through here."

§

"Agent Donovan? Could I have a word with you?"

Donovan looked up from his paper work. Before him stood a large-framed man in a jacket and tie. Out of years of habit, Donovan took the man's measure, noting the unremarkable face devoid of emotion, the clean cut hair. What stood out to Donovan immediately were the man's hands. They were huge and callused, incongruous for the way he was dressed. They also held out wallet containing a piece of identification marking him as an employee of the Central Intelligence Agency.

"My name is James Devlin."

Donovan's eyes narrowed. Ten years ago he and Michael O'Meara were the point men on a drug running scheme involving fishing boats out of the port of New Bedford. They teamed up with the Coast Guard and jumped a swordfisher filled with dope–and CIA operatives. The CIA had been running some central American infiltration scam, and they had been using drugs to do it. The Director himself personally called O'Meara and Donovan and told them to forget whatever it was they had been working on. Since then Donovan had nothing but spite and contempt for the CIA.

"Won't you sit down, Mr. Devlin?" said Donovan, graciously offering him a chair. "What can I do for you?"

"I understand you've had contact recently with a Rance Vaughn."

Donovan smiled. "I'm sorry, Mr. Devlin, but you're mistaken. Why would I have contact with a man wanted by the FBI and every other law enforcement agency in the area–unless, of course, I was arresting him?"

Donovan continued smiling but his eyes went steely and cold. He knew Devlin would be reading his eyes and the message he sent was: Fuck off. Devlin didn't blink, his expression unchanged.

"Agent Donovan, I don't have to tell you that this is a matter of national security–"

"Then call the NSA," Donovan interrupted. "Mr. Devlin, the door is right behind you. Walk straight through it and you'll come to the elevators. Push 'L' to get the lobby and leave the building the same way you came in." He looked back down to the report he was writing.

That time he got to Devlin. The big man seemed to recoil for a second. Then he did as Donovan had suggested. When he was gone, Donovan got up and went to the window, watching Devlin exit the building and cross the street, where he got into a car and drove away.

Twenty minutes later Donovan got off the red line branch of the MBTA, Boston's metro, at Harvard Square in Cambridge. He made his way through the crowds of students, street musicians, and freaks to a Chinese restaurant called the Hong Kong. Upstairs at the mostly empty bar he ordered a beer and made a call on his cell phone. When he discovered that Rance was no longer at his hotel in Paris, he snapped the phone closed.

§

The border guard thrust his round head into the window.

"*Rien à déclarer*," said Rance. Nothing to declare.

The guard looked at him. "30 francs. Swiss." He tapped the windshield.

Suddenly he realized. It cost 30 Swiss francs to use the highways in Switzerland. The sticker went on your windshield and was good for a year, but it cost about twenty Euros. He paid and was waived through. He had entered Basel, Switzerland.

That morning, armed only with a map, he had taken Isabelle's car and left Paris. He had mixed feelings about it, but he quickly convinced himself it was the safest and fasted way out. Rance decided that he was alive today because he had fallen asleep out on the balcony. When whoever killed Isabelle came in to the apartment, they failed to check out on the balcony, and he was spared. But taking her car was a risky proposition.

If Isabelle was murdered legitimately–that is to say by some conventional entity–then Rance figured he'd have a two or three day head start. But if she was killed by the same people who managed to fill the lobby of the Hotel Lyon-Mulhouse with local police and foreign agents, his chances were worse, because whoever killed Isabelle would make a call to the police and let them know, probably with the hopes of pinning it on him. And his fingerprints were all over her apartment.

Taking side streets and back roads, Rance made his way slowly out of Paris. An hour later he picked up the Autoroute A6 which, five and a half hours after that, brought him to the Swiss border. During the long drive he was careful to observe the speed limit, not a difficult thing given that in France the speed limit on highways was 85 miles per hour.

Now he was in Switzerland, and he had to make a decision about continuing with Isabelle's car. His pockets were fat with money; he had stopped at an ATM near Isabelle's and maxed out his credit cards. And since his cards were gold, that translated into a lot of Euros. But the cash would have to last him, for he knew that credits cards left an electronic trail that a blind man could follow.

If he kept driving her car, he risked being identified by the Swiss police. Some kind of bulletin would surely be posted concerning a stolen vehicle of French registration–if he was linked to the murder scene. The answer to that question was obvious; less obvious was the time frame. If he abandoned the car it would surely be discovered and traced back, thus tipping off his movement to Switzerland. He had an idea.

Doubling back, he made his way to the Basel airport, a facility that was split down the middle by the French-Swiss border. Staying on the Swiss side, he went to the large, long-term parking lot. Finding an out of the way corner, he nosed Isabelle's car in. After a quick check around, Rance skulked out of the car and stole the front license plate off a Swiss car. He then replaced Isabelle's rear plate with the Swiss one. He removed her front plate and buried it in the trunk, then walked to the car rental counter where, under the name of Albert Cummin, French businessman, he rented a car with cash and drove to Zurich.

To anyone checking car tags in the garage, Isabelle's car would appear to be of Swiss registration. Since the lot was long term, it could be weeks before anyone became suspicious enough to run the registration on the car. And by then he planned on being back in the States.

The Swiss highways were in excellent shape, and the countryside was magnificent, right out of *The Sound of Music*, but Rance was concentrating on other things. Among them how to find Franz Hurlimann, Katarina's erstwhile husband.

A feeling swept over him then, the same feeling he had upon landing in Paris two days earlier, that events were beyond his control, that he was just a marionette manipulated by some thrill-seeking gods somewhere with too much time on their hands. He thought that if he let go of the steering wheel and closed his eyes he would wake up on Hurlimann's doorstep-or in heaven.

Another feeling crept over him, too. It was the feeling that this was all somehow staged, a production performed for his benefit alone. It was fiction, just as his literary career had been too much to believe.

In an attempt to seize his racing mind, he clenched the steering wheel tightly and focused his mind's eye. There he saw Michael's darkened and lifeless face. There he saw his promise.

§

It was easier than he thought.

The offices of Uberbank Suisse were located one block off of the Bahnhofstrasse, Zurich's Rodeo Drive. According to Isabelle, Hurlimann was a VP with Uberbank, so Rance figured his place of work was a good place to start looking for him.

But Rance's clouded and exhausted mind forget to tell him how to get beyond the phalanx of security personnel in the lobby. It was four p.m. Why not just ask? he thought.

"Excuse me," he said in French to one of the guards. "I have an appointment with Mr. Hurlimann. Could you direct me to his offices?"

Though the Swiss all spoke at least four languages–German, English, French and their native Swiss-German–Rance was wary of giving himself up as an American. His French was probably accented enough to define him only as a native speaker of English, giving him a little breathing room with the possibility of being taken for a British subject. The guard frowned.

"Mr. Hurlimann?" the man said almost rudely. The Swiss-at least the native German speakers, which included Zurich-were notorious for their disdain of the French, and in fact preferred speaking English. "Mr. Hurlimann has left for the day." The guard turned and walked away from Rance before he could be thanked.

Frustrated, his next stop was a phone directory. Among the many Hurlimann's living in this part of Switzerland, only one had the first initial F. Thirty minutes later he pulled into the little hamlet of Unterageri.

The village was nestled along the northern shores of the Agerisee, the lake of Ageri, a stunning mountain lake in the foothills of the Alps. The Alps themselves were jagged white ghosts tearing up into the pale southern sky. Whether due to the crispness of the air, the lack of sleep or the excitement of moving closer to Katarina, Rance felt a pleasant lightheadedness began to buoy him.

Even the small mountain roads were well marked in Switzerland, and after consulting the map of the village and its environs, which was posted in the town square, Rance made his way to Seestrasse, Number 38. A sprawling brown chalet-style house carved into the side of the hill that overlooked the Agerisee marked Hurlimann's residence. As he drove up Rance saw a man bent over in a large garden located on one side of the chalet.

The closing of the car door brought the man's head up. Squat and dirty, the man looked to be some sort of laborer probably hired to tend to Herr Hurlimann's tomatoes.

"Excuse me," Rance said in English this time. "I'm trying to find Franz Hurlimann."

The man removed his gloves and walked to the fence that enclosed the busy garden. He produced a handkerchief and wiped his brow and balding head, then looked up in such a way that Rance suddenly realized he was not talking to a lowly gardener.

"You have found him," he said in German-accented but otherwise perfect English.

Forgoing any ruse aimed at protecting his identity, Rance introduced himself as Katarina's ex-husband. This man, he decided, would be able to see through that. But when he added that he was also Michelle's father, Hurlimann's demeanor changed, going from closely guarded to ingratiating.

"Won't you join me for some iced tea, Mr. Vaughn?" Hurlimann motioned toward the deck attached to the chalet.

On the deck a short, angry looking woman appeared with a tray containing a pitcher of iced tea and some butter cookies.

"I'm sorry I don't have something more substantial to offer you, Mr. Vaughn," Hurlimann said graciously. "Will you be staying for dinner?"

Rance was thrown off by the man's hospitality toward a complete stranger.

"No, but thank you for offering."

"Such a wonderful little girl, Michelle. How is she doing?"

Another checking move. "I haven't actually seen her...yet."

"So, you are trying to find Katarina, too, yes?"

Rance nodded and sipped the iced tea, which tasted delicious after the events of the last twenty-four hours.

"Devil of a woman. I'd like to find her myself. She 'borrowed' some of my money and disappeared some time ago. I've had no luck in tracking her down."

"So you're still officially married."

"As you are well aware, it takes two parties to sign divorce papers."

Sensing that Hurlimann chose his words carefully no matter what language he spoke, he carefully began admitting morsels of truth.

"I only recently discovered that Michelle was my daughter, Mr. Hurlimann. When I tried to contact Katarina about seeing–maybe even getting custody of–my daughter, I learned that she had once again vanished."

"Then it was Isabelle who sent you here."

He hesitated. This would link him from Isabelle to Switzerland-but he had no choice.

"You were the only one she could think of that might know of her whereabouts."

"Lovely woman, Isabelle." Hurlimann smiled and looked out over the peaceful lake. A cold shill blew up Rance's back. "But I'm afraid I can't be of must service to you."

"You said she stole some money from you when she left?"

Hurlimann sipped his iced tea thoughtfully.

"As I'm sure you are aware, Mr. Vaughn, Katarina travels in...clandestined circles. I don't know what exactly she does, but I do know that it is illegal and that the governments of several nations-including your own-would like to find her."

"Isn't there anything she did that might tell you where she has gone to?"

"She left me over a year ago. I tried to follow her, but the trail ended at the airport. Or, I should say, at the airport where she landed. Kazakhstan."

Rance drew a deep breath and rose.

"Thank you very much, Mr. Hurlimann. You've been of great assistance to me."

The two men shook hands and Rance walked back to his car. After the car had turned out of the driveway, Hurlimann picked up a cell phone and made a call.

§

Kazakhstan. The name festered in his head like a deeply buried splinter.

In his rear view mirror, Rance saw Ageri fade away. Though it was mid-summer in Europe and readable light would be available until ten p.m., the sun had already disappeared behind the high Swiss hills, setting the place with bright blue sky and deeply shadowed swales.

Fatigue began to drain him, and he found himself rubbing his eyes as he tired to navigate his way out of the hills. A sign appeared, advertising the city of Zug below. He took the turn and hoped to find a hotel for the night.

And then he didn't know what.

First he would try to call Jenny and Donovan. Perhaps they had come upon something more substantial than the cold shadow he was chasing. Kazakhstan was someplace he didn't know the first thing about.

But maybe Donovan did. Maybe, as he had done already, he could provide Rance with a contact, someone who knew the lay of the land.

In the same breath that thought fizzled as he remembered Francoise. Though he still wasn't totally convinced that she had turned on him, his experiences with her had been less than exemplary. True, she had located Isabelle for him, but beyond that...

There was more to her. He knew that by profession she was enigmatic, but there was a deeper dimension to her, something that she hadn't shown him, something she had thus far only betrayed with her eyes. And in those eyes Rance saw something true.

The shadows of the hills across the road contrasted the brightness of the western sky, playing tricks with his burning eyes. He found himself stepping on the brake over nothing, incurring the wrath of the locals who negotiated these switch-back stretches of pavement at breakneck speed.

As he slowed to enter another hairpin turn, he saw a large car appear suddenly in his rear mirror. It sat on his bumper and mimicked his moves.

"Okay, buddy, give me a second to get through this turn-"

The smash of metal cut him short. He felt the rear end of his car fishtail, and before he could apply any brakes the car had gone over the edge of a steep bank, skidding to a stop only when it lodged itself in a stand of saplings.

The shock of the crash was the worst of it. His seatbelt held him fast, saving him from a trip through the windshield, though it did leave his chest with an aching bruise.

"Son of a bitch!"

Rance swore angrily as he extracted himself from the car. The ramifications of the accident were for the moment lost on him. Right now he wanted to get out and pound whoever had hit him into-

The bright sky silhouetted the figure of a man, and for a terrifying second he experienced a horrific deja-vu, taking him to the marsh in Duxbury. The man standing on the edge of the embankment above him held a gun in his outstretched hand. It pointed at Rance.

It wasn't Big Red. That mattered little right now. What did matter was the fact that he was once more looking down the wrong end of a gun barrel-again. If it weren't so deadly a situation, he'd feel irritated.

But vexation took a back seat to the fear that crimped his throat. Who the hell was this, and how did he-

Hurlimann.

"Son of a bitch," Rance said for the second time in as many minutes.

"You should have stuck to booze and books, Mr. Vaughn," the man said. His accent was mid-European nowhere, cultured and non-descript, and though Rance couldn't see his face clearly, he thought the man smiled.

"Yeah?" Rance answered. "You should have let me."

For a second the smile left the man's face and he brought the gun up. Just as Rance saw the barrel level itself with him, the man's head exploded. That's funny, Rance thought as the semi-headless body crumpled to the ground. His head didn't look like it was going to explode.

As suddenly as it all happened, it was over, the peace of the Swiss hills returning to the forefront of the atmosphere. Overwhelmed by a liquid feeling in his joints, Rance sank to his knees and began to shiver. This was getting out of hand, and he decided on the spot that if he could get out of this, he was done, gone. Already he was thinking about getting very, very drunk. Sorry, Michael.

Then he saw Francoise.

She kept her gun trained on the dead man for good measure as she approached. With a high heeled foot she kicked the body, but it didn't move. Replacing her pistol into a bag at her side, she came awkwardly down the slope to Rance.

"Are you all right?" She was there, kneeling beside him, looking at him with eyes that held real concern.

And tears.

"Francoise," he said. "Jesus Christ, what the hell are you doing here?"

With a soft hand she caressed his face. Then she smiled. "Someone had to keep an eye on you."

§

Thankfully, the road was not heavily traveled.

Rance's car had ended up on its wheels, coming to rest on a shelf about fifty feet below the road. A few feet from the car's wheels there was a drastic drop off of at least a hundred feet. Only upon second look did Rance realize how close he had come to dying–again. But the situation also held advantages.

Putting the car in neutral and giving it a shove, Rance and Francoise watched it plummeted into the dark thicket below. Next they did the same for the other man's car. Before placing his dead body in the driver's seat, they searched him for identification, but he had none. He did, however, have a gun that would no longer be of any use to him, and Rance convinced Francoise that if so many people were going to try to kill him, he should at least be able to defend himself.

"It is a Glock 10 millimeter," Francoise said, expertly inspecting the weapon's action. "Fully automatic with a 15 round chamber." Along with it came two extra clips of ammunition. "Here, take this instead." She reached inside her leather jacket and Produced her own gun, a sleek looking French model. "Be careful with this," she said, reluctantly handing him the gun.

The man's car went down the slope, smashing into the first car. They quickly smoothed over the blood stains and tired tracks in the dirt and sped away.

"Who do you think he was?"

"What?" Rance replied incredulously.

"That man who tried to kill you. Who was he?"

He was dumbfounded. "You mean that you followed him to me and you don't know who he was?"

She smiled at that and gave him a sultry look that was at once endearing and condescending.

"No, Rance, I was following you."

Now he was lost. She explained.

"When I left you in Paris it was at Isabelle's. We were supposed to meet later that night, but you must have obviously seen what happened at the hotel and gone back to the only place you could think of–Isabelle's."

"And what did go on at the hotel?" He was not looking at her, instead to keeping his gaze locked on the road before him.

"I don't really know. I thought you might tell me."

"Are you joking?"

Her plain stare told him she wasn't.

"I received a call from your CIA that they were going to apprehend an American fugitive. They knew the French were involved in this case, so the call was one of courtesy. I called your hotel room immediately, but there was no answer."

"Then who was that man I saw you talking to in front of the hotel? The big red-headed man?"

For a moment she frowned.

"Ah, you mean Agent Jackson? Why, he was with the CIA of course."

Rance's face fell ashen, giving him away. She touched his arm.

"Are you all right?"

"Francoise, that man is the man who tried to execute me back home before I came over here. He's the one I saw at the airport when I arrived in France."

"*Mon dieu.* Rance, you must think I had something to do with that, but it is not true, I swear. He said he was with the CIA, and that they were seeking you for questioning. The Paris police were co-operating with them, that is how they came to know your hotel."

In the fading light her eyes became deeper and darker and as Rance looked into them he was sure that they could not lie.

"Where are we going now?" he asked.

"Back to France."

"What! Are you crazy? Every cop in the country must be after me because-"

"Because why? Because they think you killed Isabelle?"

"How did you know I was there?"

"Rance, you're fingerprints were everywhere. If you are asking me do I believe you killed Isabelle, the answer is no. I don't believe that you are capable of killing unless you yourself are faced with death. Besides, whoever killed Isabelle was a professional, quite possibly the man who tried to kill you today."

"You mean that I may have been followed...?"

"That is exactly what I mean."

"And how did you find me?"

"Mostly luck. In Isabelle's address book was the name of Franz Hurlimann. The address was the same as Katarina's last known address. Since you really couldn't stay in Paris, it occurred to me that your next step might be to find this man who was sharing his address-"

"Married. They were married."

"I drove to his address and waited, calculating the time it would take for you to arrive."

"I didn't know I was so predictable. What about my friend back there?"

She shrugged. "He pulled out in front of me as you drove away."

"Jesus." His hands began to shake. Taking a deep breath, he grabbed his knees in an effort to quiet them.

"There was nothing you could do." She reached over and took his hand, immediately quelling the trembling. "Be happy that you are alive and with me."

Her smile cut through the surrounding dusk, and in the passing headlights Rance caught flashes of her beauty: the soft line of her neck; her long legs, slightly uncrossed, jutting from her skirt; and her hands, delicate but so strong and so cold, he knew. He was beginning to relax.

"And now you're taking me back to France."

"Alsace," she corrected. "To a place where you will be safe for some days, a place where we can formulate a plan."

"Kazakhstan," Rance said.

"Kazakhstan?"

Relating to her the story that Hurlimann told her about Katarina's last address, Rance added that it could have been a false lead.

"That is one of the things we must determine in the next few days."

Rance wondered what else might be determined.

§

Francoise left him to scale a fence in the dark.

"It is far too dangerous for you to attempt a border cross-ing. Coming in from Germany would be easy-the customs sta-tions are all deserted now. But the Swiss are very difficult, so everyone else is difficult back to them, and that means that entering and exiting Switzerland is not a good idea."

So Francoise had deposited him at the gate to an unused truck depot a half a mile from the border station. She would identify herself to the guards and try to find out what the situation regarding Rance the fugitive was. Before dropping him off, she told him what to do. Her instructions had been explicit, and she made him repeat them to her verbatim:

In the back of the depot was a ten foot fence. Climb it and walk north along an old service road, keeping the lights of the border station on your left. The road will end with a small barricade. Proceed past this for about a hundred meters. You will see my car waiting.

"And I'm supposed to trust you?" he asked.

She smiled. "You don't have a choice, do you?" Rance felt a chill upon hearing those words, but the chill turned to a burn when she leaned across the seat and kissed him on the cheek.

"Now go, *vas-y! Je t'attendrais*. I will be waiting for you."

She was.

"Do you always smuggle men across the Swiss border at night?" Rance asked as he climbed into the car.

"A good agent knows how to get in and out Switzerland," she replied.

An agent. The term rung in his ear. He had once thought

of himself as an agent, though now he knew he had been nothing more than a low-level field monkey. There seemed to be a lot of agents running around these days, none of them of the field-monkey variety, and they all seemed to be after Rance.

"Where are you taking me?"

"To a village called Riquwihr. It is a small village at the base of the Vosages, a touristy place where you should be safely unnoticed. My grandmother runs a small restaurant there."

An hour later, just after midnight, they drove through the walls of the tiny medieval city. Francoise pulled the car into a dark alley and they entered a darkened building through a side door. She showed him to his room.

"Sleep as late as you want," she told him. "I know you must be exhausted."

"You're not going to vanish on me again, are you."

"No, Rance. It is too much trouble to go chasing you around Europe."

He collapsed on the small bed and fell quickly into a dreamless sleep.

§

Riquewihr was crowded before nine a.m.

The window in Rance's bedroom overlooked the end of an alley that opened into a small, yard used by a pottery maker. The first busload of German tourists were hustled into the tiny yard, where the artisan gave them a performance on the wheel. Afterwards they were shown more finished product, which they eagerly bought.

Though he did not speak German with any fluency, Rance knew enough of it to be able to identify the nationality of the first crowd. To his ears they were practically screaming. And the French complained about American tourists? The next group was British, and Rance was driven out of bed into his unfamiliar surroundings.

The first thing that struck him was the sensation that he was going to tip over. He was listing badly to port, and he had to reach out for the wall as he walked down the hallway. Then he realized that it was the structure, not him, that was leaning badly. At the bottom of the stairs was a tiny kitchen.

A small woman was hunched over a huge griddle emitting a raucous sizzling sound. Beside the stove was a radio, its volume turned up high, playing old Edith Piaf songs. The woman sang to a few of the words, hummed the rest. Only when she turned away from the stove did see Rance standing in the doorway.

"O! Ye!" she exclaimed, using the Alsatian language equivalent of blasphemy. "*Vous êtes bien sûr le copain de Francoise. Allez, elle vous attend dehors.*"

Bolstered though it was this last week through near constant use, Rance's French comprehension suddenly failed him. The woman was speaking French, wasn't she? He followed her only because she gave him the universal hand wave that meant "follow me."

He found Francoise sitting out on a balcony flooded with bright yellow morning sunlight. For a moment, he thought he might be looking at a stranger.

Recalling the first time they had met, Rance remembered

Francoise as a dour, poutingly beautiful Frenchwoman in the classic, stereotypical sense. Her aura changed only slightly when she became a trained agent capable of killing another human being without blinking an eye, as she had done yesterday. Again, another role. But what he beheld now defied explanation.

It was still Francoise, he saw. But gone was the severity, the austere professionalism. In its place was simple beauty. That was the only word he could think of: beautiful.

When they met a week ago, her sexuality aroused him primitively. But today he saw a different person, a natural, fluid person free from pretension and the dogma that must engulf those in her line of work. He felt he was meeting the real Francoise.

"Good morning," she said as he came out onto the patio. "Did you sleep well?"

She was wearing a dress, a real dress, not some latex-fabricated body suit, but a cotton dress, string straps and yellow trimmed, not too long, but long enough to wear to church. It would have been wholesome on someone else; on her it was mildly erotic.

She was smiling, and even that was different, Rance noticed. For the first time since he'd met her, she let her teeth show through, almost laughing as she did. Rising up, she took him by the elbow and guided him to his seat, the consummate hostess.

"The only thing wrong with my sleep was the German tourists the morning."

"Ah, yes, going to Uncle Gerard's. He is the village's potter. Coffee?"

"Uncle Gerard?" he asked, watching her pour the coffee from a silver urn. "And the old lady that just brought me out here...?"

"Mémé Arlette. She is my maternal grandmother. In a month she will be 95 years old."

"I couldn't understand her. And here I was thinking I spoke French just fine." He sipped the coffee. Good and strong and black.

"She wasn't speaking French. She was speaking Alsatian, her native language."

"Aren't we in France?"

Francoise laughed, letting her head tilt slightly to one side. "France is not one homogenous country, Rance. Instead it is made up of many different countries and many different peoples–les Bretons in Brittany, les Dauphinois in the Alps, and the Alsatians, here in the northeast part of the country. There are many more, all with their own languages and customs."

"And all a part of France. Interesting."

"I know it is a concept that would not work in your country, am I correct? Americans are...individualists. Though they have very little to culturally separate them–certainly they don't have separate, indigenous peoples claiming certain sections of the country as their ancestral homes–they still find ways to alienate one another. They have a great dislike of a strong central government, where as we here in France realize that it is the only thing keeping us from total anarchy."

There was a future for her as a diplomat, he thought. Francoise could insult someone and they would go away thinking they were in love. He thought about that for a second and finished off his first cup of coffee.

Set into the foothills of the Vosages mountains, the town of Riquewihr was one of steep grades. The patio where Rance and Francoise sat was on one side crowded with the village buildings leading up the mountainous slope; but on the other side, the town fell away, allowing them a view over the walls that ringed the city, down onto the alluvial plain of the Rhine river valley.

Looking out onto the patched squares of farmland, fields of corn and rape, he wondered how many armies had marched across it, how many men had fought died defending it, and did any of it matter now. Francoise's grandmother had lived in this building all of her 95 years and she spoke neither French nor the language of France's arch enemy, German, the country that was easily visible a few miles in the distance. She spoke something else, something that worked in this place.

"What's our next move?" he asked, turning back to Francoise.

"How do you feel about mixing business and pleasure?" she replied, the corners of her mouth twisting up coyly.

Rance's heart jumped, his palms becoming instantly clammy.

"Ah, probably not a very good idea," he heard himself say.

"I agree. In that case, business will be suspended, at least for a few days."

Francoise explained. Before he had come down this morning, she had been in touch with the central office of the SDECE. Having told them that she and Rance were safe, she went on to relate the events surrounding Franz Hurlimann in Switzerland and the man who nearly killed Rance. An agent was being assigned the case and would report back in two days' time.

Meanwhile, field operators with experience in Kazakhstan were being contacted. It would take a day or two to make contact and explore the possibility that Katarina Favergé might be in that country.

Until then, they would enjoy the Alsatian summer.

"But first, we must eat something," Francoise said, taking a tray filled with toasted baguette and bowls of fresh fruit from Mémé. "Then I will show you my village."

§

"I never would have guessed..."

Francoise was smiling, her arm linked through Rance's. Together they walked along with the flow of the crowd moving up the rue du General de Gaulle, which bisected the walled village of Riquewihr.

"That I grew up in Alsace?" she asked playfully.

"Yes. It's just that, well, you look so, so...French. I mean Parisian."

Her head went back and she laughed. People passing them on the street gave them the warm smiles reserved for obvious couples enjoying each other's company.

"Just because we here have a different heritage does not mean that we don't recognize the importance of our capital city-especially when it comes to fashion. O la la!"

"Why are there so many images of storks everywhere?" Rance asked.

"Storks? Ah, you mean *cigognes*. The people of Alsace believe that they are a bird of good luck. They spend their springs and summers here in Alsace, then they migrate for the winter to Africa. If a cigogne nests on your roof, you will have a good wine harvest. If there is a cigogne on the roof of the church when you get married, then you will have many children."

"That must be where the legend about the storks brining the babies comes from. It's a very picturesque village, Francoise. Has it always been an attraction for tourists?" She nodded enthusiastically.

Without turning his head he could see Germans, Italians, Americans, Dutch, Japanese and English people all meandering within a few feet of one another, staring at the beauty of the medieval village.

Behind the village–itself already at an elevation of over 1,000 feet–rose the Vosages Mountains, cloaked in a shawl of thick, dark pines. Some 50 kilometers due east, the mountains of Germany's Black Forest rose up into the humid summer sky, sisters to the Vosages. Together they guided the mighty Rhine northward on its journey to the North Sea.

Rance felt puny. The timelessness of the land, the virtual density of the history that had preceded him here, it was all overwhelming. When you detached yourself from the normal motions of the tourist, Rance thought, something happened. It became real.

"This is one of the oldest original structures of the village," Francoise was saying. They stood before a four-sided tower of about five stories in height. A huge arch and tunnel had been cut into it, and tourists as well as local drivers crowded underneath.

"It is the Dolled, and it was built in 1291. There is a museum inside, but it's not terribly interesting."

Good God, thought Rance. Seven hundred years old.

The area around his home of Green Harbor was one of the oldest settlements in the New World. His town had recently celebrated its 350th founding anniversary. But this place was twice as old as that. And that is just this particular building. People have been living here-

"Forever," Francoise said, as if she were reading his mind. He didn't know how it happened, but he felt her hand in his. "People have been living in this part of the world for thousands of years. Just down the road is Strasbourg. The Romans under Julius Caesar gave it the name-it means strong city at the crossroads. And before them all this place was the heart of the Celtic kingdom."

"I thought the Celts were-"

"Only Irish? No, that is a mistake that most Americans make. The Celts originated in the Bohemian Forest far to the east. Their migration and loose form of rule spread their culture down through the Iberian peninsula, into northern Italy, throughout most of Germany, across France and up into Holland. By 1000 B.C. they reached the zenith of their empire, with territories that included most of western Europe, and they migrated to the British Isles. But as soon as they reached their pinnacle, they imploded. The Romans soon arrived, and though they weren't the match of the Celtic warrior, they were better trained and more highly disciplined. By 100 B.C. the Celts had disappeared, except for England and Ireland."

They had made their way back to the front terrace of Mémé Arlette's restaurant, called the Petite Cigogne, already crowded with lunch diners.

"But I haven't yet showed you the best part of Alsace," Francoise said.

"Oh? And what is the best part of Alsace."

"The vineyards."

§

"It's called the *Route du Vin*," Francoise said.

"Route du Vin?"

"It means 'wine road.'"

Of course, he thought. Only in France could you find a term that meant "wine road." In temperate America, merely thinking of such a term would be enough to lose your license for 90 days.

Currently Francoise was doing about seventy miles per hour down the Route du Vin, which in no way resembled an interstate highway. What it was the basic two lane, twisty country road. That she was tearing down the narrow road at breakneck speed didn't cause him to grip the underside of the front seat; that the road was crowded with other motorists driving in the exact same fashion was another story altogether.

"Where are we going?" he asked as the car screeched around a corner. A huge white wall appeared suddenly in front of them. Rance closed his eyes and braced himself for the crash. An instant later he heard the crunch of gravel and felt the car come to a stop.

"Right here," she answered. With a violent upward jerk she set the tiny sports car's emergency brake and jumped out.

They had stopped at some kind of farm. To their left a large, ancient house rose up out of the scorching summer dust. Connected to it via a rickety breezeway was an equally decrepit barn, with a small shed-like building tacked on at the far side.

"Come!" she called, nearly dancing up to the small structure attached to the barn. By the time he caught up to her she was standing before a large, non-descript door. She pounded three times. A moment later the door was opened by tiny, withered woman who recognized Francoise instantly.

"*Ah, Francoise, ma p'tite, comment tu va? Entrez, entrezy, il fait assez chaud, entrez.*"

After exchanging kisses, Francoise introduced Rance to Ilsa Doppf.

"*Ah, m'sieu parle francaise,*" Ilsa observed upon hearing Rance's greeting. "*Il a soif, bien sûr.*" He must be thirsty.

"Yes he is," Francoise answered, leading him into the building.

When his eyes finally adjusted to the darkness inside, Rance saw that they were standing in a long, low room, filled with several picnic tables. There were no lights and it was about forty degrees cooler. On their left was a high wooden bar. Ilsa moved behind it.

"*Muscat, cherie?*" she asked without looking up.

"*Oui, Mémé,*" Francoise answered. She and Rance sat at one of the picnic tables.

"Is she your mémé, too?"

"In this part of the world, any woman over sixty is my mémé."

Presently Ilsa arrived at the table with a cool looking bottle of wine and two glasses. She thumped them down and smiled.

"*À lá votre,*" she said, and returned back to her bar.

Francoise uncorked the bottle, thin and tall and slowly tapered toward its neck, and poured two glasses.

"Muscat d'Alsace," she explained. "One of the wines produced in this region. Ilsa's vineyard, Frau Doppf, is renowned for its production of Muscat d'Alsace. It is said to be the finest in all Alsace."

A half a bottle later he agreed.

"Good," Francoise said, saying her good-byes to Meme Ilsa. "Next we go to the vineyards of the Hansis, my cousins, for the best pinots in France: blanc, gris, and noir."

And so it went for the balance of the afternoon. Each vineyard had its specialty, a particular Alsatian wine it made better than anyone else, from Sylvaner to Riesling and finally to the cellars of Wolfberger to taste the finest Gewurztraminer in the land.

By the time they had returned to Riquewihr, at nine p.m. and just in time for dinner, Rance was happy Alsace had run out of wines for them to taste.

§

"Any word from your headquarters?"

The western sky was a fading shade of fuchsia. Outlined obscurely before it were the sleeping Vosages, elephantine enigmas sighing under the night's descent. To the east, above the blackened plain of the Rhine, the first stars blinked.

There were still several couples seated out on Mémé Arlette's patio. The amber flicker of the candles between them was the only light. Before him, Rance could only see the dancing yellow reflection of the candle on Francoise's face. Her hands were entwined under her chin, and her head rested at slight angle as she smiled at him.

"No," she said, still smiling. "And I don't expect to hear from them for a day or two. But let's not talk of that. Soon that will be all we have."

"And what do we have now?"

"The best choucroute in all of Alsace. Is something wrong?"

"No. I mean, the first time I came to France with Katarina, she took me to an Alsatian restaurant in Paris-Au Gare des Alsatians. Katarina enjoyed Alsatian food. She blamed her weakness for comfort food on her Slavic heritage."

Francoise looked down quickly. "I know the restaurant. It is across from the Gare de l'Est. The owner is Jean Kleber."

"You know the owner?"

"Rance, Alsace is still a small place. When a son leaves for the bright lights of Paris, everybody knows."

"And when a daughter leaves for the big world of international espionage?"

She laughed and took a sip of her wine.

"I never thought of it that way. To me, I was just doing something that was right. I was doing something for my country, giving back something to my people."

"And that is why you must find Katarina? Because she betrayed her country?"

"Because she betrayed me. I told you, we were friends. Not acquaintances, or friends as people in the United States call themselves. No, we were almost sisters. What I feel goes beyond words. But I can't let my emotions cloud my objective. There will be time for that later."

Francoise had been talking to the dancing flame of the candle more than she had been addressing Rance. Now her eyes came up, brown mirrors bouncing the flame's image back up to him.

"And you, Rance. You have your own pain. Your own reasons."

"I told you already," he said softly. "I made a promise to a dying friend. And maybe I made a promise to myself, too. A promise to change, to go back and begin again where I left off, before all this, before..."

He gestured vaguely and she took his hand, gently stroking his fingers.

"Tell me about your Katarina. Tell me what made you two so good that you have a daughter."

Now he drank, his quirky looking green Alsatian wine glass filled with crisp, racy Riesling. How much wine have we drunk tonight? he wondered. It didn't matter. Everything was good, so good, and even though the invocation of Katarina's memory was difficult, the wine helped him manage it.

"It was her passion. She was so intense, so full of life. She was a real, very real person to me, the first one I had ever met. She had a verve that cured me like a tonic. And she loved Shakespeare."

"Ah yes," Francoise said, taking a sip of her wine. "That is Katarina. Everywhere all at once. But tell me about Shakespeare."

"In the summertime in London there are so many companies that perform Shakespeare...we just fell into it. That summer *Othello* was our favorite. We must have seen it ten times, each time discovering something new that we had missed before."

She was listening intently, leaning forward on her elbows, hanging on his words.

"*Othello*," she repeated. "Tell me."

Rance laughed, more to himself.

"It seems so obvious to me now. But then..."

"What?"

"Iago," he said. "It was always Iago with Katarina. She seemed almost obsessed by his character, how he manipulated people to his own means. She said that Iago had supreme insight into the frailties of human nature. That he had the ability to turn the world on its head and laugh his way through it.

"Now I see why she was so fascinated with Iago. 'Honest Iago,' she would repeat. 'True genius surrounded by a cast of fools.' Perhaps she was using Iago as her inspiration."

"It's not as crazy as it sounds, Rance. It is something we should think about. Maybe it will give us some insight into he she will act and react.

"But now we will eat."

§

With each step Rance felt his throat tighten a notch.

Underfoot the ancient stairs creaked out their broadcast as the two sets of feet mounted them. Their width was not enough to accommodate both Rance and Francoise, so he walked behind her, hearing the soft swish of her dress.

At the top of the stairs, in front of his door, Francoise stopped and turned to face him as he rose up to her. His chest ached with the slamming of his heart. It only took a fraction of a second to read the look on her face as her eyes found his. In one motion he gathered her up in his arms and kissed her. She responded in kind, pulling him fervently against her lips. As their hungry mouths probed each other, the door opened and they tumbled into his bedroom.

§

There was no breeze.

With his right eye Rance could see through the small opened window. The night was quiet, and in the swatch of sky he could see there were no stars. There was only Francoise.

§

A small blue square with the number 15 hung above the door.

The doorway was set into the buildings lining the street. On one side was a jeweler's shop. On the other was a sporting goods store. The street was not unlike most streets in Paris' 16th Arrondissment: a line of cars parked up and down each side, two more lines of traffic dodging pedestrians and students on mopeds, shops up and down the street, residences above them. James Devlin walked down the rue des Poissonieres and entered number 15.

He walked up one flight of stairs to the second floor, and knocked on the only door there. A second later the locking mechanism buzzed softly, unlocking, and Devlin proceeded down a long hallway. At the end of the hall he passed into a tiny cubicle of an office. There was a woman sitting at a desk. He spoke with her, and a minute later she led him up another flight of stairs.

"He'll be right with you," the woman said, opening a door into an office. She left him.

Devlin looked around. There was one window, and it looked out over an inner courtyard. It looked very normal, all of it, except for the one inch thick steel bars which lined the window. The office held a computer but other than that looked almost generic, as if it were reserved for visiting executives needing a place to get some work done.

"Ah, you must be Devlin."

Devlin turned around calmly. He had heard the approach of the man seconds ago, and now he was pleased to se that he had been correct in guessing the man's size: at least six-four, 220 pounds and wearing cotton trousers. The only thing he hadn't been able to guess was that the man had bright red hair. And that the fingers of his right hand were twirling a rubber band.

§

She kissed him.

It was fully morning now, and the stillness of the light portended another scalding day. Rance's chest heaved with the weight of Francoise atop him, and he thought that she really didn't weigh anything at all.

His hands reveled in the luxury of her velvety solid body. Some sense that he didn't know existed was bathed in Epicurean delight, lifting his soul out of its physical shackles and teleporting it far away. It was the dance of two as one, he thought, and he had never experienced it like this.

She was pressing into him, almost maniacally, almost too softly to be perceived, simultaneously breezy and forceful. He surrendered himself to her, a canvas to her inspiration, and she painted with the intense brilliance of a master.

"We've missed breakfast," she whispered into his ear later.

"No we haven't."

She laughed.

"You're scandalous, Rance Vaughn. What will Meme think?"

"The same thing that I think: that you're woman."

"Is that your compliment to me?" Her tone was scolding, but her nuzzling betrayed her emotions.

"You hardly need compliments. But if you think your honor has been compromised then believe me when I tell you that I could never have imagined anything so beautiful."

The bed was a tangle of damp sheets and entwined limbs, hanging over themselves in a way that suggested a total lack of inhibition. Not ten feet below the open window various nationalities paraded by, cameras whirring. He ran a hand through her short, jet hair and kissed her again.

"So much energy for one who has not eaten," she said, pulling him over.

"How will you deal with that?"

"Lunch," she said. "But first I will make you work for it."

"Suits me." With a practiced ease he caused her to gasp with a delicate erotic pleasure that he felt electrically pass through her skin into him.

§

"You didn't tell me this is what you meant by 'working.'"

Rance was gasping again, but this time Francoise was twenty yards away from him, standing on an exposed section of trail, her hands on her hips, smiling, the merciless midday sun illuminating her flatly. The air he breathed was hot and though he knew it contained the oxygen needed to feed his screaming muscles, sucking it into his lungs was a task nearly as difficult as ascending this mountain she had taken him to.

"Let's rest a minute," she said, coming back down the trail and handing him a bottle of water from her pack. Son of a bitch, he thought. She isn't even breathing hard.

"*Le Bonhomme*," Francoise responded to his question, asked earlier that morning, of where were they going. When he posed it she had been tearing up a narrow switchback mountain road cut into the thick black firs which blanketed the Vosages mountains.

"The good man," he translated. "*Le bon homme*." But they had stopped at the tiny mountain village of le Bonhomme long enough only to park the car and begin hiking up a dark forest path lined with decaying pine needles.

In the beginning the path was gentle and she told him where their ultimate destination was.

"Le Brezouard."

"Sorry. I can't translate that one."

"It is one of the peaks of the Vosages. The view is magnificent, and there is not a better place in all of Alsace to have a picnic lunch."

That was something he looked forward to, if only because it meant the load coming down would be considerably lighter than the load going up. That included all their water, a bottle of Edelzwicker wrapped in foam to keep it cold, a sack filled with meats and cheeses courtesy of Mémé, and the necessary utensils to eat it all. Though they had divided the load equally between them, Rance thought sandwiches would have been a better idea.

Rance took a long pull from the water bottle, still cool. Francoise sat down beside him on a rock. The view was limited to the trail and the forest that guarded it, though now they had climbed high enough so that the trees were smallish and withered. What was left was sun, an abundance of bright sunshine.

He looked at her and felt something deep stirring inside, something pure and uncluttered, and he wondered just what it was.

"You know, a week ago I was sitting on my boat minding my own business. Now..." He gestured at his surroundings, his eyes resting on her.

"And now...?"

"Now we better get to the top before I expire."

The last hour was the worst, but the destination was worth the effort. The trail ended in a field of short grass. In the middle of the field was an outcropping of stone, in the middle of which was mounted a bronze plaque that identified the place as le Brezouard, altitude 1,228 meters, or 3,991 feet.

Visibility was at least 60 miles in every direction.

As she spread the blanket out, Rance noticed that they were the only ones up there.

"Don't you think the climb is enough to keep the casual hikers away?" Francoise responded to his observation. "Now, aren't you hungry?"

They fell on the food and wine with a vengeance, not slowing until they reached the cheeses. Rance poured the last of the bottle of Edelzwicker, feeling it rush his head.

"You haven't heard from your office?" he asked.

She shook her head. "I will call tonight. Are you becoming impatient?"

"In a way, yes. So much has happened so fast, and for everything to stop...I don't know."

"I thought writers cherished their ability to step back and look at it all."

"Sometimes. But sometimes it's so frustrating. You see things and you want to change them, and the only vehicle you have is your ability as an author, but that influence is so slow in taking shape."

"Do you think you influenced some people with your first book?"

"What do you think?"

She was thoughtful for a moment. "I think you did a very difficult thing with *Jungle Water*. You re-invented the action-adventure genre, for starters. Many people have written novels with a strong female protagonist, but these have been classified as romances.

"But by sharing the center stage with an equally strong man, I think that you accomplished something special. You brought the man-woman relationship to a different level. I think one of the reviews I read said that you have created a new genre-'romantic adventure.'"

He felt himself redden at so heavy a mantle.

"But what made it so extraordinary, Rance, was that you did what you did in that format while at the same time offering a succinct commentary on how a large government loses touch with the ideals of the people. How individual rights are trampled when we become too blasé about our lives."

Rance stared open mouthed. It wasn't until he had finished *Jungle Water*, revised it a dozen times, had the manuscript rejected by 30 agents and publishers, succeeded finally in having it published and read it again in its first hardback edition that he realized what exactly he had done.

And what he had done was precisely what Francoise just said.

"It just came out of me," he heard himself saying. "A lot of things were happening, and I found that book just oozing from my pores. *Jungle Water* wrote itself."

"And *Snake Ranch* did not?"

"I think *Snake Ranch* showed how much perspiration I had. The story was so good, but the words...it just didn't resonate like *Jungle Water*."

"It sold well, the movie was a huge success."

"You seem to know an awful lot about my past."

She leaned over and kissed him and he could taste the sweet tang of the wine on her tongue.

"Do you think," she said, pulling him down onto the blanket, "that I would sleep with a man about whom I knew nothing?"

And with only the sun as a witness, they made love in the afternoon on a blanket high above it all.

§

Francoise emerged from the basement wearing her glasses.

She looks almost like a teacher, Rance thought. Though she was still dressed in the hiking boots and walking shorts from earlier in the day, her face wore a stern, professional look that Rance had not seen since they were in Paris together.

He found his mind racing with the images of her body and his locked together, rolling through the alpine meadow, tangled in the sheets, bathed in a glow that came from within each of them, twisting up slowly like a perfume, mingling in the atmosphere. He swallowed once, hard.

Clutched in both her hands was a huge sheaf of papers, some in manila folders, some loose. She brought them over to the table and plunked them down before him. She took off her glasses and looked at him.

"This is all we know," she said. "About Katarina and what she might possibly be involved in. The lead that her ex-husband-Hurlimann?-gave you was good. The MIT scientist that was kidnapped from Michael O'Meara-"

She began shuffling through the papers, seizing one finally.

"Mr. Gengi," she continued. "He has ties to an organization called Inlan. They are sort of a freelance terrorist organization, but they operate out of Kazakhstan."

"Why Kazakhstan?" Rance wondered aloud.

She shrugged. "It's a little bit like the wild west out there now. Underground organizations like that are flourishing in an atmosphere of permissivity."

Rance shook his head. "How could someone like that be involved in a government software development project-especially something having to do with national security?"

She put her glasses back on and looked down at some of

the papers.

"A new missile jamming system, to be more precise. Using satellite based lasers and a global tracking network, this new software would be able to detect and destroy not only inter-continental ballistic missiles, but also air to air missiles, SAMs, even shoulder held rocket launchers."

"What?" Rance was incredulous. "That's impossible!"

"Not according to our intelligence. France has even helped in its development in the hopes of sharing the benefits of such a system when–and if–it comes to fruition."

"And this guy Gengi was the point man on the R & D side of the whole thing. No wonder someone wanted him. With his knowledge, he could hold the free world hostage. What is the name of this software that would coordinated something as complicated as this?"

Francoise looked up at him.

"SHAKESPEARE."

§

"It makes sense when you think about it," he said.

"I guess that the master of the English language is a good metaphor for something so complex, so powerful."

"A bit ironic, no?" she said. "That you and Katarina should have shared a passion for Shakespeare."

"You don't think...?"

"It could be possible."

"And what exactly is Katarina's stake in all this?"

"I don't know, Rance, because she is not acting conven-tionally–speaking from the point of view of an agent of the

SDECE, that is. I mean that in espionage, an agent reacts to his environment, tries to place himself in the position of collecting information. But..."

"What is it?"

"I just spent a lot of time on the phone with our director of operations. He had an interesting theory. He thought that perhaps she was acting instead of reacting. That somehow she was able to place this Gengi fellow in the right place, and now she is going to deliver him-at least his work-to the highest bidder."

"The highest bidder?"

"Yes. Iran, more than likely. Besides Israel and Saudi Arabia, they're the only functioning state left in the Middle East. They might even be bankrolled by some Americans."

Rance frowned. Terrorism was a new hobby of some of his fellow citizens. The World Trade Center, the Oklahoma City Federal Building-both served as convenient message senders, and though the perpetrators of the World Trade Center bombing had ties ostensibly overseas with Muslim terrorist organizations, they couldn't have pulled it off without domestic help. Hate was a dish overflowing.

"So she is essentially the coordinator of all this," Rance thought aloud. "But the FBI tripped over Gengi first, by accident. The CIA wants him, too, but Michael said the FBI was taking him to a maximum security lockup. That's when they were ambushed. Gengi turned on Katarina and she had to get him first.

"So she is working with the big red-head."

"Maybe," said Francoise. "Maybe not. They could be working against each other, too. Right now we are running the description of him through all our field offices. If he is active in the business someone should be able to place him."

Rance sat forward intently. He couldn't remember the last time his mind had been so clear, so focused. It was the danger, he thought. Or maybe it was Francoise.

"So, theoretically speaking, what could someone do with this software? Could they use it offensively?"

"In a certain way, yes," she answered. "More probable is some kind of jamming of national defense systems combined with a small number of attacks, then a withdrawal. An infusion of chaos. Enough to do damage to the United States and its allies, then hold them hostage with their own defense system. Terrorist states like Iran or North Korea would never be able to threaten the United States militarily, but they can step up the level of misery that they have been working on for years. This would bring them up onto the field with the 'big boys,' as you say in America."

"Now I know what Michael meant."

"What?"

Rance looked at her. "He knew how big this whole thing was–or at least he smelled it. We have to cut off the head of this dog, not just the tail, and that means we have to stop Katarina, and we have to do it fast."

Francoise reached across the table and took his hand and once again he saw that magical transformation sweep over her, softening her edges, radiating from within her.

"I think you should go back home," she said to him. "What is going to happen next is something that you are not prepared for. You have been very lucky up until now, and I...I don't know what I will do if your luck runs out."

She was looking at him and her eyes were big, bigger, and wet and she didn't look away, she just kept it up, the truth flowing out of her eyes, telling him more than her words ever could. Rance understood.

"Come here," he said, and he gathered her into his arms. He spoke low, in a gruff whisper, his words staggering out into her ear, his lips touching.

"You know I have to. I made a promise, and it was the first rational thing I've done in years. I told Michael I'd do what I could to stop her. I know how she thinks. And I have to see her myself. I want to know about my daughter, and if someone else gets to her first...well, I might never get that chance.

"So what's next?" he asked.

Francoise pulled back a little and wiped a tear from her eye, looking down. Her hands still held his tightly. "We start in Kazakhstan," she said, looking up at him. "We will pose as a French couple on vacation. A passport will be here for you in the morning."

He smiled. "You knew I wouldn't leave you."

She smiled back.

"A French couple is it?" he asked, pulling her again to him. But this time she turned her head away slightly.

"Rance, the next few days or weeks will be dangerous and difficult. I think we should wait until..."

"All right. For you, all right."

She kissed him once more quickly on the lips, then led him down into the basement where a small corner served as her office.

"Come," she said. "Before we leave, you must be prepared."

Part III

Kazakhstan

Aeroflot flight number 7416 from Moscow banked sharply.

Rance opened his eyes and looked out the window. The city of Almaty, Kazakhstan's capital, was bathed in the orange flame of the sunrise. Behind the city, the jagged Tian Shan mountains thrust their glaciered peaks high, lifting the sun into another day.

It was one thing to travel, he thought. It was another thing to go off the beaten track to a place that really should not be there. Exotic vacation destinations like the remote Amazon in Brazil or the tropical forests of New Guinea came with pre-suppositions about their lack of visitors.

But Kazakhstan had been forbidden for so long, shuttered behind the Iron Curtain, that the sheer enigma of the place, even twenty years after the fall of the Soviet Union, drew visitors in waves. He nudged Francoise. It had already been so long a journey, but in a real sense, it was just beginning.

From Alsace they had driven through Germany, the Czech Republic and Slovakia. Though they were both impatient, they knew only patience would avoid the arousal of suspicion. After entering the Ukraine they stayed a day in Kiev, then flew to Moscow.

Though they were made up to be tourists, neither Rance nor Francoise felt very much like sightseeing. Both were tense and quiet during the few days of their journey. Rance wondered if it was the sexual tension between them, for although they abstained from lovemaking they did not cut back on the intimate contact. It was a heavy weight on his chest and he felt that now he knew Francoise well enough to recognize the same symptoms in her.

So they both used the time to learn a little about Kazakhstan and though the place was largely unremarkable, they both understood the character traits it possessed as making it a ripe place to do business. Any kind of business.

As they exited the plane onto the tarmac a fresh breeze washed down from the mountains, taking the edge off the heat and turning the day into a splendid example of summer on the steppes. Rance and Francoise collected their bags and left the airport, finding themselves in the middle of a totally foreign city, asking the question, "What's next?"

"I will call Anatoly," Francoise said, referring to the French Intelligence operative who had briefed her over the phone before they left France.

"Hey! Joe!"

Both Rance and Francoise snapped their heads around at

the shout. They saw nothing but the crowds of people moving in and out of the airport terminal. A smallish boy ran up to them, smiling, and Rance could hear himself sucking the air into his lungs sharply.

"Hey, Joe!" the boy said again.

That a Kazakhstani boy could speak English did not immediately register on them. They were left speechless because of the shock they felt when looking at the boy. He was horribly deformed.

Of all the things they read about Kazakhstan in the last few days, there was one thing that was repeated over and over, in article after article. It was the horrific legacy of the Soviet reaction to the Cold War.

Between 1949 and 1991 nearly 600 nuclear devices were detonated both in the skies and under the ground of northeast Kazakhstan. But the most appalling aspect to the Semipalatinsk nuclear research and development sight, which the Soviets denied even existed, was that the detonations took place not in isolated wastelands, but right in the middle of a large population. Hundreds of thousands of people lived within a 50 mile radius of the test sights.

Reading about the horrible results of long term exposure to radiation, they were discovering, did little in the way of preparing for the eventuality of its reality.

Rance guessed that the boy was about five feet tall. He was skinny and grubbily dressed, and with features that belied the Mongol influence in the ethnic Kazakhstani population. But that was as far as Rance got.

The boy had no right eye.

It wasn't that he had lost it in some kind of accident; this boy had never had a right eye. Where the boy's right eye socket and eyeball should have been there was only a smooth extension of his cheek bone running up to his forehead. It was as if he had been a clay sculpture, and the artist only had time to carve out and detail the left eye, leaving the right side of his face a blank.

And he had no left arm.

Well, that wasn't exactly true. But what he did have was too incredible to believe. What substituted for a left arm jutted out about a foot from his left shoulder. Instead of a hand on the end of the appendage there was something that resembled the crusher claw of a lobster. The comparison was all too clear in Rance's mind. The boy had a lobster claw.

"I am Marat," he said enthusiastically. His smile was broad and straight and his teeth were unusually white and even, as if his creator tried to make up for the physical defects he suffered by giving him a million dollar smile.

"I am your guide and I am at your service. You will not find a better boy in all of Almaty. I will take your bags."

Rance and Francoise exchanged cautionary looks, reading each other's minds. Why did this boy come to them out of all the other passengers? And why did he assume that they spoke English?

"Wait," Rance said, making the decision. "Who are you?"

"I am Marat," the boy said brightly.

Francoise took Rance's hand. "All right, Marat. Where are we going?"

"You are going to visit Kazakhstan, yes? Welcome to my country. I am your best boy at your service. You are lucky because Marat is honest and true. I will find you a good taxi.

Come."

Despite his handicap the boy made off with both their bags and Rance and Francoise had a job to keep up with them. He ran past the taxi stand.

"Marat!" Rance called. "Aren't those taxis there?"

Marat's smile disappeared. "Those are criminals. They will steal you blind! Come!"

Parked around the corner was a decrepit, rusted out Lada, a Soviet make that embodied the fruits of communism. Marat opened the trunk, deposited their bags and held the back door open.

"This is the taxi of Berik, the brother of my mother. He is honest and fair."

Reluctantly they climbed in the back of the dirty car. Uncle Berik rattled off something to Marat, who was sitting beside him in front.

"Where would you like to go?" Marat asked, his smile still big and bright.

They gave him the address of the Holiday Inn.

"I know it well. It is where I learned my English. Yes, you are wondering how Marat speaks so well? The Texas oil men come here now to Kazakhstan. For two years I am the best boy of Chester W. McCloud, the biggest baddest oil man in all of Texas."

For as entertaining as the boy was, they could not get past his deformity. Nor could they override the suspicion they felt at the convenience of Marat's appearance.

"Just until the hotel lobby," Francoise whispered in Rance's ear.

When they arrived at the Holiday Inn, after Marat chatted

his way through a quick tour of Almaty, Rance tried to pay him.

"Oh, no!" said Marat. "You don't pay until the end. Only when you have seen that Marat is the best boy in all of Almaty will you pay. Then you will realize how lucky you are. But now you must be tired. When you need anything, you will call the front desk and Marat will be ready."

The boy trotted outside and sat down on the curb, watching the traffic pass by.

§

Washington, D.C., was climatically a southern city.

Jenny Ryan was thankful that she had opted for the T-shirt and shorts. Deciding that she would raise fewer eyebrows if people thought she was a law student, Jenny had forgone her power suits. An unexpected benefit of that choice was that even in her mid 30s she was fit and youthful enough to pull it off.

She was worried about Rance.

It had been almost a week since she last spoke to him, and the conversation had been strained and hurried. Something was going on that she wasn't being told about. It was his voice that gave him away; his voice always gave him away. That little byte of personal information made her smile.

Like most people who had never visited Washington, Jenny was surprised to discover that there was a city that functioned outside of Capitol Hill. Antipodally removed from federal Washington, the city was not attractive, and most of it was to be avoided after sunset.

There, she thought, there it is. From her fanny pack she produced a notebook. Inside it was a name and an address that had taken her considerable time to research. The building was boxy and nondescript, and Jenny once again was amazed that there seemed to be two Washingtons; one for the tourists, one for the residents.

She had never visited Washington in part because she was one of "apathetic" citizens periodically decried in the press. Jenny was a tax lawyer, and she paid attention to Congress insofar as it affected the current tax codes. And it did, year to year. Fortunately the changes were tracked and shouted about in the three separate newsletters she subscribed to. Beyond that she knew little of the players, and she was always taken by surprise when foreign policy grabbed the headlines.

Thankfully, the office building she entered was air-conditioned. She lingered for a moment in the lobby as she searched the marquis for the name. She found it and frowned when she saw the office was on the fifteenth floor of the building. Oh well, she thought, some work on the stairs wouldn't kill me. Elevators were out of the question.

It was a trip in the elevator that had brought her here in the first place.

"Look to the offense," the man in the elevator had told her.

As she trotted up the steps, the sound of her sneakers squeaking on the treads bounced off the cool concrete. The offense, she knew, was the prosecutors, and in the case of *United States v. Katarina Favergé*, the lead prosecutor for the government in the case had his offices in Washington, D.C.

The receptionist smiled when Jenny entered a little breathless.

"It's so hot out!" Jenny said.

"Glad I'm not out there," the secretary said. "Can I help you?"

"Yes. My name is Jenny Ryan, and I'm a law student at Georgetown. Anyway, I'm working on a case, one that he prosecuted some years ago and, well, I was wondering if it would be possible to set up an appointment with-"

"Mr. Armstrong?" She smiled. "That might be a little difficult."

"Oh, really?"

"Mr. Armstrong won't be back in the office for at least two years. If you'd like to meet with him, you'll have to call the White House. He's the President's National Security Advisor."

§

The markets that lined the streets were byzantine.

Not in a cultural sense, but in a myriad, wild and reckless sense. Vendors leaned over their wares and practically dragged Rance and Francoise back with them. The fact that they were dressed as tourists (jeans, cameras, wide-eyed looks) made matters worse.

The café was at the end of an alley, and it comprised nothing more than several tables sitting in the dust and shade by the front door. Rance and Francoise smiled and through a combination of pointing and body language they ordered two bottles of beer.

"How do you like it?" Francoise asked.

"It's a little overwhelming. And so different from Europe.

Seeing the boy was disturbing."

Marat had led them to the market, and only after promising to let the boy show them around some more later were they able to shake him.

"The Soviet Union showed a pathetic disconcern for human life, didn't they?" she asked.

"There are some Polynesians who would say the same of our countries."

A man entered the alley. Though he wore a flowing white drape, Rance could tell he was small and skinny. And old. His face had the weathered and grizzled look of a sailor, something Rance guessed was directly attributable to the harsh life out on the steppes. He sat at the table beside them and ordered tea.

"I hear the weather in Europe is fine," he said after a while, not looking at them when he spoke.

"Everywhere except England," Francoise replied. "You know the English."

"Almost as bad as the Americans." The man smiled at the wall he was staring at. "How are you, Chaumont?"

"I am well, Anatoly. Have you had any success since we last spoke?" Francoise did not look at him either. To the casual passerby it looked as though she were speaking with Rance, and Anatoly with the wall.

"The success I have had has made things all the more unclear. Our lady is here, though."

Rance leaned forward. "She's here? Katarina is here in Almaty?"

"Rance!" Francoise hissed. "Sit back and do not make a spectacle."

He leaned back in his chair but his eyes did not leave Anatoly.

"Yes, she is here. I remembered her right away when I put the two names together."

"Two names?"

"Yes. You see, I did not know her as Katarina Favergé. But in spy circles in this part of the world she is well know by the name Venus. Just looking at her is enough to understand how she got the name. A very beautiful woman and not afraid to use her beauty, either."

"What is the stake of the Kazakhs in all this?"

Anatoly shrugged. "Officially they ignore it all. Unofficially they are extracting a fee for letting people have a place to do business. This fee involves arms suppliers, among other things."

"Arms suppliers?" Rance asked.

"Kazakhstan perceives itself as having a lot of catching up to do."

"Tell me who Katarina-'Venus'-is doing business with here," Francoise said.

Anatoly darkened. "That is the subject of much debate among my suppliers of information. The general consensus is that Nabu Mohammed is the reason. He is here representing the interests of several states."

Nabu Mohammed. The name shivered Rance's spine. Not since Atilla the Hun, then Adolph Hitler, had overrun Europe had any one man evoked so much fear and hate. But at least Atilla and Hitler showed themselves on the battlefield. Nabu was not so gentlemanly.

He had sprung into the limelight as the organizer behind

the massacre at the Munich Olympics in 1972. Since then he has left a trail of destruction and grief. Choosing his targets for the maximum exposure, Nabu has been responsible for commercial airliner bombings, assassination of heads of state- he was even suspected as having something to do with the bombing of the federal building in Oklahoma City in 1995. He had allegedly recruited and inspired Osama bin Laden to commit the atrocities of 9/11.

Beside him Rance saw Francoise bristle at the sound of his name. Her reasons for loathing Nabu, however, were considerably more specific.

"Let me guess," Francoise said with great control. "Iran, North Korea."

"Among others," Anatoly said. "Whatever it is she is selling, it must be the crown jewel, for never before have these countries been able to agree to anything. It seems as though they have now done just that."

Rance and Francoise exchanged quick looks.

"When is this going to happen, Anatoly?"

"This meeting?" He shrugged. "A day, maybe two."

"Do you have any idea where she is?"

"Ah, now that I can help you with. She is staying in the yurt of my horde leader." He smiled. "I anticipated your interest in her. Now, will you need a guide?"

Both Rance and Francoise thought instantly of Marat and declined. They would get little sleep tonight.

§

"You're thinking exactly what I'm thinking," said Rance.

The guests of the Holiday Inn were mostly western, and they all seemed to be eating in that evening. Rance and Francoise had to wait for a table.

"Yes. If we can get to her first, we can stop this whole madness. Do you realize what those countries would do if they possessed the technology to cripple the nuclear power of the United States and its allies?"

Rance thought she looked pale. She had said almost nothing to him since their meeting with Anatoly, as if she were pushing him away.

"What's wrong?" he said finally, taking her hand in his. "You've looked distant since our meeting with Anatoly. Is something bothering you?"

She smiled sheepishly. "Nothing. I'm fine."

A tall man strode up beside them and looked impatiently at his watch.

"Waiter!" he said in a drawling Texas accent. "Waiter! I'm Jeb McCoy, I reserved a table."

McCoy noticed Rance and Francoise and smiled at them. "You folks been waiting long?"

"Long enough," said Rance. McCoy seemed to light up upon hearing his voice.

"Well, the least one American can do for another is ask them to join him for dinner. Would you?"

As they dined with McCoy, a modern day wildcatter negotiating development claims with the Kazakhstani government, several things struck Rance.

First was his accent. Though Rance was not a geographical accent expert, McCoy seemed to have a queer intonation when he spoke, as if he had been away from Texas for a long time.

But he told them that he had arrived only yesterday for the first time and was still jet lagged.

The other thing that Rance found strange was the way McCoy kept the focus on them. He seemed endlessly interested in an American who had married a Frenchwoman and was taking an unconventional honeymoon. It was the first time he had ever met a Texan-let alone an American-who didn't spend the whole time blustering about himself.

And there was one other thing that Rance noted-McCoy's hands. They were as big as catcher's mitts, almost too big to be human. He thought he would not like to have those things clamped around his neck.

§

Anatoly was comfortable with the darkness.

As he made his way home through the darkened back alleys, his concern about the American grew. There was obviously some prior knowledge of Venus-Katarina Favergé-with him. It might be a problem.

What also worried him was that he was not an agent-of any country. Anatoly had known Francoise for some time, held only the highest respect for her, but he questioned her bringing the American with her.

These thoughts were swimming through his head as he exited an alley onto the street, preoccupying him long enough to cloud his normally careful routine for just a moment. He didn't see the car until the door was open.

Huge hands gripped him and dragged him into the back before he could utter a sound. When the car was underway,

Anatoly was let go. He couldn't see his kidnapper very well except to note that he was a big man with huge hands.

"Well, now," James Devlin said, still employing his phony Texas accent. "What do you say you and me go have a little talk."

§

"What did you think of our company at dinner?"

"Mr. McCoy?" Francoise said. "Your typical American-sorry."

She was somewhere else, Rance could see. Her eyes were clouded with something from the past, and Rance wondered how much it hurt her. But there was nothing he could do.

He took her in his arms and drew her close.

"I don't know if you want to hear this, but I care about you. If something's bothering you, then something's bothering me."

She looked back at him in the fuzzy darkness of the room and let herself stay folded in his arms.

"I'm sorry," she said. "It was the mention of the name of Nabu Mohammed. "You've obviously crossed paths."

"Many years ago I was engaged to be married to a man who was killed by Nabu. It just brought back some painful memories."

Rance swallowed at the news. But his soft caressing of her neck let her know that the past was the past. He urged her to go on.

"He was a colonel in the French military, a dynamic and dashing young man, the leader of a crack anti-terrorist unit created specifically to deal with the Nabu Mohammeds of the world.

"For once Nabu had made a mistake. Having hijacked an Air France jet, Nabu planned on taking it to Algeria and ransoming its passengers. But a French Mirage fighter appeared and began shooting out the jet's engines with precisely controlled fire, telling Nabu that the French government would be happy to sacrifice 132 patriots for the chance at terminating the bloody reign of Nabu.

"Badly damaged, the jet was forced to land at Marseilles, where Dominique and his men were waiting. They stormed the plane and killed or subdued all the hijackers, capturing Nabu, but the price they paid was dear. Dominique was killed in the raid.

"As a final insult, Nabu escaped when he was being transferred from Marseilles. So you see, I have a vested interest in Nabu."

"And Katarina."

Silence spread through the darkness, enveloping them. Tomorrow they would rise well before the sun and go see Katarina. Rance and Francoise, hugging each other in the dark, fell asleep without saying good-night.

§

Richard Armstrong stepped lightly into the Oval Office.

For the first time since he was a boy, he felt a slight wave of panic. It wasn't as if he had orchestrated all this. Things had simply fallen into place without his trying. Certainly nothing had been planned.

Armstrong sated his angst by reminding himself that the circumstances that dictated the chain of events were still unfolding. Whatever the case, it was well beyond the reach of his control now. He grimaced and wished he had never met her.

The President looked up from his desk.

"Dick, perhaps you can tell me what in the hell is going on with SHAKESPEARE."

Armstrong frowned.

"I'm sorry, sir, I don't know what's–"

"Don't bullshit me, Dick. I thought this flap was a temporary thing. But that's not what I'm hearing now."

Son of a bitch! Armstrong thought. Why did I ever agree to this? Senile old women could be better trusted with secrets than anyone around this town.

"Sir, I can assure you–"

The President's fist came down on the desk with a crash. "Don't lie to me, Dick! Don't you stand there and lie to me!"

Armstrong bit his lip. "Sir, it's not something that you need to know about. It could be dangerous. Sir, we're talking about your political future here, your chance at re-election in two years."

To Armstrong's relief, the probe hit its target. He saw the President waver as he thought about the consequences of his knowing too much. Armstrong kept the pleading look on his face.

"Let's get some air."

Despite the scorching temperatures, the Rose Garden was always refreshing and cool. Armstrong knew that it was an addiction that the President could not refuse, and after a few minutes of fragrant strolling, Armstrong spoke.

"Mr. President, the law enforcement agencies of this country are currently engaged in an investigation that could have national security ramifications." Armstrong knew that the President loved that kind of dramatic movie talk, so he gave it to him with both barrels.

"National security!" said the President.

"Sir, your satellite defense system is based upon a highly developed network of computers. Those computers need a program of software to run them. That program was developed at the Massachusetts Institute of Technology within the last year. It was code named SHAKESPEARE.

"There's been a security breech with one of the people that worked on that project, and we are working now to correct it."

The President stopped and looked at him.

"That's it?"

"Yes, sir."

He shook his head. "I can't believe-I mean...Dick, you're doing a fine job. Just let me know if you run into any problems, OK?"

The President turned and walked back into the Oval Office. Alone now, Armstrong breathed a sigh of relief and wondered how in the hell he had ever gotten involved with Katarina Favergé.

§

Marty Donovan hung up the phone and looked around.

"Everything OK, Da?" Seamus asked from behind the bar. Donovan smiled and waved his youngest son off. He took a seat at the end of the bar.

From inside his jacket pocket he fished out a pack of Lucky Strikes and lit one. He hadn't smoked in years, but recently, he had a wild urge to smoke two packs a day. He saw Jenny emerge from the sunshine outdoors, spot him and come over.

There was something between those two, Donovan thought as he watched her approach. He had been a cop for too many years not to be able to recognize it. Jenny changed when it came to Rance–either that or she changed when it came to the rest of the world.

"Hey, shark lady," Donovan cracked as she took a stool beside him. "Where's the power suit?"

"I'm not due back to work until tomorrow," she said.

"How'd it go?"

"Interesting. Very interesting."

"Did you follow your Deep Throat's tip?"

"The person who prosecuted the case for the government was a guy named Armstrong."

"Armstrong," Donovan said, his face clouding.

"As in Richard Armstrong, National Security Advisor to the President."

"Armstrong! Jesus H. Christ! I thought he made his pile in computers or something?"

"He's also a lawyer. Passed the bar in Virginia. Funny thing is, he's only practiced once his entire life. Care to guess the name of the case?"

"No shit!" he cried. "This is better than a fucking John Grisham novel–pardon my language. I become profane when I become excited. Seamus! A couple of big cold ones down here! What else did you find out?"

"That's it. I called the White House, but they laughed when I asked to see him."

Donovan snorted. "They won't be laughing soon enough. By the way, I just got off the phone with our boy."

"Rance? How is he? Is he all right?"

Jenny nearly knocked the beer out of Donovan's hands.

"He's fine. He's in Kazakhstan. They think that Katarina might be there too."

Jenny sat back, a bit deflated. "What about you? Have you come across anything else?"

"Not since that assassin came to my office. I ran his prints through the system-nothing. Doesn't exist. Claimed he was CIA, but there ain't a government employee who isn't finger-printed-that includes the President."

"Who do you think he was?"

"Probably buddies with the clown that tried to rub out Rance-the same people who killed Michael. I'll tell you this, he was one mean looking son of a bitch. The hands on that guy-good Christ!"

§

Jeb McCoy, a.k.a. James Devlin, washed his huge hands in the sink.

Even he realized that they were huge, and their propor-tions demanded greater care when washing. He started with the base of the palms first, then moving to the backs of the hands. The knuckles on the tops of his fingers were particu-larly bad-he refused to were dusters when he worked-and he spent some extra time scrubbing them.

For his fingers and nails he used a soft bristled brush, carefully scrubbing each finger and the small white crescent under each nail. When he was finished his hands looked like they had just received a professional manicure.

Picking up the plastic bag at his feet, he tied it and left it by the door. With one final look back at the limp and lifeless body of Anatoly he smiled. Then he walked out into the pre-dawn darkness.

He had a meeting to attend.

§

The sun was a ball of fuchsia fire.

It had cleared a valley between two of the jagged peaks that made up the Tian Shan mountain range, and the light that oozed down onto the steppe was eerie and liquid.

Marat said something to his uncle and the car stopped.

"It is here, just beyond the hill."

Rance and Francoise couldn't see very well, but they guessed he meant the hulking shadow before them. They got out of the car and the chill of the morning air enveloped them.

"Marat will come," Marat said.

"No," said Rance. "Marat will stay with his uncle and wait. Tell your uncle he will be well paid. And wait. OK?"

Marat looked disappointed, but only for a moment.

"OK," he said brightly.

Rance and Francoise said nothing as they mounted the hill in the dim light. When they reached the crest they could see down into a shallow valley. A lone yurt stood in the calm.

There was no sign of activity.

"Wait," Francoise said, holding Rance's arm before he could go. "We have a long walk down there, and we will be exposed." She drew out her weapon and checked the clip. He followed her lead. "If it comes to this, let me shoot first. I'm probably a better shot than you."

"Probably."

"Rance?"

He looked back at her and saw suddenly that she had quite changed. Gone was her severe demeanor of the last few days. It was replaced by the look he had come to fall in love with during their time in Alsace. She was soft again, and it caused a dry lump to form in his throat.

"If I haven't been very pleasant these last few days then I want to apologize now," she said.

There was a foreboding in her voice that raised an alarm within him. He assumed that she had developed a sort of sixth sense for danger, and now it was manifesting itself clearly on her face.

"I just want you to know that after this I think I am going to retire from my work."

The implications of her statement were not lost on him. For a moment his head swam. She saw this and turned away from him.

"Come," she said. They walked down to the yurt.

Having approached the tented structure in absolute silence, they stopped, one on each side of the entrance. Francoise motioned that she would go in first. In one smooth movement she ducked into the tent. Rance was behind her.

It was empty.

There were no signs that anyone had been inside the yurt for some time.

"Where's Anatoly?" Rance asked.

"Oh, he won't be able to make it."

At the sound of Jeb McCoy's voice they wheeled back to the entrance. They found themselves staring down the ugly barrel of a large gun.

"And from the looks of things," Devlin continued, abandoning his phony accent, "neither will you."

Rance was about to open his mouth, to say something, anything to distract him, when there was a movement behind Devlin.

"Marat is here!"

The boy let out a yelp and threw himself with no effect into Devlin's knees. Kicking him aside, Devlin leveled the gun and fired three rounds into the boy.

As fast as Francoise was, Rance was faster. He began firing his gun at Devlin. The big man turned and looked surprised. Otherwise it appeared that either Rance was missing him with his shots or the bullets were having no effect on him.

As Rance continued firing into Devlin's chest he saw the big hands level the gun at him. He squeezed off his last shot and was about to close his eyes when Devlin's head vaporized before him.

Francoise had fired one shot. Devlin's body crumpled to the ground, smothering Marat.

For a moment neither of them moved. Time was arrested. Francoise went over and rolled Devlin off Marat's body.

"He's dead," she said.

"Jesus Christ," Rance said. "What happened?"

Francoise was going through Devlin's jacket.

"I don't know," she said. She held up folder of paper. "What is it?"

"An airline ticket. To Vienna."

§

Neither of them used the dead man's ticket.

Instead they caught the first Lufthansa flight from Almaty. In Frankfort they connected with a flight to Vienna. The flight arrived 30 minutes before the dead man's flight was scheduled to arrive. Rance and Francoise were standing on one of the concourses looking up at the arrival board. Francoise was walking in an aimless fashion, weaving in and out of the crowd, never wandering far from the dead man's arrival gate.

"Do you mind if I ask what you're doing?" Rance said.

It was Francoise the French intelligence agent again, the one that had been with him throughout much of Kazakhstan, the one he had first met in a Parisian Café. She seemed only peripherally aware of him, her focus somewhere else. Then Rance got it.

"Wait a minute. You don't think-I mean, you don't think that..."

"What else do we have?" She stopped and looked at him. "If nothing comes of this now, we might as well go home and sit by the phone, because we will have nothing else to go on."

"Do you really think Katarina is here?"

"She wasn't in Kazakhstan, was she? The only thing we found in Kazakhstan was...death."

Devlin's flight was announced as having arrived on time.

She took his hand and led him to a small bar just off the main concourse. They sat on the opposite side in a place where Rance didn't think the view was very good.

"Our view is fine–if she behaves the way I believe she will behave." They ordered coffee and waited.

A few minutes later the passengers began filing through the double doors and into the concourse. Small crowds had gathered up against the retaining ropes, waiting and waving. It was a reasonably large flight. Twenty minutes later the passengers coming through the double doors slowed to a trickle.

Rance had seen nothing. While he sat there he tried to picture her in his mind, what she would look like. He tried to remember his last image of her, but the best he could do was Isabelle lying dead in her own bed. Francoise's fingers were suddenly digging into his hand.

"There," she said in a voice so low that her lips didn't move when she spoke. Rance saw nothing but the same crowds, now a little thinner. His eyes struggled to find something to focus on, near or far.

"I don't see–"

"The telephones."

There were several men at the bank of computer-charging stations opposite the double doors, their backs to Francoise and Rance. In their midst was one woman. Unplugging her phone she turned and began walking down the concourse toward the main terminal. Quickly Rance evaluated her. Long, straight hair, trendy sunglasses–

The woman turned her head for an instant toward the double doors as she passed and Rance had a glimpse of her face. It was unmistakable and he nearly choked. The square, model-caliber jaw, the full lips. For the first time in ten years Rance laid eyes on Katarina Favergé.

Neither Rance nor Francoise moved; Rance didn't even breathe. Katarina passed by and continued down the busy concourse and if she had seen them she was playing it ultra cool but Rance didn't think she saw anything.

"Come on."

Francoise had grabbed his hand and dragged him away from the bar and out onto the concourse. They were moving fast and he couldn't see Katarina ahead of them, if that's where she was, but Francoise seemed to have drawn a bead on her so he followed. Suddenly Francoise stopped short, then cut left out a door which led to a taxi stand. A second later Rance saw Katarina emerge from the next set of doors ahead and cross the road to the parking area.

They got into a cab.

"I don't know where we are going yet," Francoise said to the cab driver in perfect German. "Please drive to the end of the airport road and wait." The driver did as he was told. After only a moment Francoise ordered him to continue.

Though Rance tried to see which car they were following, it was useless. He sat back and for the first time felt his heart racing in his chest. Francoise was leaning forward and giving the driver directions.

"Turn right just ahead."

"Left here."

"Continue on."

To Rance it sounded more like she was thinking out loud than anything else. Inside he felt a mixed welter of emotion course through his veins. Fear mingled freely now that they were so close. Closing his eyes, he remembered why he was here, what this was all about. Michael O'Meara's face was quite clear. So was everything else.

"Right here, this is fine."

The taxi stopped and Rance opened his eyes. He thought he must have fallen asleep for they were far out of the city of Vienna now, parked alongside a stunning mountain lake. Getting out of the car Rance noticed an opulent hotel sitting on the edge of the forest which came down the mountainside to the lake.

"Where are we?" he asked.

"*Neusiedler See*," she said. "Lake Neusiedler. It's a ways from Vienna and quite beautiful, wouldn't you agree?"

"Is she..."

"Yes. Up there." Francoise pointed to the opulent hotel on the mountainside. Rance could see now that it was named the Alpenstrasse. When he turned around Francoise was walking away from him, down a small hill. He caught up.

"Where are we going now?" He felt childish for the question but he couldn't help it.

"To another hotel, or course."

The Hotel Leopold was about a half mile and a couple of hundred schillings a night away from the Alpenstrasse, which Rance learned from the front desk clerk was one of the finest and expensive resort spas in all of Austria. Rich people came there to get better. From what? Rance asked. The clerk blushed and Francoise took his hand and led him to their room. She was smiling when she closed the door.

"One does not ask such questions in Europe, Rance."

"If it will make you smile like that then I'll ask those questions all the time."

Now it was her turn to blush, and she did so magnificently, her porcelain skin reddening intensely on the peaks of
her cheeks. He took a tentative step toward her and she came
to him and they embraced for a long, silent time. In his arms
he felt her shake.

"What's wrong?" he asked.

"Too little sleep, too much adventure. Let's just hold for a
while."

She stopped shaking and sat on the edge of the bed.

"We're close," he said. "Is that it?"

"Yes."

"I know. I felt it already."

"We mustn't look beyond. That almost got us killed."

"No, we mustn't," he agreed.

She stood, looking more solid now.

"There are things waiting afterward, no?"

"Yes." He smiled up at her.

"I am going to see the French ambassador in Vienna," she
said. "Try to get some rest, and whatever you do, don't leave
this hotel. All right?"

"All right."

She was almost to the door when he caught her by the
arm. Her cry of surprise was muffled by his lips covering hers,
and she quickly wrapped her arms around him tightly. They
stayed like that for a long time. Not long enough, thought
Rance.

"Rance," she said, kissing his cheek. "Rance."

"These are some of the things waiting."

"Yes, darling." She kissed him again. "Now I must go or we

can forget everything." She pulled away. "Remember, don't leave the hotel. Try to get some rest."

She was gone and he was left there with that feeling so he looked around. He turned on the television and there was a rugby match. That should do it, he thought. A gang of men, muddied and sweating. That should do it.

§

"*Bonjour*," Francoise said to the receptionists.

The receptionist, a beautiful but severe-demeanored blond, looked up as Francoise entered.

"*Bonjour madame*," the receptionist said in perfect French. "*Je peux vous aider?*" Can I help you?

In an instant the Gallic blood began to boil in Francoise's veins. She had been harried and haggard for the last two weeks. She had nearly been killed twice, and despite advertising of the opposite, the life of a foreign agent was not usually so Bond-ish. Sleep was a distant dream, and now she had to stand here and put up with the inanity of this perfect woman who knew exactly who Francoise was. It was the ultimate test of her professionalism.

"I am Francoise Chaumont," she said in English. "But of course you know that, my dear. Would you please run along and fetch Mr. de Lourdes for me?" A patronizing smile completed the broadside, and Francoise saw the anger mottle the receptionist's cheeks. After a quick phone call, the woman motioned for Francoise to enter through the wide double doors.

Alexandre de Lourdes was seated behind a large desk. It looked ridiculous, thought Francoise, for it was massive, yet there was almost nothing atop it: a fountain pen holder, one framed picture and a telephone. Behind de Lourdes was a floor to ceiling window, on either side of which was a flag: one French, one Austrian. The flag of the European community hung quietly in the corner.

"Francoise!"

De Lourdes rose dramatically from behind his desk, coming around with a flourish and embracing her, giving her four kisses instead of the usual two.

Alexandre was not a bad looking man, she thought. A little thicker than the last time she had seen him, but in that way that men get, making them more attractive as they aged.

"Honestly, Alexandre, must keep your trophies out on display?" she said. "It is so unprofessional."

"But you are mistaken, Francoise," he replied, offering her a seat. "It has been over between her and I for months now."

His eyes took a shameless tour of her body as she sat down and crossed her legs. Letting his look linger on her dazzling appendages, Alexandre made no false pretenses regarding his attraction to her.

"But you, Francoise, you are as beautiful as ever. Tell me, when are you going to retire and come live with me here in this beautiful country?"

"Please, Alexandre, I did not come here to flirt–"

"A pity."

"Katarina is here."

Just as quickly as he had become endearingly ingratiating and sexually overt, Alexandre changed, darkening instantly, his thick brows furrowing, lips vanishing into a dark, staid line.

"Where?"

Francoise drew a cigarette from her purse, examined it for a moment, then placed it between her lips. She let her eyes rise up to meet his. Then she cocked an eyebrow.

Alexandre rose, but not with a rush. He calmly walked over to the credenza and returned with a lighter. Lighting her cigarette, he did not take his eyes from hers.

It was a dance that Francoise detested, but one she knew she excelled at. She also knew that the formalities of diplomacy, which extended all the way down to the scene being played out in this office, demanded it. She blew the smoke out above his head.

"I will need some help."

"You will have my best people. I have several Foreign Legionaries with a raging thirst for blood–"

"We need her alive, Alexandre."

Katarina's tentacles stretched so far, Francoise marveled. As if they knew no boundaries, no frontiers, no limits, no discriminations. Alexandre's quick offer to smote Katarina betrayed a past between them. Francoise could easily imagine the script, for she had seen the hurt on Rance's face day after day. She counted herself lucky to be a woman–and lucky that Katarina was demonstrably heterosexual.

Alexandre blinked and sat back. "Yes, of course we do. You will have all the resources you need. I am at your service. And the American? You have him?"

She looked down. "He is here."

"Good. Bring him in as soon as you can."

"Bring him in?"

"Of course. He is still wanted for murder, and as a courtesy to the Paris police–"

"But he is innocent. I know it for a fact."

Alexandre smiled, his eyes taking on a new shine.

"What is this? Do I detect something in your voice, my dear? Don't tell me that you and the American..."

She stood up quickly.

"I am at this hotel," she said, handing him a card. "I will be there the rest of the afternoon. Send your people over when they are ready."

She turned and left quickly, not wishing to see the smirk on his face.

§

Rance entered the Hotel Alpenstrasse.

A heavy load descended on his shoulders. The weight of the knowledge that he and Katarina were both under the same roof again was almost unbearable. That's funny, he thought. For most of the last ten years he hadn't devoted tremendous amounts of thought to her, and yet suddenly, her she was, controlling the direction in which his life went with an almighty indifference.

It was true that he had been heartbroken after their relationship ended. But after several of his long letters had gone unanswered, after it became obvious that he would never see her again, she began to fade. The sharpness of her features dulled, and Rance was eventually left with only her essence. But this was Katarina, and her essence was a concentrated and volatile concoction of steamy sexuality and single minded manipulation.

Stopping in the lobby for a moment, he laughed to himself. She really was Shakespeare's Iago incarnate–poured in the body of a Venus.

He approached the front desk. A thin, drawn out man stood there, plain faced and unnervingly steady. Rance smiled.

"Excuse me," he said. "Do you speak English."

The man smiled so fraudulently that Rance wished he had powers of arrest. "Yes, sir. How may I help you?"

Venturing a quick glance down behind the counter, Rance saw the object of his game: the hotel's registration book.

"My name is Hathaway," he lied, "and I am supposed to meet one of your guests, Mr. Rodney Idle. Could you tell me if he's checked in yet?"

The man looked down carefully at his book and began slowly shaking his head.

"I'm sorry, Mr. Hathaway, I don't see his name here. In fact, there is no record of his having reserved a room here."

"Oh, dear. This is the Hotel Alpenstrasse, am I correct? Oh dear. I wonder what could have gone wrong. Is there a phone I could use?"

"Just around the corner, sir."

Rance found the phones, walked past them down a long hall way and entered the kitchen. There was no activity, so he passed through and exited by a door on the opposite side. There he found himself in another hallway that contained two elevators. He entered one of the elevators.

The hotel had ten floors. Above the button for the tenth floor was the elevator car's control panel. As he popped it open, a vision of Jack Ryan, Jenny's father, flashed before him, and his heart beat a heavy thud with the memory of the dead elevator man.

But he also remembered Jack Ryan's stories about working on elevators in Boston's high rises. And those stories included tips on how to fix any elevator you happened to be stuck in. Now Rance hoped he remembered enough to break an elevator.

Inside the panel was a tangle of wires leading to three switches. Sticking his foot in the door of the elevator to prevent it from closing before he could get out, he then drew out two wires, pushed the button for the tenth floor, and crossed the wires. As he jumped back out of the elevator car, he hit the big red emergency button. The doors closed and the elevator took off on what he hoped was a long, crazy ride. Then he retraced his steps through the kitchen and back out into the lobby. He was just in time to see the desk manager disappear around the corner, responding to the elevator alarm.

Rance wasted no time. He went behind the desk and opened the registration book. But he was quickly disappointed to see that Katarina had either not registered, or was using an alias. He checked the list again and saw it. In room 713 there was a K. Desdemona. Of course, he thought. Othello's poor wife. He wondered if she knew she was betraying herself at every step. His reverie was broken by the footsteps of the returning desk clerk.

"What are you doing!" the man barked in German. "Get away from there!"

"I just spoke to Mr. Idle and he says he's booked here–"

"Get away! I don't have time for you now! There is an emergency! Now leave at once!"

Rance didn't argue. Instead he made sure that the desk manager was sufficiently distracted before he ducked into the stairwell, exiting on at the seventh floor. His luck held, and as he rounded a corner, he saw a maid approaching him. She must have been Phillipino, he thought. When she was a few steps away, Rance stumbled into the woman, apologized, and continued down to room 713. With the keys to the hotel in his hand, he paused in front of the door.

He was here. The temptation to pause and weigh the gravity of the moment was enormous, but he resisted. Instead he drew the gun from his jacket, slipped the key into the door and entered the room.

§

A guest entered the hotel.

He looked around with discrete but practiced thoroughness. Outside, the front drive was jammed with rescue equipment. Danger alarms sounded in his head when he saw them, but as soon as he determined that they were rescue vehicles his nerves calmed. He had been jumpy.

And that's why he was here. Twice now he had been forced into the game. That was no longer his way. If he had stepped back to critique himself he might even have seen the rust that had formed. But there was no time for that. He was back for good now, until the whole thing was resolved.

As he approached the desk in the lobby he saw that he was all alone. Around the corner there was some kind of commotion, and he snuck a look to see the backs of several emergency personnel. Some problem with the elevators.

Back at the desk, he leaned over and looked at the registration book. As usual she did not use her own name. As usual she would have used something cute and esoteric. He looked impatiently at his watch. He didn't have time for this.

"Can I help you?"

The desk manager had returned, a worried and haggard look on his face.

"My name is Tralfargar. You have a message for me?"

The manager rummaged through his papers.

"Ah, yes. Madame Desdemona would like you to go straight up to her room, number 713. But there will be a few minutes' delay–the lift is out of service and the fire department wants no one using the stairs in case there is another emergency." The manager smiled. "I'm terribly sorry. If you'd like to wait in the lounge your drinks will be on the house."

The man retreated to the lounge and took a seat which allowed him a view of the lobby and the front drive. The delay bothered him. The thing was getting close. She was supposed to have already delivered, but an endless array of snags kept blossoming. He accepted a drink and found that it relaxed him. From his coat pocket the big red-headed man removed a rubber band and began twirling it with his fingers.

§

As Rance entered Katarina's hotel room, Francoise entered his a few miles down the road.

She was accompanied by two agents, one French, one Austrian. The Frenchman she knew from Paris. He was named Guy Leclerc and he looked like anything but a foreign agent. Short, dark and permanently ruffled, Leclerc had greasy hair and a chronic case of dandruff.

The Austrian, Rheinhardt Waroschitz, she didn't know. Alexandre had assured her that he was to be trusted, but Francoise trusted almost no one; it was how one survived in an occupation such as this.

The room was empty. Francoise knew immediately where he was. "*Merde*," she said.

§

The shower was running.

Inside number 713 Rance found an opulent suite. Immediately on his left was a kitchenette. Before him was a vast living room, complete with leather furniture, an entertainment center and a huge balcony that overlooked the Neusiedler See. The sound of the shower came from his left, and he was about to walk toward it when it suddenly stopped.

His heart felt like screaming, screaming and tossing his gun out the window and going straight back to Green Harbor to his boat (oops! No boat anymore, Rance) and getting drunk and staying that way until everything was gone again.

He didn't because he couldn't. For Rance had discovered that not only could time not be reversed, but it couldn't be obscured either. To bury the pain of the past was to plant a tree that would bear unbelievably terrible fruit in the future. The fact that he was standing in a hotel room in Austria with a gun was testament to that.

So he slunk back into the shadows. Bright sunshine bathed the living room in a yellow fluorescence, but the kitchenette had no windows and was dark. He backed into it, his eyes and the barrel of the gun peeking around the corner.

A door opened. From his position he had a clear view of the entire suite, except the closed doors of the bedroom, and behind the door that just opened he could see more space, a light in a bathroom. And Katarina.

Though she was completely naked it was her hair that Rance saw first. Wet and long and combed back, it was exactly the way he remembered it so long ago. So strong was the pull of the past that he found himself physically hanging onto the door jamb in an effort to remain still.

As she strode across the living room, Katarina showed very little signs of aging. Her body was as firm and curvy as it was ten years ago, and her beauty radiated out and touched Rance. He swallowed hard. At the bar, she fixed herself a drink, then went over to the balcony. A warm afternoon breeze wafted in and stroked her skin.

As Rance crept from his hiding spot, he had to step carefully, for the past was spilling out everywhere, strewing the floor before him with memories good and bad, threatening to topple him. He blinked once, twice, and raised his gun. The bead at the end of the barrel rested between Katarina's bare shoulders. He thought about a daughter he didn't know. He thought about Michael. He thought about Francoise and cocked the hammer back.

§

Francoise didn't want to think about it.

As their car sped out of the parking lot and on to the main road, there were a lot of things she did not want to think about. She didn't want to think about the potential danger Rance might be in, and she didn't want to think about how that made her feel.

Instead she concentrated on what she would do: take Katarina. The diplomats could work out the details later. Maybe it would never get that far. Maybe this whole thing would remain covert. That would suit Francoise fine. In her opinion, Katarina did not deserve the formalities of justice, international or otherwise.

The car came up to a crest, then Rhienhardt, who had been driving, slammed on the brakes. The car skidded wildly to one side of the road, then the other, as he fought for control. They stopped just shy of a pile of manure.

A farmer had been crossing the road with a wagon load of manure for one of his fields when one of his cart's axles snapped, dumping two tons of cow manure in the middle of the road, the only road to the Hotel Alpenstrasse.

As Francoise got out of the car, she could see the hotel off in the distance, rising spectrally in the forest above the lake.

"We could continue on foot," Rheinhardt suggested.

Francoise waved him off. It was not an option. She lit a cigarette and hoped things could wait.

§

Katarina spun around at the sound of the gun's hammer cocking.

Though he had watched her walk from the bedroom to the balcony, it was only when she looked directly at him that Rance realized again her true beauty. Her body was an exquisite creation, a classic for the ages, and he remembered what

Anatoly had said: they called her Venus, but Venus de Milo probably wasn't as beautiful as Katarina.

"So you finally caught up to me, Rance."

Nothing about her showed surprise or the least amount of discomfort at being totally nude and having a gun pointed at her. Not her breathing, not her skin, not her eyes. She looked at him as if they had seen each other only a minute earlier in the bedroom.

His eyes flashed to the bedroom door.

"Don't worry," she said, "I am all alone here. Can I fix you a drink?"

Without waiting for an answer she walked over to the bar. "Irish whiskey, wasn't it, Rance?" She poured from a bottle of Jameson. He held the gun on her, redoubling his grip. She held up the drink for him and smiled. Just like yesterday, he thought. Just like yesterday.

He approached her. On the back of the couch there was a robe. He picked it up and tossed it to her.

"Have we become bashful?" she teased, but Rance was not amused. She's dangerous, he kept telling himself. Dangerous. Don't listen. She's a siren on the rocks.

"Just put it on, Katarina."

"Must you point that ugly weapon at me?" She put down the two glasses and pulled the robe on. As she did, Rance felt a wave of relief sweep through him. With her naked in front of him, they had been equally armed. Now, with her robed and covered, he had an advantage of firepower. How many, he wondered, have fallen in her sights?

"What don't you sit down, Katarina? While we're waiting for your freedom to come to a screeching halt, let's have a little chat–catch up on old times, shall we?"

His voice sounded cool and even and her face reacted with an almost imperceptible shift. But he saw it, saw the line of her lips change as she sat. He remained where he was, commanding the room with his gun.

She sipped her drink. "What should we talk about?"

"I don't know where to start. How about stealing American defense systems technology and selling it to third world terrorists? Or having Michael O'Meara killed? Or trying to have me killed? Gosh, I don't know where to start."

She was someone used to getting her own way, that much Rance knew. And right now, she was not getting her own way. In fact, she was being bossed and manipulated, and she didn't like it. She opened her mouth to speak but Rance cut her short.

"But all that can wait," he said. "Let's start by talking about our daughter, Michelle."

§

Jenny's cell phone rang.

At first she couldn't believe it. She had sacrificed the air conditioning that evening for open windows. To compromise for the roar of the road, her stereo, a six speaker, 100 watt Blaupunkt, was turned all the way up, sending the soulful strains of Melissa Etheridge crashing out into the night.

She hadn't really wanted the phone; she'd been the last person she knew to get one. But after continued complaints by her partners that she could never be reached on the sometimes hour and a half commute into and out of Boston, she had broken down and gotten one. She hated it precisely for that reason: only people from work ever called her. Jenny couldn't even remember the thing's phone number without checking the settings.

And now the car phone's most annoying feature was rearing its ugly head. It was a feature the salesman insisted she have, and it was called a cut off. No matter how high the stereo was turned up, the volume was automatically muted when the car phone rang. As if someone had cut the cord to her electric guitar Melissa Etheridge went silent and Jenny was left with the annoying chirp of the cellular phone. She frowned.

"Hello?"

"So what do you think of the United States attorney who prosecuted Ms. Favergé?"

Jenny's eyes went wide. It was the man who had trapped her in the elevator, the "Deep Throat" who told her to investigate the prosecution, not the defense.

"Who is this? How did you get this number?"

"Please, Ms. Ryan. That really isn't important. What's important is how far you've gotten."

"You mean have I discovered that Richard Armstrong, the current National Security Advisor was the chief counsel for the United States in their case against Katarina Favergé? And did Mr. Armstrong not see me? I think you can answer those questions for yourself, whoever you are."

"Call me Walter."

"Listen 'Walter,' you gave me a dead end. What does who prosecuted Katarina Favergé have to do with what's going on right now."

"Now we get to the heart of the matter. What is going on

right now? A matter of national security, if I'm not mistaken. Software technology, U.S. defense systems, thing of that nature."

"How do you know–"

"That's not important. What is important is that nobody know who I am, or I would involuntarily cease being a source for you."

Jenny noted again how carefully the man spoke, as if he chose his words for a living. A lawyer, she guessed. Could it be Schwartz himself? He had been known for his dramatics in other areas of the law. But the voice was obviously disguised, enough so that she couldn't be certain. She tried a different tactic.

"Did you come to tout your intimate knowledge of this thing, or are you going to give me some useful information?"

There was a long moment of silence and Jenny was tempted to hang up.

"What do you know about Mr. Armstrong?" Walter asked.

"About as much as anybody. Made millions with his own software company selling operating systems to big corporations like Boeing, Raytheon, General Electric–"

"Exactly. Boeing, Raytheon, GE. They just happen to be three of the biggest defense contractors in the country, right? And now Mr. Armstrong's name has surfaced amidst this intriguing case that your friend is persuing, a case that involves–surprise! The software that will coordinate and operate the United States' laser-based defense system in the next century. Some coincidence."

"Wait a minute. Are you suggesting–"

"I'm suggesting that you go take a look at Dynaware, Inc.,

Mr. Armstrong's old money maker. Maybe you'll bump into someone as chatty as me."

The line went dead.

"Son of a-" Jenny looked around at the cars on the highway, but it was too dark to see any of them. Nonetheless it was another level to take things to. And it was becoming increasingly complicated and dangerous.

She didn't notice the resumption of the Melissa Etheridge CD, even at full volume.

§

"Pardon me, sir?"

It was the desk manager. The big red-head stopped twirling his rubber band and looked up. His facial expression was blank and indifferent and the manager seemed taken aback by it. He straightened up.

"The lifts are back in service, sir."

The big red-head thanked him and entered one of the cars, pushing the button for the seventh floor.

§

Jerry Abel was smiling from one ear to the next.

Maybe I'll screw Senator Jessup's daughter tonight, he thought. Or maybe I'll screw Mrs. Jessup. Abel's golf partner, the President of the United States, had just shot a 77 at the Potomac Country Club, and he had given Abel all of the credit. Shit, Abel thought, maybe I'll screw both Mrs. Jessup and her daughter at the same time.

Not even the sight of Richard Armstrong, the little prick on a power trip, could dampen the ebullient mood of Jerry Abel.

"How did he do?" Armstrong asked. Abel lit a cigarette and considered Armstrong through the blue smoke that hung around his face in the still, humid air.

"He's ready to sell guns to the Ayatollah."

Armstrong frowned but inside he rejoiced. Dismissing Abel with a nod, he calculated the best tack to take with the President. When he was happy, Armstrong knew, he was careless. And nothing could make him happier than shooting a 77. His life's quest. No we'll all have to listen to him bitch about breaking par.

"Dick, you're not going to believe it," the President gushed, walking up to Armstrong and pumping his outstretched hand vigorously. "You're just not going to believe it."

"Congratulations, sir. Jerry just told me the good news. And a 77 at that. They can't say you didn't smash it, sir, can they."

"You should have seen it, Dick." The President clapped an arm around Armstrong, leading him into the clubhouse. "I didn't even have a good day off the tees. But I was consistent, Dick, consistent. The secret is don't screw up. That's all. Just don't screw up."

"That's just great, sir." Then, looking around surreptitiously, seeing nothing but a half dozen Secret Service agents, Armstrong led him off to a corner. "If I could have a moment of your time. It's about SHAKESPEARE."

The President became all business. "I'm glad you brought that up, Dick. I've been meaning to ask you about that."

"You are aware, of course of the mid-level meetings about to take place in Italy. Well, instead of sending the Undersecretary of State, I'd like to go, sir."

"But why, Dick? That's only to begin working on the next round of accords–all legal mumbo jumbo."

Armstrong looked around to emphasize his gravity.

"Sir, to be quite frank, one of the Israelis attending the talks is an old friend from Harvard who might be of some use to me. I'd like to get my finger right on the pulse of this situation concerning SHAKESPEARE. I'm afraid our people sometimes get so bogged down in protocol that, well, I'd just rather see if I could get on it myself."

The President rubbed his chin. "You think so? Well, I guess, but please, Dick, be discreet. A commercial flight, OK. And get right back to me on this."

"Yes, sir." Armstrong allowed himself a smile as he turned and walked away.

And as he did, the President's gaze followed Armstrong out of the clubhouse. If Armstrong had bothered to turn around, he would have found a narrow, almost cynical look on his boss's face.

§

With Katarina, one had to watch very carefully.

So expert was she at this game that she had to be watched with minute attention. Rance was becoming expert at that. His mind strained at its constraints, begging to return to their time together and analyze it, dissect it, try to discover all the things he had missed. But he held it fast, letting the barrel of the gun serve as its metaphor: hold the gun steady, keep the mind steady.

"Then you know," she said theatrically. She looked down and let her face sadden. That is what he had prepared himself for. She was letting the emotion manifest itself. She was controlling it. Willing it to be. Don't be fooled.

"Why didn't you ever tell me?"

"And what purpose would that serve? You would have taken an active interest in her then? No, it would have only meant more pain."

"More than you're already responsible for?"

He saw the surprise flash on her face and only then realized that he had taken a step toward her, his teeth grinding together. Taking a deep breath, he relaxed.

"You may not approve of what I'm doing but I have my reasons."

"Oh, you do? And what reasons are those? Greed? Is that it? Or do you fancy yourself some Bond-esque ruler of the world according to your prophecy? What is it, Katarina? Because I have to know. Before I kill you, I have to know. I have to know how I could have been so completely manipulated. It may sound silly to you but I actually thought you cared about me–about us. But I guess that's the way it goes in the spy business, right?"

It welled within him, an unpredictable anger, flashing violently up like heartburn, tensing the muscles of his body, increasing the pressure exerted by his trigger finger.

"Oh, Rance, you mustn't think that way. Did it feel real to you? Because it was real, and Michelle is the proof of it. You know of course her middle name. I didn't have to name her

Michelle Vaughn Favergé. But I did because she is a part of you as well as me. You must believe that."

Rance suddenly realized that he didn't have a plan. He had Katarina right where he wanted her, but he had no idea what his next move would be-except to kill her.

"I know I haven't been a good mother, and for that I have no excuse. But you must hear my side of the story, Rance. There is a reason for this, please believe me. When this is all over, you will see. We will be reunited with Michelle. I thank God for Isabelle-"

"Isabelle's dead."

This time he got her. Real shock painted her face as her hand flew to her mouth, her eyes wide with horror. Perhaps he should have saved that card, he reasoned. Perhaps he would need it in the future to manipulate her the way she had manipulated so many others.

"You really are Iago, aren't you, Katarina? You really are the supreme manipulator, the true incarnation of evil."

"Rance, please listen to me-"

"And all that time I thought that Shakespeare was just a pleasant diversion for you. I didn't know that you were a malicious student of Iago."

"Rance, turn around right now, please-"

"You can stop it now, Katarina. You can st-"

Rance crumpled to the floor. Behind him stood the big red-head, a short length of pipe clutched in his fist.

"Well now," he said, not bothering to disguise his Irish accent. "Isn't this lovely. I've got you both."

§

The last of the manure was pushed out of the way and they sped past.

Checking her gun one final time, Francoise hoped that Rance had not decided to be heroic. She had admitted to herself that she cared deeply for this man. His story was poetic to her, stirring her to depths she thought had been dried up forever. Yes, she thought to herself, I love you Rance Vaughn. Please don't get yourself killed, because I don't think I could stand it.

They skidded to a halt in front of the hotel. Bursting through the front door, Waroschitz flashed his Austrian police identification and took the registration book. While he questioned the desk manager, he handed the book to Francoise and Leclerc.

As she frantically went down the list of guests, she tried to put herself in Rance's shoes. If he had come here, what would he have done? Try to find Katarina and confront her was the answer, but she did not want it to be. Francoise recognized none of the names in the book–

Then she saw it: K. Desdemona. Othello's wife. Room 713.

Leclerc was dispatched to the stairs with orders to meet them on the seventh floor. Francoise and Rheinhardt went to the elevators and impatiently pushed the up button.

There were two cars. Above each car was an old fashioned dial mechanism which showed each car's location. The car on the left was currently descending past the sixth floor. The car on the right was descending past the third. The doors to the car on the right opened, and Francoise and Rheinhardt had to step aside to let people out.

Meanwhile the left car was nearly at the lobby level. its doors opened just as Francoise stepped into the right car. A porter wheeling a large travel trunk exited the left car first, followed by Katarina and the big red-head. The door to Francoise's elevator car closed just as she saw the porter wheeling the trunk.

In room 713 they saw that they were too late. Whoever had been in here had beaten a hasty retreat, leaving clothes in the closet, window opened, stereo on. Francoise knelt and found a small spot of blood.

"Nom de dieu."

Part IV

Ireland

It was dark, damp, and wet.

Not inside, but he could definitely feel his bones aching with the weather. Since he had turned thirty, Rance began to noticed that his body was affected by weather. Though he hated to admit it, the cold, wet winters in New England were getting to him.

At first he was in total denial. It had always been a badge of honor to chide those who fled New England in the winter for the warmer climes of Florida and Arizona. Rance was among the toughies that welcomed the driving rain of the nor'easters that relentlessly whipped the coastline in winter. Best time to walk the beach, he said, and he was often joined by other lunatics, bundled up against a gale that drove raindrops like spikes into them, slogging up and down the foam blistered beach. It justified the heavy drinking.

But as he abused himself into his thirties, Rance began to notice a creaking quality to his joints. And when the weather turned really sour, he would roll out of bed stiff and toxic, taking over an hour and a full pot of coffee to get loose enough to do some really serious lunchtime drinking.

The worst were the summer storms. Along the coast of New England, once or twice a summer, an ocean storm would lash them with cold rain and high winds. In the last few years Rance had begun to notice that these storms, striking in the middle of his summer looseness, hurt the most. At least in the winter, he reasoned, you had the benefit of thick blood.

That was how he felt right now: as if he had been plucked from the middle of a hot and humid summer and deposited into an ocean gale, the wet wind pushing through the pores of his skin and invading his marrow with rusting effect.

But there was another feeling, too. This one, he knew, had been introduced from outside. He was sure that he had been given some drug that was only now wearing off. He could feel the forced lethargy of his muscles, a drunken feeling that he was powerless over. His eyelids, on the other hand, worked just fine, and he blinked them several times.

From the edges of the window shade came cracks of light. Though he didn't have a direct view outside, he knew it was cloudy and raining out there. Then he began to wonder just where in the hell "out there" was. For Rance, time had retreated into a surreal dreamscape, liquid and loose without dimension. He closed his eyes and dreamed.

At first all he saw was his boat. Bobbing gently on a swell, it was a handsome boat. He wished he were on it right now. In his mind's eye, he could see something in his boat. But his angle of vision was low, as if he were standing in a tiny skiff some distance away. He stretched to see. Almost. A little more. There, now he could see it.

It was a body.

Without consciously leaving the skiff, he rose up, floating over the water, gliding toward his boat. It was definitely a body. He reached down and flipped it over. Then he screamed.

The body was his own.

Rance continued screaming until firm hand pushed him gently back into the bed. He opened his eyes for real this time, trying to escape the dream. The room was different, bigger and better lit. And warm. It was warm. Gone was the aching in his bones that he had–dreamed? His chest heaved and he fought to catch his breath.

"There, there, you've just a touch of the fever. Lay back, now. I'm just after putting the tea on."

He frowned and looked up at the figure before him. It was an old woman, that he could see. Her skin was white like china and healthy looking, and her smile was pressed on thin, bloodless lips. And though it was flecked and streaked with gray, her hair still shone red and fiery.

It was her accent, however, that caught him off guard. It was unmistakably Irish.

As he came more awake, he began to feel the real pain in his arms and legs. Prickly heat, pins and needles, as if he had been curled up under the covers for ages, they were stiff and achy. A massage, he thought, would do me wonders. But where in the hell am I?

He opened his mouth to speak but it was so dry, so encrusted with inactivity, that neither his tongue nor his lips could make the right motions to produce intelligible sounds. He croaked.

"There, dear," the old woman said. "Here's some tea. Just a little sip, now. There, isn't that grand, now?"

It was grand, soaking into his parched mouth, releasing it from its shackles. He wanted to gulp the entire cup down but the woman allowed him only to sip. When the cup was gone, he felt coordinated enough to speak.

"Where am I?"

"Cashel, dear."

Cashel Deer, he heard. Where the hell is that? Sounds like the fictional town in some Stephen King novel.

"Cashel Deer?" he asked.

"Cashel. In Tipperary. Where did you think you were?"

Good question, he thought. I thought I was-

Oh, God. He remembered. Austria. The hotel. Katarina. Then what? Obviously, he hadn't been watching his back. But Cashel? Tipperary? Ireland?

"You've had a long trip, darlin', and you need some rest. I'll check back in an hour or so to see if you'll take some soup."

She left him in the room and he looked around. There was a fireplace, ridiculously small by American standards, but a bright turf fire burned in it, and all the way across the room Rance could feel its heat. Otherwise, the room was spartan. A small night table beside his bed, and a window with the lace curtains drawn. The curtains looked yellow and old and they obscured his view outside. But he could see that it was raining.

He didn't have the strength to get up, so he lay back and

closed his eyes.

§

United Airlines flight 966 cruised above the darkened Atlantic.

Though most of the people in first class were by now fast asleep, Richard Armstrong was busy working. Or, at least to the casual observer, he looked like he was working. In fact, Armstrong was far away.

The events that had brought him to this flight caused him to reflect upon how it all began. Not usually a man given to reflection, Armstrong was discovering lately that he had begun to exhibit a variety of behaviors not normally attributable to him.

Flight 966 would land in Rome in a few more hours. There he was supposed to meet with the European bureau chief of the CIA, then with an Israeli envoy regarding the on-going mess in the middle east. But that wasn't what Armstrong was looking forward to.

He hadn't seen her in more than a month. The weekend before the Fourth of July she had flown in to Washington, and though it had been a busy time, he fit her in. Thinking about it, he shook his head. It would be more accurate to say that he abandoned his duties, abandoned his family, to be with her.

And now he had created this bogus agenda in Rome as an excuse to see her again. He had to. Things were happening very quickly now, and he needed to be brought up to speed. There would be arrangements, for sure. He needed to know the timing. Because once completed, there would be a chance of his discovery, and he would have to move. Fast.

If his punishment was to spend the rest of his life with her, however, it would be a small price to pay. And with that kind of money...he thought about buying an island somewhere. That's the kind of money he was thinking about.

Richard Armstrong closed his eyes and saw her. The wait would be over soon, and then he would have Katarina Favergé all to himself.

§

Rance wasn't completely asleep.

Whatever kind of sedative he had been given was finally wearing off. Rance guessed that it was the night after he first woke up. He remembered the woman and the tea, and then he fell back asleep. Now it was fully night, and his eyes popped wide open. There were voices in the hall.

"Claire?"

Rance frowned. Was that Katarina? It certainly wasn't anyone Irish.

"Oh, hello dear." The Irish woman who had given Rance tea. "Aren't you up awfully late."

"I've just arrived. How is he?"

There was no doubt about Katarina's voice.

"Oh, he's doing just fine. A little groggy."

"Good. Would you see that he gets his breakfast? I've got a busy day tomorrow. I've got to be somewhere, but I'll be back the following morning."

"Will Jackie be up in the morning?"

"Yes, I expect him."

"That's fine. He hasn't been home for a good long time now. I'm really looking forward to seeing him. How long will he stay?"

"Oh, not long. We're going out to Derrynane for a few days as soon as I get back."

"Must you travel so much?"

"A consequence of the modern world I'm afraid. But I'm looking forward to getting away."

"Derrynane's grand. Lovely this time of year."

Their voices faded down the hallway. Rance was doubly confused now. Why am I in Ireland? Of all places, why here? And who is Jackie? Could they have been talking about the big read-head? It would make sense-a little. But was that sweet little old lady-his mother? And Derrynane-Katarina said they would be going there. Did that mean me too?

The big read-head. It must have been him who knocked Rance out while he was standing there talking to Katarina-was it two days ago? Somehow, Katarina and this guy are involved with something together. Maybe he is her lover, or business partner. Rance suddenly wondered why he was alive. The big red-head had tried to kill me on several occasions, and he obviously had me in the hotel room, but he only knocked me out, Rance thought. The only explanation was Katarina. For some reason, she wanted me alive. That somehow didn't fit. Why try so hard to kill me, then once you have me let me go?

Quietly Rance stole from his bed, trying to ignore the protest of his aching muscles. He tried the door in the dark. Locked. Though it was pitch dark inside the room, his eyes adjusted and he found the dresser. Bingo! My clothes. Dressing as quietly as possible, Rance tried to think of a way out.

There was only a window, and it was a long way down.

Poking his head outside, Rance saw his break. Thick ivy vines covered the walls of the place, and he was able to lower himself without much difficulty. Unfortunately, he noticed, it was not raining. Instead a brilliant moon shone down on the Irish landscape, illuminating everything brightly.

Once on the ground he stuck to the side of the building and got his bearings. A long driveway led up to the house. In the moonlight Rance could see sheep everywhere, along the drive, in the huge yard to either side, they were even sleep next to the two cars parked in the driveway.

There were no lights on inside the house. As he skirted the bushes surrounding the lawn, Rance hoped that the collies had been put in for the night. Twenty minutes later he scaled a wall and found himself on a narrow country road. One way looked as good as another, and without a clue as to what to do next, Rance began walking.

§

It was a slow morning.

Lately, everything about her job seemed slow. Unhurried. Geological in its measurement of time. Even the view looked slow. Down State Street, past the Customs Tower, she could see the Central Artery, a.k.a. Interstate 93, three lanes in each direction going right through the center of the city-at least in spirit, because right now it had become the world's biggest parking lot. Everywhere she looked, on every city street, the highway ramps, tiny side streets, traffic was locked up tight. There'd be shootings reported on the 10 o'clock news tonight.

Iago's Fool

Though there was a stack of work on her desk, Jenny had no ambition to approach it. She was flat, and had been since Rance fled over two weeks ago. The bastard, she thought. I can't get him out of my head. A combination of frustration, affection and confusion rattled through her, and she could feel her face flush despite the air conditioning.

She stood. The clock read only a quarter of ten in the morning, but she had had enough already. A workout was what she needed, a hard, punishing couple of hours of running under the hot sun on the beach in front of her house. She'd pack up this work and try to–

Her ringing phone interrupted the thought.

"Jenny Ryan," she said.

"My God, you should see the sunrise over here, all cloaked in mist and red orange. Damn poetic is what it is. Makes you wonder why our grandfathers ever left."

"Rance?"

"Do you miss me?"

"Rance, where have you been? Marty and I haven't heard from you for days. What the hell is going on?"

"I was hoping you could help me out with that."

"Did something happen? Where are you? Are you still in Kazakhstan?"

"Ireland."

"Ireland? What's in Ireland?"

"A lot of damp weather, for one thing. My shoulder's killing me. You remember the time I dislocated it in high school–"

"Rance! What are you doing in Ireland?"

"You'll have to read the book. But I sure could use some

help."

"What happened to the French agent you were with?"

Rance felt a lump grow in his throat. What's the matter, big boy? he thought. Feeling a little slimy? How come? There's nothing between you and Jenny. Besides, I thought you loved Francoise...

"Ah, we got separated," he said. At least it was the truth. Rance didn't even know if Jenny knew Francoise was a woman, much less a beautiful one. "Listen, I need to get in touch with Marty."

"Isn't he at his office?"

"I forgot the number. Yours is the only number I can remember. Have you dug up anything for me?"

"You could say that. Ever hear of Richard Armstrong?"

"First man on the moon?"

"Current national security advisor."

"Sorry. I was drunk. What's so special about him?"

"The software that his company helped develop is the stuff that everybody's killing themselves over."

"Correct me if I'm wrong, but that sounds like conflict of interest to me."

"I'm going to do a little checking at his old company, Dynaware. Maybe I'll find something that will tie him to all this. How are things going with you?"

"Things have been better. That's why I need to get in touch with Marty as soon as possible." Rance looked down at the credit card he had lifted from a tipsy pub patron the night before when he walked into Cashel.

"Hang on just a second, Rance, I'll see if I can get him on a conference call." There was silence for a moment as he was put on hold. "Rance? Are you still there? I've got Marty."

"Marty?" said Rance.

"Hey, it's Mr. Crimestopper."

"Marty, I'm in a bad way over here-"

"Wait a minute-where the hell are you?"

"Ireland."

"Ireland? How the hell did you end up there?"

"Katarina."

"Katarina?"

"Katarina?" said Jenny. "Did you find her?"

"Yeah, you could say that. I caught up to her in Austria. Then somebody jumped me and when I opened my eyes, bingo, welcome to Ireland. Anyway, I managed to escape, but they'll be out for me any minute now, and I have no place to go."

"What happened to Francoise?" asked Marty.

"We got separated. I don't think she knows what happened to me."

"Where are you now?"

"Cashel."

"Can you get to Shannon International Airport?"

Rance glanced down at the credit card. "Sure, no problem. But why-"

"Because you've staggered around long enough. I'm coming over and we're going to wrap this thing up."

"But how-"

"Listen, sunshine, I'm related to half of that damn country, and a few of them are cops, right? So you just get your butt to Shannon. I'll see if there's an afternoon flight. Jenny?"

"Yes."

"Come pick me up at my office. You're going to be running the point back here so we need to straighten things out. And Rance?"

"Yes, dear."

"Try not to commit any crimes while you're in Cashel. I have an Uncle Bill that lives there."

Rance looked down at the name on the credit card.

"Bill O'Connell?"

"Yeah, that's him."

"Too late, Marty."

§

It was the part of the job that Francoise detested.

Actually, she thought to herself while sitting in the lounge and waiting to see the director of operations for the SDECE, this whole episode had been draining, emotionally as well as physically. I'm burning out, she thought. Never before have I let something like this happen...

Never before have you felt this way about a man, she reminded herself. Not since Dominique's death had she even touched another man. But eight years of grieving was enough, she told herself. Rance had come and all that had changed in the beat of a heart. His heart.

She lit a cigarette to try and distract herself.

There was a way, she knew. She could simply go in there, have her interview, complete her report and drop her gun off at the front door. Air France flew direct to Boston...

But Rance wasn't in Boston. She had lost him in Austria. When they entered the hotel room, one of the seat cushions on the couch was still warm. The front desk confirmed that they had checked out minutes earlier, though without anyone answering to Rance's description. Sealing off all the major ports of entry to the country was futile, and there had been nothing since.

But Francoise refused to let herself believe that Rance was dead. Not because of some childish hope, but because if they had killed him, they would have displayed their work, and there had been nothing to suggest that Rance or anyone else was killed in that hotel room.

So now what? Surely she would be reassigned, maybe even to someplace far enough away so that the continuation of her search for him would be impossible.

"Madame?"

The secretary showed Francoise into the offices of Edourd Dessin. She had been in here only one other time, when she was decorated for bravery by the prime minister himself. Dessin was on the phone and he gestured for her to seat herself.

"Francoise," he said, as if they were old friends. Dessin's charm was legendary, and Francoise felt the temperature of the room rise several degrees.

"Please accept my apologies regarding the incident in Austria. I know you invested a lot of time in this case, and it must be terribly disappointing to see it end in that fashion."

Here it comes, she thought. Sri Lanka? Tahiti? Argentina?

"Be assured that we will continue the investigation as much as humanly possible. But there are other pressing matters. Francoise, you are one of my most versatile people, and your reputation precedes you. That is a matter of some urgency that I need you to assist with in Ireland."

He handed her a folder. Ireland? she thought. Nothing happens in Ireland. Did he say Ireland? Not Northern Ireland but Ireland?

Dessin looked at her with a mixture of lust and respect. She had been one of his most faithful employees for a long time. It was curious that the Director General himself would specifically recall an agent. Highly unusual. No matter, he, Dessin, knew his people best. And Dougherty had been adamant, reminding Dessin that he was owed a favor. Dessin remembered the cooperation he had received from the Irish several years back regarding a hijacked flight and quickly acquiesced.

"You will meet Inspector Colm Dougherty of the Irish Guardia. He will brief you on the case there. You are to take the next flight to Shannon Airport where you will be met. If you have any question between now and then, please contact me through our normal channels."

Outside now, she still couldn't believe it.

Ireland.

§

Airports could be good, and airports could be bad.

As he eyed a rack filled with Irish coffee mugs, paperback novels by Irish authors and Irish crystal, Rance mulled the dilemma. On the one hand, airports were like big shopping malls, busy places filled with distracted people where you could lose yourself in an instant. That was good. On the other hand, there were high concentrations of security personnel wandering around, and they could be alerted to be on the lookout for a baggage-less American carrying Uncle Bill's stolen credit card. That was bad.

"Having a hard time finding the right thing?"

Rance turned and found himself staring at more freckles and red hair than he had ever seen in his life. The girl was probably in her teens and she probably worked there because Ireland had an image to live up to.

"I'm not sure I'm even looking for anything," he said.

"It can be just dreadful shopping for someone else. Now, on the other hand, shopping for yourself is a breeze. What do you think of these?"

The girl was holding out a pair of garish yellow and green plaid shorts.

"Perfect for golf," she said. Rance was sure she had a dazzling career as a used car saleswoman ahead of her.

"If you'd like to try them on," she continued, "we've some fitting rooms over there."

"Thanks, but I think I'll pass." He walked quickly from the boutique. Right now he wanted a little solitude.

The bus ride from Cashel had been thankfully uneventful. Nobody had questioned him when he purchased the ticket, and he took a seat in the back, where he could observe the rest of the passengers. Two hours later, the bus rolled to a stop in front of the large terminal building that was Shannon International Airport.

It was a bright and beautiful day, but cool, definitely not something that could pass for summer, with temperatures barely reaching 60 degrees. Shannon was busy, and Rance observed that many of the jumbo jets landing stayed only long enough to refuel. In the main terminal lobby he checked the arrival board. There was an Aer Lingus flight from Boston due to arrive at 6:30 p.m. With three hours to kill he decided to familiarize himself with the lay of the terminal, for by now he was surely missed by those in Cashel.

Rance found a coffee shop that overlooked most of the traffic in the terminal and ordered something to eat. Still he couldn't figure out why he was here in Ireland. The connection was obviously Katarina. But who was Claire, the sweet, red haired old lady? And what possible connection could Katarina have in Ireland? The big red-head who kept appearing with near death results? Did they both have something to do with each other? Or with another terrorist group–the IRA?

He was sure that he and Francoise had interrupted something that was going on in Kazakhstan. If Anatoly was right, then the place was some sort of open air trading center, with the participants suffering no rules, no conscience, no particular allegiance.

The thought of Francoise brought a pain to the center of his chest. He wanted desperately to call her, to at least try and get in touch with her, to tell her he was all right, but that was no longer an option. After using the stolen credit card to make the phone call to the States and buy the bus ticket, he went to the post office and mailed it back to Uncle Bill.

When Marty arrived, he thought. Hell, Marty might have even heard from her.

Finishing his coffee, Rance got up. He felt better moving about, less of a target. A small Air France jet deboarding onto the tarmac caught his eye. France, he thought, was a country which had a strong pull on him. He thought about his promise to himself to buy an apartment on the Île St. Louis. Paris would be a good place to live.

Standing by the international arrivals gate, he saw a copy of the International Herald-Tribune and bought it. The news was full of the usual stuff–war in Bosnia, the Russians staggering around, back benchers raising hell in Parliament and Washington D.C. descending into bureaucratic rubble.

As he flipped the paper over, the back section spilled out and slid across the waxed floor. Without thinking he chased it, even though it had slid into the midst of a crowd of new arrivals. He gave it the effort because it was the section containing the sports, and he wanted to see how his Red Sox were doing. A woman tripped on the loose newspapers, almost losing her balance.

Though his concentration was on the escaping newspaper, Rance could see that the woman who had tripped was the owner of a very beautiful set of legs. Even in distraction he could find a moment to appreciate the opposite sex. The legs ended in high heels that stomped on the paper, trapping it for him. He looked up to thank the woman and saw–

Francoise.

"Rance!"

She dropped her bag and embraced him tightly, staggering him back several steps. All around them people smiled the way they do when they are witness to teary airport reunions. Rance was still stunned.

"Rance, my God," she said. "I thought you were dead, I thought I had let you die." She looked up at him and pressed his mouth to hers. After a long minute they pulled apart and smiled at one another.

"But what are you doing here?" she asked. "What happened?"

"Somebody had to keep an eye on you," he said.

§

There was a knock on the door.

Usually a quiet, methodical man, this time he jumped at the sound, spilling his drink. He rushed to the door of the hotel room and flung it open.

"Katarina," he said.

"Richard," she returned.

The smile that cracked her lips would have been deemed patronizing by a disinterested observer. Brief, forced, and without the benefit of the rest of her face, the smile was difficult to hold. Especially when Armstrong rushed her.

"My God, Richard," she said, turning her face to avoid his lips and pushing him back. "Can't you wait until I'm in the room at least?"

Armstrong was out of control. Under his jacket his shirt was soaked with sweat. His heart raced at an incredible rate. And the crotch of his pants strained with the sudden growth from within. His eyes narrowed and sweat slicked his brow.

Katarina escaped him and went over to one of the suite's large tables, where she threw her purse. Dramatically, she turned and faced Armstrong.

"How is your stay in Rome?" she asked.

"Tiring," he said. Seeing that what he wanted more than anything would have to wait, he walked over to the bar.

"Drink?"

"Sherry, darling."

She heard the ice cubes clinking into the glass followed by the swish of the liquid as it spread itself over the ice and filled the glass. He wasn't a terrible man to be with, she told herself. No, not devastatingly handsome, but a good-looking man. Perhaps some other time. If he were more powerful, she thought. Yes, it would be pleasant to sleep with, say, a king. Yes, a king. Real royalty, not the democratic kind. Soon enough, she thought.

"There's been a slight change," she said, taking the drink.

"Oh?"

"Yes. Mr. Farrell has changed the venue."

"To where?"

"Ireland."

Armstrong took a sip of his drink without reacting.

"Ireland," he said. "The old sod. Why?"

"Quite frankly there have been too many close calls."

"I thought our Mr. Devlin was going to take care of that."

"Your Mr. Devlin is dead." Something stirred pleasantly inside her. Now there was a devastatingly handsome man. She had enjoyed having sex with Mr. Devlin, and she was mildly disappointed that he would not be able to give any repeat performances.

"Excuse me?" Armstrong looked surprised.

"It seems that poor Mr. Devlin was no match for a drunk author and a French SDECE agent. He was killed in his own ambush."

The news visibly staggered Armstrong, clouding his face with a deep, lined frown. The mention of Rance, though not by name, disturbed her. She wished him to go away, leave forever, vanish back into his fishing and drinking. He was under control now. Perhaps he could be spared. She didn't want to kill him-that had been Farrell's idea in the first place, and a stupid one at that, a Pandora's box that plagued them throughout this, the most critical phase of the operation.

"Son of a bitch," he said softly. "Devlin was one of our best, Special Forces, everything." He sat down on the couch.

Katarina came over and sat next to him. "Don't worry, darling, we have Mr. Vaughn now, and Ms. Chaumont has been recalled by the SDECE, so she will not be our problem any longer." Katarina's eyes twinkled as she savored her enormous influence. The Director General of the SDECE had been more than happy to oblige her when she had whispered her request into his ear. Katarina hoped that lustful men continued to hold the reins of power in this world-until she could wrest them away for herself.

She put a hand on his shoulder. This was much better. With Armstrong showing weakness she might actually be able to tolerate him.

"So Farrell wants to do it in his own backyard," Armstrong said, more to himself than to Katarina.

"He's already arranged it with Nabu and Inlan."

"What!" Armstrong exploded off the couch in a fury. "What the hell's wrong with him? I've spent months setting this up! He thinks he can just go behind my back and pull all the strings he wants?"

Katarina was up, soothing him now.

"He can do whatever he wants," Armstrong continued, "but the deal we made still stands. I'm not taking all this fucking risk so that some fucking terrorist can show me up at the end. I'll have him killed, I swear it."

"Don't worry, darling, he knows. He simply wanted to speed the process up. When is you next meeting?"

"Tomorrow morning." Under the influence of her touch, he was beginning to cool. Soon he would heat up again.

"You will be contacted through the usual channels for confirmation."

"Where's it going to be?" he asked. Katarina was massaging his shoulders, and his voice was languid.

"Caher Daniel, in Kerry. At Derrynane, Daniel O'Connell's estate. Jackie-Farrell, that is, has some ties with the people that operate the place. It's secluded and access can be controlled easily."

"All right," he said finally. "Everything else remains the same?"

"Everything, darling," said Katarina, whispering into his ear.

He turned and kissed her, unbuttoning her blouse quickly. Out of his own clothes just as fast, he gently pushed her down onto the floor. As Armstrong covered her, kissing her neck, her shoulders, her breasts, Katarina laid motionless. Her eyes remained open. They looked bored.

§

The dressing room was barely big enough.

For several minutes after they found each other at the airport Rance and Francoise stayed locked together. Only when they became aware of the obvious stares did they compose themselves.

Francoise, blushing, looked up into Rance's eyes.

"I'm sorry," she said. "I don't know what to say. I thought you were..."

Rance covered her lips with a finger.

"Don't say anything. Come on."

Taking her by the hand, Rance led Francoise back to the little boutique he had been in earlier. The freckle-faced, red-headed cashier was busy with several foreigners and she didn't see Rance and Francoise slip into one of the tiny dressing rooms. As the door closed behind them Francoise understood instantly. In another second her skirt was hiked around her waist, her legs wrapped tightly around Rance, moving to his rhythm. She shuddered with delight, giving herself to him completely, and had to steady herself against the door of the room. Craning her neck down, she kissed him fiercely.

"My God," she said through sharp gasps, "I never knew that the American penchant for spontaneity could be so passionate."

"I never knew anyone could move me like you do," he answered, feeling her still clinging on to him.

Then the door flew open, and the clerk was standing there, gaping open mouthed at their public ardor.

"And I didn't know I was working in a brothel!" she said without missing a beat. "Now, if you're finished, please have your pillow talk elsewhere. And you might try one of the hotels in town. I understand they have nice beds that you might find a bit more comfortable than our little booths."

Embarrassed but thankful that only the boutique's clerk had discovered them, Rance and Francoise made a quick exit. At the airport's small coffee shop they found a table in the back.

"Now tell me what happened to you," Francoise said. "I told you not to leave the hotel room."

She was angry with him in a way he found utterly endearing. She scolded him the same way a puppy is scolded for breaking his leash and running off.

Rance shrugged. "I got curious. After all the time I had spent trying to find Katarina, it seemed a little anti-climactic to see her arrested in a hotel room and dragged away before I could talk to her. There were so many questions I had–about our daughter, about her motives. I just found myself in the lobby of the Hotel Alpenstrasse."

Francoise's ability to change quickly never ceased to amaze Rance. She had gone from wild lover to concerned friend and now to interrogating officer. Her eyes, minutes ago wide and glassy with ecstasy, were now narrow and cold.

"So you actually saw Katarina?" she asked.

Trying not to blush at the memory of Katarina's voluptuous inhibition, Rance nodded. "I broke into her hotel room. She didn't act surprised, like she was half expecting me. We were talking when BOOM! The next thing I remembered was waking up in a cold room. From the accent of the old lady who was taking care of me, I guessed one of two places: South Boston or Ireland."

"And now I suppose you are here to meet Marty Donovan, am I correct?"

Rance's mouth hung open, but had he read her eyes, he would have known.

"Yes, but how did you know?"

"Because he's walking up behind you."

§

"Jackie, dear, I'm so sorry."

Mrs. Farrell seemed to be adding gray streaks to her red hair by the moment. At the breakfast table next to her, Jackie, her son, downed a massive cooked breakfast of rashers, grilled tomatoes, porridge, eggs and tea. The whole meal was devoured with his fork in his left hand.

"Come now, Mum, it's all right. You did the best you could."

"Yes, but you asked me to watch that young man until we could get him to hospital. I feel just awful."

Jackie took a sip of tea, carefully picking up the cup with his left hand. His right hand remained on the table.

"There's nothing we can do now, Mum. Maybe he found his way home all right."

"Maybe," she echoed.

Jackie finished and rose. "I'm off now."

"When will you be back, dear?" Mrs. Farrell had a sweet but blank look on her face, a look that Jackie noticed was becoming more and more permanent with his mother. It hurt him to see her so, and he turned away.

"Can't say, Mum. But I'll call you in a day or so."

Jackie bent his six and a half foot frame and kissed his mother on the forehead. Then he turned and walked out, the rubber band still twirling through the fingers of his right hand.

§

"The last time I saw you was in the Charles St. jail drunk tank."

Rance turned at the sound of Marty's voice.

"Hello, Francoise," Marty said. "You look well."

"And you look like a man who's had enough of the FBI."

"You could say that. Mind if I sit? Actually, Rance here has aged me about ten years in the last few weeks."

"Nice to see you, too, Marty," deadpanned Rance. "Now maybe someone can tell me how it is we all ended up here?"

Francoise shrugged. "I was sent her by my deputy director."

"I got you here," said Marty. "When Rance popped up, I figured the best thing was for him to stay put-he seems to have a difficult time at that. My cousin Colm-Dougherty of the ATU branch of the Guardia-made a few phone calls to make sure you'd be here."

"What's the ATU?"

"Anti Terrorism Unit. These guys cut their teeth busting up the IRA-"

"Wait a minute," said Rance. "Are we in Ireland or Northern Ireland?"

"Listen up, sonny boy. The only people who give a shit about the IRA are the slobbering fools bellied up to the bars in Southie and Dorchester. The rest of the world-including Ireland-would just as soon see those criminals done away with. Over here they're interested in getting on with their lives-not with bombing and killing."

"OK. But how can Colm help us?"

"For starters he has a file three feet thick on Katarina. And I want you to tell him about that big red-head that keeps popping up in your nightmares. Colm's people are in active mode. Maybe they can get us the break we need, because right now, we got nothing."

"Has Jenny come up with anything else?"

"You're going to owe her lobsters for the rest of your life," Marty cracked. The body language between Rance and Francoise was not lost on the savvy agent. But hell, that wasn't his business. As long as it didn't interfere with what they had to do now.

"Yeah, she's come up with some interesting stuff. Seems as though someone keeps calling her with little tidbits of info. Fancies himself a 'Deep Throat.' Not only was Armstrong's company, Dynaware, the main contractor for this software that everybody wants, but the guy who developed it–the one they stole from Michael–this Gengi guy, he's the chief engineer of the whole thing."

"So it was planned from the get go," Rance murmured.

"It would seem that way. Real bunch of swells we got running the country."

§

Katarina waited in the pub.

Edward O'Sullivan's was brick walled and windowless. The only natural light that penetrated the place came from the small square of glass in the center of the door. The rest was incandescent.

At two in the afternoon, there were few people to keep Katarina company. That suited her fine. She detested places like this, little holes in the wall that the working stupid cherished. The place was infectious, she thought.

Jackie Farrell, the big red-head, entered and spotted Katarina at the end of the bar. He ordered a pint and sat beside her.

"Everything go all right in Rome?" he asked.

"Wonderful," she said.

"When will he arrive?"

"His plane lands in Shannon in a couple of hours."

"Very good." Jackie sipped his Guinness. "Did you arrange a lift for him down to Derrynane?"

"He insisted on driving himself. And the rest?"

Jackie looked at his watch. "They should be there by now."

"I'm not sure that Derrynane is the best place."

"Ah, now she's an expert on security. When did you learn so much–after you discovered what a stupid idea brining that bastard American here was?"

"It wasn't our fault he got away."

"No. It was my mother's. Leaving him with her–bringing him over here in the first place–stupid. You should have let me kill him in Austria."

"You've had several chances already, haven't you?"

He looked at her sharply, his blue eyes piercing and cold.

"It doesn't matter now anyway," she continued. "He hasn't got a penny. He'll be staggering around for days before he sorts himself out. By then we'll be done and gone."

Jackie pulled again on his pint, draining it. He signaled to the bar man for another.

"What is it with this fellow? I mean, you act awfully funny at the mention of him, like you were relieved I didn't kill him when I had the chance. You wouldn't have the hots for him, now, would you?"

She looked away. "Don't be so foolish. And don't worry about him. He's finished. We have only to concentrate on wrapping things up now. Then we can retire."

"Won't that be nice?"

He finished his pint and they left, but Katarina was still frowning. In her mind's eye she saw a little girl. And her father.

§

The place looked deserted.

"That's why they picked County Kerry," Marty said. "Still pretty wild."

They had been climbing a mountain range called McGilli-cuddy's Reeks for the last hour, and the little rental car sounded as if it were ready to croak. Marty had just turned off the windy road and entered a small property with a run down house and a dilapidated garage. He parked in front of the garage and waited.

None of them saw the heavily armed soldier walk up to the car. It was as if he materialized from the dust.

"Marty?" the man said while peering over a nasty looking automatic weapon.

"That's me."

The soldier nodded toward the garage door, which opened on cue. Beyond the door lay a wide open courtyard, completely obscured from the front, but opening onto a huge building which appeared to have once been part of an estate. Another soldier motioned them out of the car and walked them up to a door.

As pleasant as it was on the outside, inside the place was all business.

"Reminds me of Langley," said Rance. They were led down a series of halls and through a number of doors until they were shown into a windowless office. Colm Dougherty was behind the desk.

"Marty me boy," he said, rising. "How's your mum?"

"Daft as ever, daft as ever."

A long, thin man, Rance's first impression of Colm Dougherty was that of an Englishman. His complexion was waxy and pale, lacking the vigor of the Irish skin. Rance thought his frame might snap when they shook hands, but Dooley's grip was deceivingly strong.

"Well now," he said, "is everybody enjoying their visit to Ireland?"

"Hardly," said Marty, "but if we can clean up this mess, I promise to bring us all back for a vacation."

Francoise's eyes glittered. "I'll hold you to that, Agent Donovan."

"And you must be Francoise Chaumont. Your director was quite perplexed by my insistence that you be here. Between you and me he sounded a bit miffed."

"Miffed" was a word that Francoise had never before heard, but from the context of the statement she guessed *ennervé*, or irritated.

"And this is Rance Vaughn," said Marty wryly. "He's the cause of all this."

"Symptom would be more accurate," said Rance.

"Vaughn, Vaughn," said Dougherty, lost in thought. "Not of the Waterville Vaughns, are you?"

"Yes, my great-grandfather came over from Waterville, County Kerry, about a hundred years ago."

"Great fishermen, the Waterville Vaughns."

"Too bad the same can't be said for the Green Harbor Vaughns."

Rance smirked. "Enough banter. What have we got here?"

"Well that's a good question, Mr. Vaughn," said Dougherty. "Suppose you fill me in on what's happened."

Between Marty, Francoise and Rance, they gave Dougherty the whole story. As Dougherty listened he pulled several folders from his file cabinet and tapped in commands on the computer which dominated his desk. When they were finished Dougherty slid a file with a photo across his desk. It was the big red-head.

"Jesus Christ!" said Rance. "That's him. That's the one who shot me, the same guy I saw in Paris. Probably the same guy who whacked me in Austria. Who is he?"

"Jackie Farrell," said Dougherty. "Grew up making Molotov cocktails for the PIRA–the Provisional Wing of the Irish Republican Army. They're the bad boys, the ones Sinn Féin are always denying connections with whenever a bomb goes off in a shopping mall in London.

"But killing British soldiers wasn't sporting enough for Farrell. He fell in with some bad types in Europe, did an apprenticeship under Nabu Mohammed then opened up his own shop, so to speak. Word was that he couldn't take the hot climate of the Maghreb, where he was drilling terrorist wanna-bes, so he started his own killer camp right her on the Emerald Isle. Of course, we don't put that in the tourist brochures.

"It's a secret organization that we've been dying to penetrate. In fact, it's so secret that we don't know its name yet. What we've been able to learn from limited wiretaps and surveillance is that Farrell uses our moody weather as a base for training warfare tactics to terrorists. We suspect he has a camp up in the wilds of County Claire, but we've got nothing on him so far."

"Did you know whatever it is he's up to he's up to it with Katarina Favergé?" Rance asked.

"Now you've got my attention," said Dougherty. "She was responsible for the deaths of several of my men who were co-operating with the German government on investigating the bombing of that Lufthansa plane a few years ago. Walked them right into a trap, then she vanished."

"She's here in Ireland. I saw her–heard her–the other night."

"Where?" Dougherty was intense now.

"Cashel."

"Cashel? Fancy that. That's where Farrell is from. Mother still lives there, I believe."

Dooley's phone rang.

"I see," he said, and hung up. "Well now. Seems we've got a little action. One of my men just spotted Mr. Farrell and Ms. Favergé leaving a pub in Cork."

"Great," said Marty. "Now what?"

"Now we go for a little ride to see what our friends are up to."

"Wait," said Rance, taking Dooley's arm as he rose. "Where's Derrynane?"

Dougherty looked incredulous.

"Derrynane?" he said. "Why, every Irishman knows Derrynane. That is the home of O'Connell the Liberator. It's in Caher Daniel in County Kerry."

Rance recalled the conversation he overheard between Katarina and the old lady.

"They're going to Derrynane."

§

The Irish countryside startled Richard Armstrong.

He knew his family had come from Ireland originally, heard the stories his mother and father had told, but his roots had never been a major interest in his 52 years. His life had been devoted to the amassing of money and its direct corollary: power.

About the current deal Armstrong had mixed feelings, but not because he was committing treason against his country. Rather, the dilemma stemmed from his perception of his role in the big picture. In his opinion he was the one who had risked the most, he was the one who had invested the most time and effort into the foundations.

There was no question about his compensation. The first half of the money had already been wired into an offshore account in the Bahamas. There was enough money now to live a lavish lifestyle off of the interest alone. What Armstrong questioned was the power.

Richard Armstrong had made a living out of being the silent partner. Staying in the shadows was his forte, first with his company Dynaware, then with the coordination of the President's run for the White House, and now with SHAKESPEARE. He could feel Farrell–and to a lesser extent, Katarina-squeezing him for control.

Don't think about it, he told himself. Enjoy the scenery.

Scenery was useless. All he could see was Katarina. He told himself that he should know better-going soft like that over a woman. But it was true. No woman had ever made him feel that way, invigorated him the way she did. Certainly his wife of 26 years didn't. Neither did any of the innumerable mistresses. No, he decided early on, Katarina was different. Very different.

He almost drove through the town before he saw the hotel. Though it wasn't the right hotel in the right town, Armstrong decided to stay there for the night. Caher Daniel was only a few miles up the road anyway. He turned his car into the tiny parking lot. Before he went in to the hotel he looked for a place to get a drink.

§

"Did you know that you're being followed?"

"Since the last roundabout in Cork," Farrell said.

"Who is it?" asked Katarina.

"The same bastards who've been shadowing me every time I come back to this bloody country. Some division of the Guardia."

"How did they find out about you?"

Farrell laughed. "Darlin', I haven't exactly led a quiet, righteous life."

Katarina didn't share his amusement.

"Well, it's getting dark now. Maybe we can lose him."

"Oh, we'll do better than that. Macroom is just up the

road. I'll stop there and take care of it."

Slowing as they entered the town of Macroom, Farrell tried to entice the tail to get close enough for him to have a good look. But the other driver was good, hanging back patiently, innocuously. Farrell snaked through the town square and pulled into a parking spot just before the road left the village.

"Stay here," he said to Katarina as he got out. She watched him enter a pub.

A hundred yards behind them, a young officer of the Guardia had pulled into a parking spot on the opposite side of the road and he, too, observed Farrell. Tim O'Sullivan discreetly keyed his radio and spoke into the lapel mic on his sports jacket.

"351 to 350, subject stopped in Macroom. Subject A has left the car and entered Donoghue's pub. Standing by."

O'Sullivan had no idea who he was following. His orders were to tail the man and woman who fit the description in the car ahead of him, report all activity and maintain radio contact with 350 base.

It had been a long day already, and the Tim O'Sullivan rubbed his face and tired eyes. In the split second that it took him to do so, someone darted out of an alley behind his car. O'Sullivan didn't see him; his gaze was fixed on the woman in the car and the front door of Donoghue's Pub.

§

"351 to 350, still no further activity."

Back at the secluded mountain estate that was 350 base, Matthew Madden operated the equipment in the radio room.

Sitting next to him and reading the latest edition of Horse and Hound was Lt. James Twomey.

"Roger 351," Madden acknowledged. He leaned back and fished a cigarette out of the pack in his pocket. After offering one to Twomey, who declined, Madden lit up, squinting through the blue smoke.

"McSweeney says something's afoot here."

Twomey glanced up from his magazine.

"That so? What does McSweeney know?"

Madden shrugged. "He was on duty earlier when those civvies showed up. Said one of them is FBI, from the States."

"That a fact, is it? I suppose McSweeney's had a lot of contact with the FBI–being a guard at the gate and all."

Madden smirked and took another drag of his cigarette.

"Why don't you check in with 351," Twomey suggested.

"350 base to 351, over."

Madden tapped his fingers on the console and waited.

"350 base to 351, come in, over."

He was joined by Twomey in a frown.

"Last contact?" asked Twomey. Madden consulted the log.

"Three minutes ago."

"Keep trying," Twomey said. He reached for the phone.

§

As Farrell slipped from O'Sullivan's car he heard the radio.

At this time of the evening, dusk, the streets of Macroom were quiet, affording the opportunity for quiet solicitude. Farrell wanted none of that, so he tried to double his step without looking conspicuous. There were a group of old codgers sitting on the bench below the fountain in the middle of the town square, and Farrell looked the other way as he passed them. With nothing better to do they would surely remember his face, and he would be quickly tied to the body in the car once it was found. Perhaps he would catch a break and the body of the Guardia officer with his throat cut ear to ear would not be discovered until tomorrow morning. He was at his car now.

Katarina looked over at him and smiled.

"No one saw you," she said. "Except me."

§

"What do you make of that?"

Dougherty shrugged. "Either he's left his post or his post has left him."

The road they were following was narrow and winding, dipping and rising along the hills that rolled down to the sea. The ocean itself was visible as the sun set into it. Having grown up on the east coast, Rance never had many chances to see the sun setting into the ocean. The feeling was vastly different from watching the sun rise out of the sea, perhaps because of the time of day, or maybe because the light was different. He made a mental not to study the phenomenon more closely out at the tip of Cape Cod. Truro, maybe.

Dougherty turned the car off the road, following a gravel drive for about a mile. It ended in a circular drive in front of a low, ramshackle farmhouse. As they got out of the car Rance could taste the salt in the air and his eyes instinctively found the ocean.

"This is as far as we go tonight," said Dougherty. "Below us is Caher Daniel. If you look along the shoreline you'll see Derrynane-O'Connell's estate. Take a good look because the next time you see it you'll be in it."

Dougherty led them to the front door and knocked. A moment later a small, stooped woman answered. Recognizing Dougherty, she smiled.

"Come in, come in," she said. "And don't be dragging you muddy boots through here. Give them a good wipe." They dutifully made a show of wiping the shoe bottoms on the mat. Ushering them into a long, dark hallway, she then led them into a parlor incongruously ornate compared with the building's exterior. Dougherty moved about the place as if it were his home. In the corner of the parlor was a highboy, which he opened to reveal a well-stocked bar.

"Donovan, are you still drinking that horrible bourbon?"

Marty smiled. "Considering the soil, I'll make an exception this time. Make mine Jameson's."

Dougherty nodded without smiling, as if it were the proper thing to do. He looked to Francoise.

"The same would be fine," she said, eliciting a raised eyebrow from Dougherty.

"Mr. Vaughn, you don't have a choice."

A moment later Dougherty brought a tray with the bottle of Jameson and four glasses over to the coffee table around which they all sat. He poured the whiskey and distributed the glasses, then he spoke.

"Well," Dougherty said, "I'd like to be able to tell you I know what we're going into tomorrow, what this is all about, but I haven't the faintest idea. But this is what I do know:

"Jackie Farrell is the leader of a very discreet terrorist organization we now believe is called The Boyne. Those familiar with Irish history need no explanation for Farrell's inspiration for founding The Boyne, and in fact they began life a decade ago as a tougher version of the PIRA-the Provisional Wing of the IRA, the bad guys. Farrell and his thugs were so bad that even the IRA didn't want anything to do with them, so Farrell set out on his own.

"He met Nabu Mohammed and together they molded today's version of The Boyne: a terrorist training organization bent on building a world wide web of madmen capable of operating harmoniously in globe-spanning acts of terrorism.

"Farrell runs some foul weather camps up on the wild coast of County Claire, and we've busted them up a few times, but come up with nothing. No arms, no documents, nothing. Apparently its all tactics and exposure training, so our hands are tied. Farrell's never done anything on Irish soil, and connecting him to the random acts of violence around the world...well, that's usually the job of some novelist.

"But not this time. This time we're going to take them all-that includes Nabu, who was seen yesterday at a hotel in Dingle. And-" Dougherty put a pair of spectacles on and consulted a notebook. "-Jay Kaplan and Boris Nubrikev."

"What!" Marty exclaimed. Francoise shook her head slowly.

"Somebody want to fill me in?" asked Rance.

"Jay Kaplan," explained Marty, "is an American trained in the Israeli army. After he was cleared for the highest level of security he disappeared. Ten years later he turned up as one of the Middle East's biggest arms dealers, serving as a middle man for clowns like Kaddafi and Sadaam before their downfalls. Now he freelances: Venezuela, North Korea-he's even available to legitimate states who need dirty deeds done dirt cheap. A real deal maker, without a conscience."

"And I have had experience-too much-with Boris Nubrikev," said Francoise. "He was a KGB agent who defected to West Germany. After the fall of communism, he found himself without much value-except to the emerging underworld in Russia. He has used his domination there to expand into world terrorism, especially in Asia, where you don't hear so much about it."

"So all these guys, all these international heavyweights, they're all here in Caher Daniel?" Rance asked.

Dougherty sat back. "More or less."

"And Farrell's on his way-with Katarina."

"And I think you know why."

"It's the software," Rance mumbled.

"SHAKESPEARE," said Marty.

§

Marty explained what Jenny had found out.

"Who do you think this 'Deep Throat' is?" asked Rance.

"If I had to guess," said Marty, "I'd say it was Schwartz. An investigation would point to him, even if he weren't involved. It would be in his own interest to turn the heat away from himself. Surreptitiously whispering in Jenny's ear would suit that dramatic weasel."

"So Dynaware was actually the vehicle of inception for this whole new type of national defense? One company?"

"Dozens, actually," said Marty. "But all with the same connection-which, by the way, Jenny is diligently documenting even as we speak. Armstrong is the connection."

Rance swallowed hard at the thought of Jenny pouring over long documents, trying to assemble a paper trail with which to thwart this thing which was daily proving more unstoppable. Not wanting to give his emotions away, he fought the urge to look at Francoise sitting beside him. She snuck her hand under the table and squeezed his, extracting another measure of guilt.

"And the United States government's code name for the project is 'SHAKESPEARE'?" asked Francoise.

Marty nodded.

"How prophetic," said Rance.

"How's that?" asked Dougherty.

Rance cleared his throat. "I don't know if Marty told you, but Katarina and I were once...well, we were married, briefly, ten years ago, and we have a daughter."

Dougherty raised an eyebrow, then his glass.

"Anyway, one of the things both Katarina and I enjoyed was going to the theater when we lived in London. We practically lived at the West End. Shakespeare was our favorite. *Othello* was the best, and we would spend hours talking about the characters, the performances of the actors. We just loved it. Now it seems a little too convenient that this software that she's hawking-which will be the key to the national defense of the United States-is named SHAKESPEARE. It's almost as if she had something to do with it."

§

Her powerful computer didn't make the task any easier.

Jenny still had to sift through endless articles, legal documents and government records. What the computer on her desk allowed her to do was look for everything without moving out of her office.

And by using the Internet, Jenny could also access just about anything in the world. It was a mixed blessing.

The same ability which allowed her to access legal briefs filed in Kentucky ten years ago, then download them and print them out, also made her slog through piles of electronic muck, a bog of bytes that threatened to strangle her search for more connections between Richard Armstrong and Dynaware and the drama that was unfolding across the ocean.

Currently, Jenny had somehow managed to get lost in the Washington Daily News, a tabloid style daily that went under years ago. None of the commands on her toolbar menu were working, so Jenny was doomed to click through the entire edition of the newspaper, with hopes of exiting when there was nothing left to browse.

As she clicked the "Next Page" command rotely, Jenny hardly noticed the contents of the newspaper as it flashed by. Screaming headlines and endless box scores were a huge news turn-off to her. So too was the five pages of gossip the paper printed. But, hey, it was Washington, right?

Color caught her eye.

Jenny clicked back three pages. There it was, a color photo amidst a desert of black and white. When she looked at it more closely, her eyes widened.

It was one of the society columns, and the paper was dated almost a year earlier. Just before they folded, Jenny thought.

The night before this edition had hit the streets there had been some kind of gala state dinner. There, smack in the middle of the page was a huge, four-color photo of Richard Armstrong.

That there should be a photo of Richard Armstrong in a Washington tabloid was not in and of itself remarkable. Nor was it so unbelievable that a woman should be on his arm. What was so interesting to Jenny was that the woman was not his wife. The caption under the photo explained:

And who could that be escorting the dashing-but-still-married-as-far-as- we-know Richard Armstrong to the State dinner at the White House last evening? When they look this happy, does it really matter?

Evidently, Mr. Armstrong had been caught stepping out on his wife. Though the newspaper didn't know the woman's identity, Jenny was pretty sure she did. It had been a long time, and Jenny had only met her once when she visited Rance in London, but the woman's beauty was unmistakable then, and it was unmistakable in the year old photo.

It was Katarina Favergé.

§

FBI Agent Martin Donovan's cellular phone rang.

"I didn't know this thing would work over here," he said with some disgust, "or I would have left it in Boston." To the phone: "Donovan."

Marty grunted for a couple of seconds, then looked up at Dougherty. "You got a printer in this place, cousin?"

Dougherty gave Marty the fax number, who relayed it into

the phone, ending the conversation with "Thanks, sweet lips."

"Sweet lips?" asked Rance.

"That was Jenny. Says she has an interesting fax for us to look at."

"Over here," said Dougherty, motioning to a huge set of double doors. A fully equipped office lay behind them, the printer busy already, printing out the document sent from Jenny. A few seconds later, neither Rance nor Francoise could believe their eyes.

"That's Katarina," Rance said, pointing to the woman in the photo.

"And that," said Marty, pointing to the man, "is the National Security Advisor to the President of the United States. Also known as Richard Armstrong."

§

Dougherty left them.

For the balance of the night, until they moved out before dawn, Colm Dougherty would spend his time in preparation for tomorrow. His first order of business was a debriefing concerning the murder of Guardia officer Timothy O'Sullivan.

Deciding not to share that information with the others, Dougherty had to play ignorant until he left them. That Farrell had killed O'Sullivan was obvious; law enforcement officials' throats aren't spontaneously slit from ear to in while shadowing a subject. Proving it, however, would be a different story.

But prove it they would, Dougherty swore to himself, regardless of tomorrow's outcome. Somebody in Macroom saw something–he knew the kind of people that lived there, they'd've noticed a person like Farrell. And if Katarina Favergé were there, God, she'd stick out like Jesus Christ himself.

And if nobody saw anything, if nobody in Macroom would come forward to connect Farrell to the crime then by God they'd invent somebody who saw something.

After the debriefing Dougherty sat alone in the kitchen and rubbed his eyes in thought. He had devoted his life to the battle against people who want to change the world through violent, stupid means. There may be times when armed revolution was the only way justice could be served and the wrongs against a people could be righted, but this wasn't one of them.

In the last 200 years revolution had become a cheap and sexy term, the argot of violence-for-fun asocial hoodlums who hid easily behind the veneer of popular fear and exploited it for the advancement of their own violent agenda. Anybody anywhere could find something imperfect with any society and use it as a flag to fan the fires of insurgency.

Except Dougherty called those people terrorists, and had devoted his life to ridding the world of them. For those who wanted to sow anarchy, for those who defaulted to chaos and disorder, for those who lacked the courage to do nothing but kill, he had one philosophy: fuck you.

The American made him nervous. He was a wildcard, an unpredictable factor in the equation, not in any way equipped for what would happen tomorrow, yet somehow both Marty Donovan and Francoise Chaumont had placed enormous trust in him. Dougherty would think about it. And sometime before dawn, in a few hours' time, he would make a decision.

§

Donovan refilled their glasses.

"I don't have to tell you what Michael O'Meara was to me," Marty said. "Or that he is the reason I'm here. His life, it was worth more than all this, this shit." Marty looked down into his drink and pursed his lips. "I'm not here to save the country, or the world, or anything like that. That's hopeless.

"It's only been–what?–a few weeks since this whole thing started? Michael's dead for three weeks...feels like three years already."

Marty was looking into the soft flames of the turf fire burning in a blue ceramic fireplace. His eyes didn't reflect the flames' undulation; instead they became it.

"We were in the academy together, just a couple of young guys, both of us educated at good schools, Michael at Holy Cross, me at Boston College, and the FBI recruited us. Can you imagine? The FBI came to us? We thought we were something special.

"So it's the last week of the academy, and we're just waiting for our field assignments–heard all the stories about being sent to Butte, Montana to investigate coal mine espionage, or being sent to Texarkana to chase interstate trade violators–and we all kind of half expected to end up in some godforsaken hole. But not Michael.

"'We're going to Boston, buddy. Home,' he said. Like he had an inside line. I laughed at him, but he was serious. 'It's the IRA,' he said. 'They're operating a large, well greased organization in the Boston area. Hey, we all know it, every clown from the Speaker of the Massachusetts House of Representatives to the guy pulling drafts at the corner gin mill is helping the IRA out in Boston. Shit, where do you think they get all their money from. Certainly not the Irish–they could care less about "The Cause."'"

Marty refilled his glass and Rance's; Francoise declined.

"Michael was right. Back then, the fever for the Irish cause was hot in Boston. Hats were being passed at every level of Irish-American society. But Michael saw it differently. Michael didn't see freedom fighters struggling to reunite their unjustly divided country. Michael saw terrorists. Killers. Murderers or innocent people. Cowards. And it made him ashamed of the blood that coursed in his veins.

"So they threw us into the Boston office, O'Meara and Donovan, a couple of local kids bent on getting it right. I think, for Michael, that's when this thing really started.

"Our first case was a biggie. Speaker of the House. Guy from South Boston, Emmit McCarthy, friend of the people, champion of the poor, dictator of the law in the Commonwealth of Massachusetts. That fucker didn't serve. He ruled."

Rance remembered the scandal. McCarthy, a second generation Irish-American rags-to-political riches story, was the de facto governor of Massachusetts, surpassing even the elected governor (who actually had to be endorsed both publicly and privately by McCarthy in order to win the election) in terms of real political power.

For years McCarthy had been under investigation for almost everything imaginable, from kickbacks and bribes to tax fraud to illegal use of state funds. And none of it had stuck. Around South Boston, they say that Emmit McCarthy was

Teflon before Ronald Reagan and John Gotti.

Then came the Irish scandal. In a different twist, the FBI had been able to turn one of the Sinn Fein representatives visiting America on a clandestined fund raising tour of the pubs of Boston and New York. They established a paper trail, thanks mostly to the diligent work of two young agents named Donovan and O'Meara, that led to Speaker McCarthy.

"Should have been a glorious day for us," said Marty, recalling the day in question. "We had everything on McCarthy, witnesses willing to talk, the numbers to offshore bank accounts, and the documentation that Speaker of the Massachusetts House, the honorable Emmit McCarthy, had been diverting-stealing-state money and sending it to the Irish Republican Army.

"Michael wanted to take him down while the legislature was in session. I'm serious. He wanted to burst into the House chamber, shackle McCarthy and drag him out, photographers a blazing. Instead we decided to take him at his South Boston townhouse."

Marty paused, took a deep breath and finished the rest of his drink.

"We knocked first. No answer. Finally got McCarthy's man servant up out of bed. Said he didn't know where his boss was. All he knew was that Mr. McCarthy was having dinner alone with one of his 'Irish' friends, and that he, the man servant, had been given the night off.

"Kicked in the door of McCarthy's dining room. There he was, still in his seat at the head of the long, empty table, dead." Marty tapped the center of his forehead. "Neat little hole right here." He shrugged.

"Worst part? Worst part was that we found out who did it. McCarthy, dictator that he was, had hidden security cameras everywhere on his property. Hidden microphones, too. He recorded every conversation–you have to remember, this was the seventies, and political leaders surreptitiously recording their conversations was all the rage–including the one he had as he was being murdered. We also had a description from the man servant, who let the killer in. Guess who?"

Francoise and Rance shook their heads. Rance had never heard that they caught the killer, only that the case remained unsolved.

"John Francis Farrell, a.k.a. Jackie Farrell."

Rance's face fell. "You mean–"

"Yup. Same guy that we're going to get tomorrow. Same guy that killed Michael. The one and only. He's all ours."

Marty put down his empty glass and walked unsteadily toward the door. Before he got there he stopped, and without turning around he spoke to them once more.

"I'm here because Michael O'Meara's life meant something. I'm here because his death meant something, too. I just wanted to tell you that."

§

For a long time they said nothing.

The turf fire seemed to have a life of its own, burning endlessly. But slowly, the flames began to shorten their lick, the light grew softer, and the fire began to burn down.

"I only met Michael once," said Francoise. "I was in the States with my agency and Michael and Martin briefed me on the movements of someone we wanted. He was very nice, and very intense. His eyes seemed to glow."

Rance shook his head and looked at her. With the flames of the fire in them, her eyes became a rich, decadent butterscotch that he wanted to devour.

"With all the chances our paths had to cross," he said, "I can't believe it ever took so long for us to meet. You were with Katarina, and you've met Michael..."

"Well, I've met you now."

"Francoise, what will you do? I mean after tomorrow."

His sudden directness surprised even himself. She looked back to the fire.

"I don't know, really. I hadn't really thought about it. Well, that's not entirely true. Before I came to Ireland I thought I'd had enough."

"And now?"

She sighed. "And now I still think I've had enough." Leaning her head into the crook of his arm, she pulled her feet up beneath her and snuggled against him in a way that nearly arrested his heartbeat. "I'm not a young woman any more."

"I couldn't tell by looking at you."

"You're sweet but somewhat prejudiced, Mr. Vaughn. Do you really want to know what I'd like to do?"

"Tell me."

"I would like to be the caretaker of a little inn. Maybe a nice little *auberge* like this one. Or a place by the sea."

"You mean a bed and breakfast?"

"Yes, exactly. Someplace quiet and peaceful, in nature, away from the city, away from the direct influence of society. People on vacation are so much nicer to deal with."

Up until now, in his mind, Rance had a vision of who Francoise Chaumont was: dark, long legged beauty, with high heels and a gun, cigarette, oozing sex from every pore. It was a vision that sometimes scared him. But Francoise had shown many sides of herself to him, a compassionate side that recalled an old friendship, a caring side that had wept when they were reunited in Ireland, a traditional side that had shared with him her people, an honest side that told him she was woman, yes, but a human being too, susceptible to all the afflictions, physical and emotional, that a human being is.

"I know a great place," he said. "Far out of the way, facing the ocean. On one side is a sheltered bay with warm water. Beaches stretch for miles up and down on both sides. It's an old inn that has been there for years, just down the street from where I grew up. Now the family that runs it wants to sell it and retire."

She closed her eyes and smiled, happy in his embrace.

"It sounds so wonderful," she said, and fell asleep.

§

Rance carried her to her bed.

Taking off only her shoes, he slid her between the sheets, tucked her in and slipped out of the room. Downstairs he fetched the rest of the bottle and a glass and stole out into the night.

§

Their story had made the Boston Globe.

Rance remembered that neither he nor Michael O'Meara knew that yet. The early city editions were just hitting the streets, and the second and third editions wouldn't make it down to Green Harbor for another hour. It was two-thirty in the morning, the day after their high school team won the state hockey championship.

In front of them, the ocean was angry. March was like that, cold and blowing along the coast. Rance and Michael didn't seem to notice. The cigars and beer muffled them from the foul weather as much as their heavy winter jackets. Four hours ago they had won the state hockey tournament at the Boston Garden.

"South Shore Prep," Michael said. "I can't believe it."

"Me neither," agreed Rance. They both stared out at the dark ocean, the drone of the wind and the crash of the waves their only company.

"They gotta respect us now. They gotta."

"Michael, do it again."

"What?"

"The play. Tell me again."

"OK. Allen scoops the puck around the net and Leclair picks it up. You're up on your wing and as soon as I get to the blue line, Leclair hits me with a beauty of a pass, right on my tape. Then you go, exploding past the defenseman on a clear break, and I give you a blistering pass, but that defenseman, man, he gets lucky, just gets the tip of his stick on the puck and it goes spinning into the corner, your corner. But does that bother Rance Vaughn, leading scorer in the state? No way.

"Now it's a footrace between you and that Catholic Memorial goon, Anderson. The sound you guys make when you go into the boards is like thunder, man, just crashing, exploding, and I'm all alone in the slot, that's how fast we broke away, and I'm screaming my head off, but this goon Anderson is punching the shit out of you, I mean just belting you, and that ref, that homer, he ain't calling nothing, and I have to go over and help you, but I'm all alone, so I scream once more, and then it happens.

"I don't know how you got that puck out to me. Anderson was laying the lumber on your head bad. Did you look in the mirror yet? Don't. That pass was perfect. That was your goal, Rance. I just told it where to go. That goalie never saw the puck, never saw the shot, it just floated between his legs and stretched the net. Rance, I never touched that puck, I swear it just curved on its own.

"And we beat Catholic Memorial, we did it, little South Shore Prep, with the hottest goalie in the state, we beat 'em in OT, state champs, how to go."

"That's sweet, man," Rance said. "We should be going to school together. It ain't right to break us up, Michael. You led the league in assists, that's why I scored so many. You should be coming to Boston University with me."

"No way. You're going to win national championships at BU. You're going to play in the pros. I peaked, man. Holy Cross is giving me a ride, I'm taking it."

"I'm going to Holy Cross with you."

Michael laughed. "You ain't that smart!"

"And you ain't a good enough player to go to BU!"

"Asshole!"

"Asshole!"

"Champion!"

"State champion!"

"Drink up, buddy!"

§

"Drink up, buddy," Rance said softly to the stars, and the tears rolled down his cheeks.

The Irish night was damp and cold, the stars already beginning to disappear as low clouds moved in from the south.

He didn't want to go back into the farmhouse. He knew that once inside, he would go to bed, sleep, and wake in the morning. And then it would happen.

It frightened him because up to now everything that had befallen him had not been anticipated; things had come to him when he did' not expect them. But now there was a plan, a formula, structure. The very stuff that had scared him into a lobster boat.

He shook his head. There was only one direction, forward, and those were the consequences, not the causes. There could be no stopping, no second guessing now. He was discovering that there were more people than him with vested interests in the events about to unfold.

Failure. It was something that he had never considered, not once, since the day he left Cape Cod and swore behind closed and tearing eyes that for Michael he would finish this thing. And if tomorrow-today, in a few hours-if they did fail?

Shit, he thought, how the hell should I know. Maybe this software-SHAKESPEARE-maybe it is as important as everyone says. But Rance knows that isn't the real reason he's here, in Ireland. For him, it's more.

The ramifications of what happens tomorrow were in fact inconsequential. He would do what he had to. He promised.

"They never should have split us up, man," he said to the stars. "Tomorrow, I'm going to fix it. I promise. I didn't forget, Michael. I promise."

Rance turned and walked back into the farmhouse.

That night he did not sleep.

§

There was coffee, tea, and Irish soda bread.

Rance had already caught Francoise looking askance at him when she came into the room. It's the eyes, he figured. Probably red and puffy from lack of sleep.

Sleep. Seemed now like such an unattainable option. Before he had spent entire weeks asleep, sleeping on his boat, in his car, anywhere. Though it was alcohol induced, it was more than he had in the last three weeks.

The room was located in the basement somewhere and it was harshly lighted by rows of fluorescent tubes. Against the back wall was a large diagram, a map of sorts. In front of it was a large table around which a dozen or more uniformed soldiers had gathered.

"All right?" Francoise whispered to him.

"Fine."

"You didn't sleep last night."

"I was thinking."

She raised her eyebrows and he looked into her face. It was such a beautiful face, he felt that it was somehow unjust that he could have fallen in love with her, but it was true. So much about her he didn't know, so much he wanted to tell her, show her.

"I'll tell you when we get to your bed and breakfast," he said. Colm Dougherty waved them over.

"This," Dougherty said, "is the layout of Derrynane. As you can see there is only one road in. The property is sort of a peninsula, and the access road is guarded on one side by boggy marshes and on the other by heavy forest. Our people are already positioned here, here and here."

Dougherty pointed to points guarding the entrance to the Derrynane access road.

"Everybody else is under surveillance. When they move in, we'll be right on their heels. We're not going to wait for anything to develop. As soon as they're in, we're taking them out. We'll start by taking out the people they post outside. Then we'll go in.

"Gas first," Dougherty continued. "We're going to tear gas the entire place, and we're going to use a new kind of gas that produces a thicker, blacker smoke. And then we're going to take them, dead preferably, alive if they feel up to it."

The shock must have registered on Rance's face, for Dougherty focused in on it.

"That bother you, Mr. Vaughn?"

Rance shrugged. "That's not my call."

"Good. I was afraid I was offending your American justice sensibilities."

Rance took a deep breath. Dougherty was watching him very closely, and Rance wondered how much Marty told him about his past with Katarina. Probably everything. Holding back would have only jeopardized the mission.

"No, you're not. Frankly, those people have spent all their fairness chips. It's time to set the record straight."

A think smile cracked Dooley's lips. "Very good. Now, let's go over what I expect of everyone here. We're going in by boat, so I hope you've all got your sea legs. We'll hit the beach one minute after the last one has arrived at Derrynane. In case you haven't noticed, we've got a dense fog and a driving drizzle out there, so we will be totally obscured when we land."

As Dougherty continued, Rance couldn't help but notice that his name was glaringly absent from any instructions. Even Marty and Francoise were out of the main action, almost in observer roles.

"What I expect of you, Mr. Vaughn, is to remain on the landing craft until I come back and tell you to do otherwise. Is that clear?"

Rance nodded. He had decided that Dougherty wasn't a man who talked tough. He was tough, and this was his op, besides, what the hell would I do but get shot? he thought.

"Good. Let's go. We've got a boat to catch."

§

She hated the whole idea.

Ireland had been Farrell's idea, Derrynane had been Farrell's idea and what could she do? He felt better on his own soil, somewhere he could be in control. So she agreed, anything to finish this terrible mess.

It had all started so nobly, so daringly. It was supposed to be the masterpiece of her career, the thing that would let her retire and vanish forever, to one of the French DOM-

TOM-overseas possessions-out in the middle of the Pacific or Indian Ocean. Reunion, perhaps.

Of course it still would. There was nothing to suggest that anything else would go wrong. Except Rance.

Damn him, and damn Farrell for opening up that Pandora's box. All he had to do was leave Rance alone, alone to drown himself in his liquor in his little town, self-absorbed with confusion and pity. But leaving things be was never Jackie's strong suit. No, he had to cover the whole field to be happy. He had to tweak the happy drunk from his reverie.

He had been cute then, but more, something more that she had never felt before or since, something she would not allow herself to feel. It explained the stupidity of a marriage. Michelle had complicated things, but Katarina loved her daughter. Michelle was, in fact, part of the reason she didn't want anything to go wrong now. Her future was as much at stake as Katarina's.

Katarina hung up her cell, disconnecting with the call she had placed to the United States. She hoped that the result would be the tidying up of the last loose string there.

Farrell turned onto the long road that led down to Derrynane. Along the way there were several armed people waving them through. That made her feel better. Maybe Farrell had this under control after all.

§

The boat sat dead in the fog.

Out beyond their sight in the eerily lightening dawn there were three other boats filled with soldiers. Rance could see that the troops on his boat were armed to the teeth: Kevlar vests, gas masks, helmets and automatic weapons. Bandoleers of ammunition weighed them down and he wondered what kind of weapons they were using; though he didn't know much about weapons, he knew enough to see that what these guys were carrying wasn't the ubiquitous Uzi or anything sexy that you see on the six o'clock news. These guys had big stuff. A couple of them looked like they were carrying rocket launchers, for Christ's sake. He wondered how the historical people that looked after Derrynane would feel about having their place razed.

A voice on Dooley's radio, very soft, very clear, very quietly ticked off the names of the guests as they arrived at Derrynane: Kaplan, Nabu. Farrell, Favergé. Nubrikev.

"OK," said Dougherty. "That sounds like everybody."
Dougherty turned and was about to give the go signal when his radio crackled again.

"There's another," came the lookout.
"What?"
"Just a minute. Cap, I don't know who the hell this guy is, but he's being waved right in."

Dougherty frowned. "All right, stand by for ten more minutes. Let's make sure they're all here."

Dougherty pulled a cellular phone from his pocket and dialed a number. "Have you got it? Good, get it to me right now."

The boat they were on was essentially a shallow draft vessel, entirely open to the weather except for the center console, where the helm was located. Dougherty went there and opened a cabinet. A second later he came back to the stern with a sheet of paper.

"Anticipating something like this we put a fellow with a big lensed camera in a place where he could get some pictures of our guests. Modern technology, what a kick. The guy faxed it to me. Recognize it?"

Obviously Dougherty knew; he just wanted to see the reaction on their faces.

"Jesus Christ," said Rance. "Armstrong. National Security Advisor to the President of the United States."

Marty shook his head. "We knew he was into it, but I don't think we thought he'd come for it."

"Katarina," said Francoise. "There's only one thing that could make a man of that stature risk everything, including his country, which doesn't seem to matter anyway, and that's Katarina."

That's one way of putting it, thought Rance. But she was probably right. They had already established a connection between Katarina and Armstrong, and when it became known what his role in this affair was...well, in the end it would all be the same.

"Mr. Armstrong, it appears, has gotten in over his head."

"You know what kind of heat will come down on you if something happens to Armstrong, don't you?" Rance asked.

Dougherty smiled and rubbed his chin.

"Mr. Vaughn, it's all shit in the morning. Now let's get going before the fog lifts and we're fucked."

§

The hood of Jenny's Lexus was still warm.

Thanks in part to her recent involvement with Marty and Rance, Jenny had been spending eighteen hours a day at the office. Just like old times, she thought, as she pulled into her driveway after midnight for the fourth night in a row.

There was no point to unwinding. She would rise again at five-thirty, so Jenny went directly to bed, leaving her clothes in a pile. Sleep was paramount, all-demanding, the center of her universe, and her eyes gratefully closed the instant her cheek touched the pillow.

Outside the house, a man removed his hand from the hood of her car. In the black light of the night, he could see that the car was one of Lexus' top sports coupes. Very nice, he thought. The kind of car he'd like to drive.

He entered her house by the door beside the garage. Earlier that day he had broken in and spent a few hours getting to know the layout of the house, which now allowed him to move quickly. Before he entered her bedroom, the man took a small bottle from a pocket, poured the contents on a handkerchief, and went to Jenny.

The chloroform never let her wake up, and her body went limp in the his arms. The man was small and wiry, and though there wasn't really an ounce of fat on Jenny, she was still a tall woman, and he had difficulty moving her downstairs and out the door to his own car.

Quietly the man cursed Jackie Farrell. Lousy fucking aim. If he coulda shot straight in the marsh that day this would have all been over a long time ago. Screw it. He grunted and laid Jenny across the backseat, climbed behind the wheel and took a breath. He had a long drive ahead of him.

§

Rance had the worst seat in the house.

Left on board the shallow draft boat with him was a rotund, red-faced man named Donnelly. The fog was too think to see anything beyond the gunnals of the boat, where a few minutes earlier Francoise, Marty, Colm Dougherty and the rest of them had disappeared into the shallow surf. After the others had been discharged, Donnelly backed the boat out beyond the gentle break of the waves. Rance guessed that they were about fifty yards from shore.

"You know," said Donnelly, in an accent so thick that Rance had to frown in order to understand him, "it's not every day that you get to run something so involved."

"What's the usual around here?"

Donnelly smiled, a large, brown-toothed smile and Rance was thankful that there was three feet and a breeze between them.

"Little guys. You know, small enclaves of IRA supporters, stockpiling arms, having secret meetings and such. We use the hounds, usually."

"Hounds?"

"The dogs. Sniff 'em out, you see."

Rance nodded.

"From Boston, are ya?"

"Kind of." Then he thought about it. "Yeah, Boston."

"The money pit."

"How's that?"

"The money pit, that's what we call it. The fucking money pit. It's where all these bastards get their money to kill people."

Donnelly's smile was gone and now he looked at Rance with his face slightly cocked. Like he was waiting for something.

Just then Donnelly did something strange. He sat down. The deck of the boat was muddy with rain and boot muck, but that didn't seem to bother Donnelly. His wide bottom made a splash as he sat heavily.

Frowning madly, he looked down at Donnelly. The same quizzical expression remained on Donnelly's face, and it wasn't until a gentle swell rocked the boat and knocked him over that Rance could see what happened.

Just before you wake up from a nightmare there is a time without calibration, a period that might stretch for hours of seconds, where you know that it's all just a bad dream and all you have to do is smile and wait for it to be over. Rance had that feeling now.

He had that feeling now, but as he kept waiting, he realized that it wasn't going to be over. This was a bad dream that wasn't going to last another nanosecond and be finished, because Donnelly just lay there, face into the puddled muck. At the base of his skull there was a small hole that looked more black than red but Rance knew that the blood rushing from it was red, red and foamy, blood meant for Donnelly's brain now mixing with the dirty water around him, around his feet, and he knew that the hole in the base of Donnelly's skull wasn't natural, wasn't a spontaneous creation of nature, was in fact man made, and there was only one thing that man made that could make that kind of hole, and it had to come from behind Donnelly, and all he had to do was lift his eyes, lift his eyes and look, beyond the gunnal of the boat, and he would see it.

Without consciously knowing it, Rance dove. He dove backwards and he dove insensibly, closing his eyes and contorting his body to avoid the boat's transom and not wanting to believe that not only had he seen Donnelly laying there with a hole in his head, but also not wanting to believe that he had seen the other men, the man in the wet suit, his SCUBA gear draped all over his body, his arm outstretched, a gun its terminus, the yellow flame licking out of the barrel.

§

He hoped he had chosen the right direction.

All was confusion. The salt had burned his eyes after he had dove in, just as it always had, as it had when he was a boy swimming at the beach at Green Harbor, as it had three weeks ago when he had for the first time dove into the water to save his own life. Now he just hoped that he was heading in to shore.

Breathing was about to become a problem. Rance was swimming a modified stroke that he always used when underwater. It was a stroke that had once won him a dollar on a bet against Eric Mantos that he couldn't swim the entire length and back of Billy Duggan's inground pool. It was kind of a breast stroke underwater, and though it worked well, it involved every major muscle group, and it chewed up a lot of oxygen.

He needn't have worried, for one thrust later his chin ground into the soft sand. Rance stuck his head above the water and sucked in two lungs full of air. Damn the lead, he thought, else I'll die anyway.

Everything was colorless gray, thick and blind. He guessed his visibility to be three feet, which was a mixed blessing. Though no one could see him, neither could he see anything. Standing in the shallow surf, catching his breath, he listened.

There was no sound but the soft fizz of the waves spending themselves on the soft sand. He moved up onto the beach.

There were a lot of things that he didn't want to think about. And by the same turn, there were a lot of things that he did want to think about right now. Trouble was, they were all too close to one another to be easily separated.

He tried to invoke the map that Colm had gone over, the diagram of Derrynane. But he kept seeing Francoise, that look on her face, just wait until we're through, you'll see, that look. Derrynane had to be in front of him; it certainly wasn't out there in the water, surrounded by armed divers, aberrations of Ian Flemming's imagination.

A large phalanx of dunes rose up from the beach, and Rance hit them blindly, arms and legs digging, pulling himself up, the sand flying into every open flap of drenched clothing, clinging to him, blinding his eyes, burning his already fatigued muscles. And then he was there.

The dunes were crested with a hard, short grass that he grabbed, propelling himself up and over, onto a flat field.

Rance ran. He ran with a wild impetuosity, the way a child runs in the dark night of a summer evening when he has the feeling of speed, unstoppable speed, super hero speed, a speed of blind joy, except he wasn't joyful at all, he was scared, running scared, running reckless, running toward, he was sure, his death.

Toward Francoise was the reality.

Whatever happened fifty yards offshore, it must have been part of something terribly wrong. Something had gone terribly wrong with the whole operation, and though Rance didn't have the time nor inclination to reflect upon it now, in the dark, subterranean reaches of his mind, in the place that never sleeps, the original 24-hour, open all night section of the brain, the consciousness that looked like somebody's college dorm room, that place knew already that only someone on the inside could have subterfuged this thing.

The field sloped down gently, helping his progress. As far as he could remember, Rance thought that Derrynane House itself must have been about five hundred yards straight back from the beach, and as the ground disappeared behind him, he tried to listen.

For what? he asked himself. For it. Death. The snapping, popping, crackling sound of death, just before it smacks into you, wet and sick sounding and indelibly impressing you in the most horrific manner known.

Visibility around him increased to about twenty or thirty yards, which did little but make him feel as though he were in a larger gray envelope than he had been in. He ran hard, trying to listen for anything, any sounds at all, his eyes closed, though he didn't know it, his eyes were closed and they didn't open until the ground came up to meet him.

Like the Irish blessing: May the wind be at your back, May the sun shine warmly upon your face, May the road rise up to meet you...

Fuck that, Rance thought as the wind left his lungs. Fuck

the ground, or the road, or any of this damn island rising up to meet me. Not until he rolled over did he realize that he had been tackled, but by then it was too late, for his attacker had subdued him expertly with some kind of inescapable grip.

It was Dougherty.

Colm Dougherty had a wild look in his eyes, the look of an animal, Rance thought, a look that had displaced the steely, cagey look of knowing, of confidence, that had always been there. Now Dougherty looked wild and almost out of control.

Dougherty put a finger to his lips. Shhhh.

Letting Rance go, Dougherty motioned to follow him, and a second later they had crawled under a low shrub.

"What the fuck are you doing?" Dougherty yelled in a barely audible whisper.

"Donnelly's dead," said Rance. "They've got divers out there and if they got Donnelly then they probably got the other guys, too."

Dougherty considered this, looking no place in particular. "Sweet Jesus help us," Dougherty said.

Not exactly the words Rance wanted to hear.

"What the fuck's going on?"

Dougherty pursed his lips and shook his head. "I don't know," he said. "Everything was as quiet as a fucking church when we came up off the beach. And visibility? You couldn't see fuck-all. Just about the house, we had just fanned out nicely, boys with the gas in position when: Bang! They were behind us. They were fucking behind us and it was a free for fucking all."

"Where's Marty and Francoise?"

"I had them back and on my left." Dougherty gestured to nowhere.

"Any radio contact?"

Dougherty looked at him evenly. "None."

Rance bit his lip and looked around. "So what do we do now?"

An explosion was his answer.

§

"Captain Dougherty?"

The radio was next to Rance's head. He and Dougherty had instinctively covered themselves at the sound of the blast, and now they both looked up. Off to their left there was the sharp crackle of gunfire, and yells, everything maddeningly muted by the pall-thick fog.

"Dougherty here, go."

"Collins here, sir. Me and team 1 just sent a rocket in, sir. We were receiving heavy automatic weapons fire from the west wing, so we let them have it, sir."

"Casualties?"

"None for us, sir, but pity the fuckers inside."

Just then there was the roar of gunfire in front of them. Was the fog thinning now? Rance could see dim orange licks of flame, moving from left to right and getting closer. Dougherty, laying prone, weapon drawn, sighted in on nothing but a sound, here it comes, closer, Rance can just make out a figure-

Boom! Boom! Boom! Boom! Dooley's gun roars and Rance wonders just what the hell kind of cannon he has in his hand.

"Jesus!" said Rance. "I couldn't even see who it was!"

"Neither could I," said Dougherty. "But whoever it was wasn't firing anything we issue. Come on."

On their bellies Rance and Colm crawled, the crackle of gunfire falling off to their left, and Rance wants to know where in the hell are Marty and Francoise? At the body and Colm rolls it over and says a word that Rance thinks is foreign at first then he gets the name.

"Nubrikev."

Somebody screamed, and it wasn't a man. Rance jumped to his feet, sprinting to the house, oblivious to the shouts of Dougherty behind him. Running so fast he almost hits the house, he trips over a body. He rolled it over but recognized nothing except a bullet hole because he'd already seen one today.

He took the two guns, one a pistol that felt like a .45 but he couldn't be sure. The other was some kind of automatic weapon with what looked to be about thirty rounds dangling off it. He stuffed the pistol into his pants, pointed the gun forward went around to the front of the house.

The fog was lifting. Under the cover of the trees, in the lee of the onshore flow, visibility was downright excellent. Rance was about to round the corner when something caught his eye. It was the perfectly round and black end of a gun, and it was about one millimeter from his right eyeball.

"What are you, crazy?" Marty said. "How the hell did you get up here?"

"Telekinesis," Rance said. "I heard Francoise scream. What happened?"

Without looking at Rance-his eyes relentlessly scanned the area-Marty spoke. "She acted stupid like you. Saw Katarina trying to make a run out the front door, so she ran up and got the drop on her. Trouble was, somebody else got the drop on her. Nabu, I think it was. They took her inside.

"Now listen. I want you to stay right here. I'm going to circle around the front and get on the other side of the door."

"Then what are you going to do?"

Marty smiled.

"Knock."

§

For a second Rance saw the Death in his eyes.

Then Marty was gone and this time Rance did as he was told, sliding back into some heavy shrubs that gave him a view of the front door. Around back the gunfire became intermittent.

God, he thought, Francoise! The thought of her in there twisted his stomach into a hot knot of acid, quivering his bowels causing a fresh round of sweat to break out on his forehead. Stay right here, he heard Marty say. But he couldn't. And let Francoise...

Against one of the walls, almost hidden buy the thick shrubbery, there was a window. By actually climbing inside the huge shrub, Rance could get up to the window's level and look in. The room was dark and empty. He looked around once, twice.

His elbow made a lot less noise breaking the glass than he thought it would, and he reached in, unlocked the window and slipped inside. After waiting and listening for several minutes he moved to a door.

Compared to the room he was in, the hallway beyond was brightly lit. With the door open a crack, Rance could hear voices. Far away, and they seemed to be arguing; one of them was a woman's voice. He was about to steal out into the hallway when, as promised, there was a knock at the front door. Approaching steps, but sounding odd, coming to him from the earlier sound of the voices. Then:

"Hey! Inside! I'm unarmed! I'm unarmed and I want to talk!"

Rance saw Francoise from the corner of his left eye. She was being held in a half-nelson, a large gun at her neck, her eyes wide and pleading, being pushed in front of a man. Rance wanted to swallow his tongue; the man was Nabu Mohammed.

As they neared, Rance wanted desperately to signal to Francoise, to let her know he was here, that she could make a move and be covered. His grip tightened around the gun and he eased the muzzle out the opened crack. They passed within a few feet of him but Rance couldn't shoot, he couldn't be sure that he'd hit only Nabu. So he waited.

Nabu didn't. On his left, hidden from Rance's view, he had his own weapon, and he brought it up, aimed at the door and fired, the sound deafening in the small hallway, the place blinded with angry bright muzzle flash, Nabu's face gritted, gritted with anger, yes, but laughing too, laughing madly, putting the hot muzzle back into Francoise's neck and then silence.

The front door, shot to splinter and sawdust, swung open.

There on the front stoop stood Marty Donovan, large smile on his face.

"I told you I was unarmed," Marty said. "I was lying."

Rance never saw the gun come into Marty's hand, only saw the flash of his muzzle and the gun's kick lift his hand up, and Nabu falling, falling down but his finger still squeezing the trigger, the gun stubbornly coming up, the bullets tracing a splintered trail up the hallway, across the threshold, to Marty's feet, then up his leg, and Rance turned away. When he looked back there was Francoise, trying to extricate herself from Nabu's lifeless-and thanks to Marty, headless-body, Marty and Nabu, both laying there, Nabu dead for sure, and Marty...

"Francoise!"

Then they are together, clung to each other, spinning on the tiled floor, Francoise sobbing and Rance sobbing right back at her, each of them squeezing the other so tight it hurts, but it's the best damn pain Rance has ever felt and then, then she pulls back and he looks at her face and he feels somebody push her from behind.

Rance felt the push translated through her body and into his. And Francoise looks just as surprised as him, looking up at him, her eyes widening, trying to ask him a question, but no words, and then he felt her body go limp in his arms, limp and wet and as Francoise's head cants over to one side, her eyes closing even then, Rance sees who pushed her.

Katarina, at the end of the hall, gun in her hand.

And for that moment, a fast moment, she has a shot at Rance. Still doped from the events of the last thirty seconds, she has him as easily as she had Francoise, the gun leveled at him, and as close as he's come already to Death, this time he feels It, feels It slipping down the front of his body, twisting Its way to the floor, trying to take him with It.

Katarina is smiling.

That terrible smile, that horrific grin, coming to him from a bad horror film. All the times he had seen that smile, in bed beside him, laughing at him in an open car, questioning him through the night, never had it looked so chilling, so lifeless, so evil. Rance thought he might expire from fright.

Then she turned and fled, gone as fast as she had appeared. He fell to his knees but he knew already that Francoise was dead, the blood bubbling from her mouth, that horrible smell of Death asserting itself everywhere in the hallway. Rance stood and followed Katarina.

The hallway led to a large meeting room with huge oil paintings on the wall. Most of them now resided on the floor, for this had been the room that was blown out by the rocket launcher. There was nobody in it. Rance went to the far door which led to a smaller room, and when he went through the door the wall beside him erupted with bullet holes.

§

"Hold him," said Katarina.

She handed Richard Armstrong the gun and turned to the fireplace. Crouching behind a sofa, they were blocked from Rance's line of sight for a moment, so Armstrong, panicked now, took the gun that he didn't want to touch. Armstrong wanted out.

"Hurry up!" he urged Katarina.

Already he was finished in any capacity as a functionary of the United States government. But that didn't matter, because now he and Katarina had everything, the software, the money, they had it all and they were going to disappear.

"Katarina!" Rance screamed. "Katarina! Wait!"

Armstrong didn't know what to do. Never having shot a gun, he was only vaguely familiar with which end needed to be pointed at the target. Behind him he could hear Katarina swearing softly under her breath.

"What should I do?" he asked.

"Shoot him!"

He tried to, but succeeded only in blowing out a window ten feet from Rance. Armstrong's arm went numb with the force of the recoil.

"Katarina, no! Wait!"

Armstrong's face contorted in confusion. Rance made his move, boldly, brashly, striding out across the empty floor, gun leveled at him. Sure I'm a bad shot, Armstrong thought, but that's really insulting. And then he sees that this guy isn't even looking at him, he's looking beyond him, to where Katarina-

Armstrong turns and sees that Katarina is gone. Vanished. Like she was never there. And then, when the bullet crashes into his chest, he falls to the floor, backward and ungracefully, arms and legs splayed stupidly in death.

§

It was a passage.

A panel next to the fireplace had been swung open on hidden hinges. That was what Katarina was doing while Armstrong tried to cover her. Rance looked at the dark opening for a moment, looked back at the empty room containing the dead body of the National Security Advisor to the President of the United States of America, then went in.

The opening was narrow, almost too narrow for his shoulders. He had to twist his torso in such a way that rendered him completely vulnerable for a second, a second that scared Rance, for before him was blackness, but then he was through.

Surprisingly, beyond the opening the space expanded and he found he could stand. His problem was that he couldn't see anything; it was pitch dark in here. Quickly he moved away from the light of the opening, to better accustom his eyes to the darkness and to erase his outline before the door. But he knew that there was nobody watching, else he would have drawn a reaction.

He almost fell down the stairs. They were wooden and damp and noisy, and by the time he reached the bottom his eyes had adjusted enough to let him see that a long corridor lay before him. At its end there was a faint light and Rance started for it.

So this is what it comes to, he thought, the fruition of his life since Katarina entered it. What had he been back then? What could have happened had she not come to him, exerting such an influence, such a motivating pain that Rance would be able to propel himself to a place he hadn't since been able to return to?

Perhaps, he considered, he would have ended up exactly where he was before this started–a lobsterman who drank too much and cared too little.

But had Katarina's influence been the sole factor in all

this? Had it been her directive to try and silence Rance before this started? Had she been that worried about what he knew or didn't know? She had, after all, allowed him to live. After killing Francoise, she had a clear and easy shot at him. But she left him. It told him something very important about her train of thought: that she preferred him alive.

But he was a different creature now. Aside from the gun thrust out before him and the one tucked into his jeans, Rance appeared to be the same person. But something had happened back there a few minutes ago, something as bad as Michael dying in his arms, something wrong.

This time he lost something that he hadn't even had a chance to have. For what hurts the most is never the loss of something permanent; what hurts the most is the loss of promise, that cheated chance for the future. Right now he hurt largely and badly.

The light came from above another staircase. Like their predecessors, these stairs were rickety and dangerous. As he climbed them, he thought his eyes were playing tricks on him, for the stairs seemed to end in the ceiling. Only when he got to the top did he realize there was a trap door which was the source of the light.

Rance took a deep breath. He had no idea how far he had traveled, nor where this tunnel could possibly come up. Nor could he imagine what was on the other side. Katarina? Who else? Was this entrance to the tunnel guarded, watched? No purpose in waiting. Just go for it.

He pushed open the door and heard the metallic clicking of a dozen guns being cocked.

The opening to the tunnel was, it turned out, guarded. But

it was Dooley's men who guarded it. Rance found himself looking down the barrels of too many guns.

Fortunately someone recognized him and waved the men off. When he was clear of the tunnel, Rance could see that he had traveled about a half a mile from Derrynane House, to a spot at the edge of the woods. He looked and saw some men making plaster casts of the ground and taking photographs.

"We were wondering where in the hell anyone could have come from," one of the officers said to Rance. "We had a report of a car pulling out of a side road, lost it I'm afraid. Fucking tourists everywhere. Couldn't figure out how in the hell anyone could've gotten away from that bloody place."

§

It was a beautiful part of the world.

Back from the sea-which was really the estuary of the Kenmare River-the land rose up sharply into two hills, Eagle Hill and Cahernageeha Mountain. Cherished by Daniel O'Connell when he made his home here, the hills held a plentiful stock of rabbits and foxes that the Liberator and his hounds hunted.

The river estuary itself, now that the fog was lifting off it, was glassy and a dark shade of black-green. Across it lay the Beara peninsula, low hilled, a string of beasts of burden slowly descending into the Atlantic Ocean.

Derrynane House, Rance could see for the first time, was a modest estate. What made it special was the property. Dunes hiding a protected beach, large, long lawn rolling back up to the house, and thick woods between Derrynane and the rest of the world.

There were dead bodies on the lawn. Six, by Rance's count, three of them, three of us. The whole southwest corner of Derrynane House was gone. Like a bad movie monster bent down and took a bite from the place, the whole bottom corner was missing, giving the structure an improbable staggering look. Rance found Colm Dougherty standing outside a circle of his men halfway to the dunes.

"I'm happy to see you, Mr. Vaughn," he said. "I'm sorry that this had to happen, but in an operation of this nature, there is always the possibility of the unexpected."

Rance shrugged and looked around. He couldn't think about it right now; the shock was too new, the adrenaline was still tearing through his veins.

Then he saw it, a stretcher bearing a body, and thinking it was Francoise he ran over to it. As he neared it he saw it was a man, Marty. Oh, Jesus, but wait, corpses generally don't blink their eyes. Marty was alive.

"Marty! Marty!"

"Hey, tough guy," Marty croaked. "Hey, I'm sorry..."

"Don't talk. You're going to be all right, you old fart. Just fine." Rance, seeing the blood stained sheet, was biting back tears.

"As long as I don't get an Irish doctor. Liable to be a fucking rummy."

Marty was loaded into a truck that sped away and Rance returned to Dougherty.

"He's a tough bird, Mr. Vaughn. Probably have a limp and some serious pain when it rains, but he'll pull through."

"What's the attraction over there?" Rance asked, nodding

toward the circle of men.

A smile broke out on Dooley's face, not a smile of happiness, but one of cunning, a chesired smile. He led Rance over.

"It's not exactly a silver lining," he said, moving his men aside, "but it's not bad."

As Rance approached he could see there was a man laying on the ground. Dooley's men were reluctant to back off, their guns pointed at the man, even though the man was thoroughly subdued. It was Jackie Farrell.

He was hog tied brutally, the arch of his back a painful looking rainbow. Around his mouth were several strips of thick duct tape, the sticky silver stuff that would remove several layers of skin when torn off. But it was his eyes that Rance saw first and clearest.

Farrell looked up at Rance and fixed him with his eyes. In a situation like this a man should be frightened, Rance thought. But this man's eyes looked calm, almost pleased. Smiling. What Rance could see of his face was cut and bruised and bleeding, but with no visible effect on Farrell's demeanor.

Those eyes spoke to Rance cordially before he was hauled away, dragged over the hard ground by his feet, all the time his eyes calmly looking out from above the tape.

"Listen, Rance" Colm said in a quieter, reflective tone, "I know you're probably busting to get back to America, but I think you should came back to headquarters with me first. There's something you should see there."

§

On the drive back to base Dougherty filled Rance in.

"They flanked us," Dougherty said bitterly. They were sitting in the back seat of an unmarked vehicle which was flying over Ireland's narrow roads.

"It was like someone fucking knew right where we were. That's not something I'm terribly excited about, and we'll have to conduct a full internal investigation."

A full internal investigation, Rance's mind echoed bitterly. Marty and Francoise will be so appreciative. But that thought was balanced by the knowledge that their business was laden with such risks, and they too had probably been in Dougherty position during their careers.

Still...

"Any sign of Katarina?"

Dougherty looked grim. "No. Apparently the tunnel she used was known to very few people, the curator of the property among them. It's obvious, however, that the tunnel was to used as an emergency escape. In fact, that's what it was built for. O'Connell put it in when he built the place to escaped the Brits, should it become necessary. Never thought it would have been used to help someone like that get out. The Liberator is surely turning in his grave."

"So we're left with nothing." He couldn't help the caustic tone that snuck out and wrapped itself around his words.

"I know that nothing can bring Francoise back and stop Marty's pain," Dougherty said, a soft warmth that Rance had not yet heard coating his voice, "but we got Nabu. He was probably the worst of them, responsible for the deaths of hundreds of innocent people a year. And he died ingloriously, a fact that will be broadcast to the world. You see, for Nabu's people, to die in battle is there preferred way to go. But we'll make sure it comes out as cowardice. We'll make it look like he got knifed by a whore or something."

Dooley's smile was not for Rance's benefit and it was steely cold, harsh as a bathroom floor.

"And we have Farrell," he continued.

"Who probably won't talk."

"Mr. Vaughn, this isn't America." The didactic edge was back in Dooley's voice. "Farrell will not only talk, he will prattle on to such an extent that we will have to ask him to please be quiet."

For Dougherty, Farrell had forfeited his rights the day his then young family was obliterated by bomb set off in Piccalilli Square and claimed by The Boyne.

Dougherty turned and looked back out the window at the splendor of the passing countryside, flora that he hadn't seen in nearly twenty years. Not now, Colm, he told himself. Concentrate on the future.

§

Far from fearful of his situation, Farrell was cocky.

His huge frame had been absorbing numbing blows since he had been thrown in the back of the closed lorry, but he could take that for ages before really feeling it. And these guys? They were company men, following orders. They didn't have any real hatred for him, and Farrell could feel it in their blows, which to him felt almost perfunctory.

What the fuck happened back there he didn't know. More than likely his director of security, a well-meaning but ultimately stupid man named Connerty, got too aggressive and attacked too fast. He should have let them get right on top of us, Farrell thought futilely. Then we could have mowed them down like so much grass.

Farrell took a gun butt to the stomach, doubling him over again. But the blows were becoming more intermittent. As he had thought, these guys were tiring of the whole ordeal. Soon, he thought, I'll make my move. Just a little longer, when their guard is–

The truck skidded to a stop, sending the unrestrained Farrell flying forward. Catching his head on one of the metal benches, he opened up a deep gash beginning on the right side of his scalp and jagging down along the line of his jaw. Bright red blood spouted everywhere and the door flew open.

"Jesus Christ McDowd!" Dougherty roared into the bloody back of the truck. "I told you to slap him around, not fucking kill him!"

McDowd shrugged and stood, stepping on Farrell's fingers, twisting his heel and grinding them into the diamond plated bed. "What the fuck, sir? He wasn't wearing no safety belt."

For the first time a quick flash of fear blew through Farrell. Quickly fighting it off, he reasserted his inner arrogance. But the fear had been there nonetheless, however brief, something he wasn't used to. Obviously these were not regular Guardia, or Farrell would be having tea and biscuits by now. He tried to look at Dougherty but a boot caught him under the chin, flipping him out of the truck and onto a patch of hard pavement.

Farrell tried to crane his neck for a look around but a hood was plunged over his neck and fastened by means of a rope around his neck. Writhing and gagging, Farrell felt the rope tightening around his neck until enough of the blood supply to his brain had been interrupted so that he passed out.

When he opened his eyes he was in an impossibly bright room. His mouth tasted bitter and of blood, his tongue thickly feeling around and tallying up the number of lost teeth. He guessed he had been out for a while, for the entire length of his body ached, belying the beating he had been given.

Fuck that, he thought. Bruises heel, and they can't hold me forever. We're still in Ireland, he thought. They've got to arrest me and charge me and that will be the end of this shit.

A morsel of doubt shimmered somewhere and though his first impulse was to ignore it, he knew he couldn't ignore anything and expect to survive. Not regular Guardia, he remembered. What that meant was that they probably operated under their own set of rules. Well fuck them. As soon as I get a hand free–

"Ah, Mr. Farrell, are we resting comfortably?"

Farrell looked up and saw the man who had earlier opened the back of the truck. Forty-five or fifty he guessed. Hard looking the way he stands, ready to pounce. Bad look about this one. Smiling, but his eyes telling me I'm dead. We'll see.

"Who the bloody fuck are you?" Farrell grunted.

Dougherty took a seat across from him, and Farrell calculated how much thrust he'd need to charge him.

"That's not important. Neither are theatrics, Mr. Farrell, so I'll spare you the James Bond drama. To get to the point, I'd like to know about Katarina Favergé and Jay Kaplan, who unfortunately escaped. You see, we only recovered half of the

SHAKESPEARE software, which means that you were working a double cross on your terrorist friends. What I need to know is where is the second half of this program, and where is Ms. Favergé and Mr. Kaplan?"

Behind Dougherty Farrell could see a window opening on to a hallway. Disinterested people passed, some looking in at him laying there, prone and bloody on the floor. What the fuck kind of place is this? he wondered. That twinkle of fear burned a little more steadily now as the wind of his bravado subsided.

"I don't know who you are," Farrell said, "but you can beat me 'till fuck-all comes and I ain't telling you shit."

Dougherty smiled. "We're through beating you, Mr. Farrell. Besides, a gentleman of your size can absorb a lot, and I've neither the time nor the inclination to waste my time softening you up. So I'll get right to the point."

Dougherty snapped his fingers and a second later two guards appeared at the window behind him. Between them they were harshly clutching a sweet but scared looking older lady with gray streaked red hair. She was the same sweet woman who Rance awoke to three days ago. She was Farrell's mother.

The guards pushed her hard up against the window and inside the room a soft thud could be heard, followed by a series of sobs.

Farrell sat bolt upright. "Mum! Jesus Christ! Mum!" With all his energy he thrust himself at Dougherty, letting out a wild scream. But he was just as quickly thrown to the floor by the heavy chain that looped around his arms and legs. Farrell screamed and struggled as the wind left him. The fear was suddenly intense, a super nova right in his face, scalding him and melting everything, every defense he had.

"Now, Mr. Farrell, either you begin talking, or I'll kill your mother." Dougherty was grave and intense, bending to look at Farrell's eyes. "And I won't kill her quickly. I'll begin by twisting her ears off with pliers. Then I'll slice open her tongue with a razor blade. Then perhaps I'll score her back with a white-hot knife. And you'll watch it all, Mr. Farrell. You'll watch it all and you'll be able to stop it just by telling me where Katarina Favergé is, and where the rest of the software is."

There was a final surge of defiance within Farrell, and he managed to spit in Dooley's face. Not seeming to mind, Dougherty produced a handkerchief and wiped himself off. He then returned to the window.

"Knock her teeth out," he said, speaking into an intercom next to the window. "Knock her teeth out by smashing her face into the window so our guest here gets a good look."

Without hesitating the two burly men pulled the old lady's head back violently, then snapped it forward with viscous speed. Mrs. Farrell's mouth pancaked into the glass, exploding in blood, her white teeth chipping, shattering, flying out of her head. Her eyes rolled back and closed before she went limp in their grasp.

"No! No! No! Not her! Don't! Please don't! She didn't know! She didn't know anything at all! God no! Oh God! Please!"

Farrell launched himself again with predictable results, but this time he didn't get up, instead twisting down onto the floor, deteriorating into a babble of sick sobs.

Dougherty again leaned close.

"Where is she, Mr. Farrell?"

Farrell spoke but the words were drowned by tears.

"I'm sorry, what did you say?"

"Boston. She went to Boston, you fuck."

§

"You can thank Dermot here," Dougherty said.

Rance was still shaken and sickened by what he had just seen. Observing Farrell's cell via closed circuit television, he had seen the whole episode.

"Went to UCLA, got a degree in cinematography but his real love was special effects, right Dermot?"

Dermot, sitting behind a huge board that resembled a television director's, smiled and nodded.

"What was the biggie you did? Remember, right before you came back? What was that big film you worked on?"

"*Jurassic Park*, sir," Dermot said cheerfully.

Dougherty snapped his fingers. "That's the one. Dinosaurs running around, just like they were next to you. Dermot is a special effects whiz, Mr. Vaughn."

Rance still couldn't believe that the whole thing had been made up.

"Of course we helped Mr. Farrell along. Gave him a little injection-two, actually. Big, tough bastard he was. Gave him enough to make elephants think they were seeing dancing martinis, eh Dermot?"

"Yes, sir."

"Then the whole thing-" Rance began.

"Everything."

Rance shook his head. "Who the hell are you guys?"

"That's not important, Mr. Vaughn. The important thing is that you're going home. This is all finished for you. We'll be contacting the authorities regarding the information given to us by Mr. Farrell and everything will be taken care of."

Boston, Rance thought. He wondered how much Farrell told them-not enough for now, Rance guessed by the way he was getting the bum's rush out of Ireland. The whole time it was right there, in my own backyard.

There was little he could do now. He was exhausted and he slept for the first time since he'd been to Ireland on the ride to Shannon Airport.

Part V

Boston

Upon deboarding his plane in Boston, Rance was immediately arrested.

Nice to see you, too, he thought, as he was led away in handcuffs by customs officials. By this time he was too...too everything, too tired, too drained, too bitter, to care about it. Let whatever happens happens, I've been pushing the destiny envelope enough for the last three weeks. Now I'm tired. As he was led into a tiny, windowless cell, his thoughts turned to Jenny.

Well, of course, one side of him chided. Good ole Jenny, always there, while the rest of them fall by the wayside, good ole Jenny's still there, rock solid, pretty enough to marry, stable enough to make your funeral arrangements.

But right now, she was all he had. Marty wouldn't be returning until tomorrow. His condition was good–stable, but he had lost a lot of blood. How he didn't lose his leg Rance couldn't guess. He had seen the rounds smacking into Marty's leg, the horrible wet sound drowned out by the roar of the gun.

He closed his eyes against it.

Back in Boston now. With Katarina. He had wanted to talk to Dougherty about that, but Dougherty was in a huge rush to get rid of him. Like I'm cursed, thought Rance. So she's here. So she is.

He was allowed a phone call and since his attorney was named Jennifer O'Grady Ryan he tried her office.

"Umm, no, Mr. Vaughn, she's, um not here," stammered Jenny's secretary. Rance frowned and looked at the customs official.

"Well, when will she be in? I need to talk to her."

"Why don't I just give you her voice mail," she said too quickly. He left a brief message, but as he did a knot formed in his gut. Replacing the receiver, he turned to the guard.

"What's for dinner?"

§

Rance wondered what special powers Customs held.

He had been in custody for over six hours, had neither seen nor spoke to anyone, and had been charged with nothing. He was simply held in a small, windowless cell with a table and two chairs. He didn't think he was going to get any dinner, which was too bad, because now that his stomach had settled down, he was hungry. Very hungry.

The door opened and a young man in a snappy jacket and tie came in. Rance thought he should have just held up a sign that said "FBI" on it.

"Rance Vaughn?" he said, producing his Bureau ID and showing it. "I'm Special Agent Ted Benson, with the Federal Bureau of Investigation."

Rance nodded. "Sorry, you're a little late. Customs got me first."

Young and athletic of build, Benson looked like a college football All-American, square jaw, big white teeth, and short thick blond hair, the kind of hair you see in shampoo commercials. In the glow of all this squeaky-clean studliness, Rance, unbathed and still suffering some mild shock, felt awful. Benson smiled, Rance winced.

"That was a mix up. Left over from the murder of Michael O'Meara. Customs had an outstanding warrant that wasn't lifted. Our mistake. You're all set."

"If I'm all set," Rance said, standing, "why did you have to come by and tell me? Are the customs guys mute?"

Benson smiled that warm smile. "Marty told me you'd be...'quick of wit.'"

"Marty Donovan has never used the phrase 'quick of wit' in his entire life. 'Smart ass' was probably what he said." They stood there for a moment, uncomfortably regarding each other. "So if you are here to tell me I'm free to go, it'll cost you dinner."

"Deal."

"Pizza," Rance said quickly. "The European, in the North End."

"Know it well."

Ten minutes later Benson and Rance were seated behind a large pitcher of Budweiser and a pepperoni pizza the size of an oriental rug.

"So Ted, tell me," Rance said through a mouthful of scalding cheese and sauce and dough, "what's up? I know Marty will be back tomorrow, so I thought everyone was finally done with me."

Benson sipped his beer thoughtfully and Rance felt that familiar knot burning in his gut.

"We'll talk after dinner."

"Ted," Rance said, plopping down his unfinished slice, wiping his hands on a paper napkin, reaching for his beer, "you're ruining my dinner. What gives?"

Benson regarded him for a moment without emotion, his left thumb tapping the table top. He could feel Benson's hesitation impregnating the moment, and though he wanted to urge Benson along, he resisted. Finally Benson sighed; slightly, but enough to change his face.

"We've been in contact with Colm Dougherty throughout this entire ordeal, so we know what happened—I mean that we know Katarina was supposed to return to Boston to somehow consummate the deal with Kaplan." Benson was hushed now, and serious, hanging his head low and peering at Rance with blue eyes. "And we know that you...you have a sense about her. What it comes down to is this: you're the closest thing we have to her."

"So this ball is back in the FBI's court now? You guys have jurisdiction over this mess? The National Security Advisor was killed while committing treason and–"

"That information hasn't been released yet."

"Not released?" Rance took a sip of his beer. The table felt solid as he thunked the mug back down upon it. Under his feet the floor of the European felt good, familiar. Rance was home. "You mean the administration is sitting on this news?"

"Pending notification of his family–"

"Oh shut up. Please. You're nauseating me. Don't you people ever get it? You keep acting like assholes and everybody is going to treat you like an asshole."

The blood left Benson's lips, whitening them, peeling them back from his teeth just enough for Rance to see his teeth.

"Look," Benson said after a minute, "we're putting a lot on the line by even telling you this, by even including you in this–"

"Did you ever think I don't want to be included anymore? Did you ever stop to think that maybe I'm tired of having my ass shot at, beaten, and left for dead?"

"It's not just Katarina Favergé anymore, Rance. Jenny Ryan has disappeared, and we think it's related to what's been taking place."

§

Marty looked good.

"For a guy who lost half the meat off his leg, you look pretty sprite," Rance said, entering the semi-private hospital room at Massachusetts General Hospital.

There were some flowers on the window sill, and the other bed in the room was empty. His color full in his cheeks, Marty shook his head.

"Hey, don't start with me," Rance said. "I think you guys

are nuts. I'm starting to think everyone's is nuts. Even me." He sat down. "Honest to God, Marty, I think I had it right when I was sitting in my boat drinking 30 beers a day. Everything was so normal-right."

"Tell it to Jenny," was Marty's reply.

"All right. All right. What do you know?"

From his lap Marty tossed Rance a file with Jenny's name on it.

"No signs of a struggle. Summertime and busy down at her house so nobody paid much attention to her car being there for a couple of days. Her office gave her a day, then started calling. They called the cops at the end of the second day. She's been missing three days."

"No prints? Nothing?"

Marty shrugged. "Jenny was contacted by this mystery guy who lead her in certain directions, but we don't know who he is."

"You suspect someone, right?"

"Melvin Schwartz."

"Schwartz? Attorney Slip-and-Fall? That ambulance chaser? What the hell does he have to do with this?"

"He was Katarina Favergé's defense counsel in a sealed case against her."

"What are you talking about?"

"*The United States of America v. Katarina Favergé.*"

"Sealed?"

"We're working on a court order to see it, but until then..."

"Why bother? Why not just take Schwartz in for questioning?"

"Because we can't find him. He's vanished too."

Rance frowned. "Marty, forgive me, but I get the feeling that you want something of me."

Marty rubbed his chin. "Rance, I know you've been through a lot of shit the last few weeks. More shit than someone should have to go through. I also know that you care about Jenny, the same way you cared about Michael, and you're not about to go back to lobster fishing, not while this thing is still laying there on the floor.

"I also know that seeing Francoise die like that isn't going to leave you anytime soon. And don't forget your daughter, Rance. Your sense of what's wrong and what's right. And your promise to Michael."

Out of Marty's hospital room window Rance could see Storrow Drive and the Charles River. Morning traffic still clogged the inbound side of Storrow Drive, traffic that he had just left behind after a night at the Guest Quarters in Allston. There was no doubt that Martin Donovan had been close to Michael O'Meara, as close as Rance, maybe even closer. He thought like Michael, talked like Michael. It was unnerving.

"So why don't you enlighten me as to what exactly it is you want from me."

§

A private car met her at the airport.

Not a limousine, not even a shiny black sedan, the car was an unremarkable minivan. Only after she got in did she realize that it wasn't an ordinary, factory-line vehicle.

The driver was an expressionless man of medium build who simply helped her with her suitcases and drove. It took her a second to realize that the tinted glass of the car was bullet-proof. And from the heavy sound of the door when it closed, she guessed armor-plated. A shotgun was mounted under the dash, and she was sure the driver was armed with various weapons he knew how to use.

She was flattered, but at the same time wary. It was an old feeling for her: powerful man strutting his testosterone before her, trying to use the aphrodisiacs at his disposal. And always she enjoyed the experience. Until the next one. She allowed herself a smile.

Though there was a lot to be done, this interlude was important to her. Not emotionally, but in an economic sense. She looked at it as a deposit, an investment. Like a good lawyer, she would never ask a question to which she didn't know the answer. And right now she was collecting answers, leaving nothing to chance.

Glowing in the glittering night, the architectural icons of the United States were awash in white light. Twenty minutes after the car left Dulles International Airport, it rolled to a stop in front of a gate. A United States Marine checked the driver's identification, then waved them through.

Maybe soon, she thought, I will enter through the front, the public entrance. Coming into the back of the mansion distressed her, reminding her exactly where her place was. Though there was a certain sexiness to manipulating from behind, she yearned to be taken for what she was. She wanted to be the one.

Taking a deep breath she stepped from the car. A young man too smartly dressed for a Sunday midnight smiled curtly and led her inside. A plain elevator took them upstairs. The young man didn't accompany her down the hall. She knew the way.

She knocked once on the door and entered. Looking up from where he was practicing his putting, the President of the United States of America smiled broadly.

"Katarina," he said.

§

They'll fucking deny everything.

Now Rance knew how the Watergate burglars felt. Pawns. Little guys. Hired dopes. Marty had tried to sell it to him as good research for his upcoming book, but Rance was worried about the Cambridge Police Department. He knew that the FBI would have to deny all knowledge of him, so he couldn't use them as his...absolution.

For the caliber of person–publicly and professional-ly–Schwartz was, his home was rather modest. Rance had fig-ured the guy to be worth gazillions, getting the rich and fa-mous off the hook for a living. But though his house was lo-cated in Harvard Square, a few steps from both his law offices and his lectern at Harvard University's law school, it was rather a modest affair: a two-family, a fact that he found dis-turbing, especially since the occupants living below Schwartz were home.

The house, located on Langdon Street, a quiet loop just off busy Massachusetts Avenue, was a three level, Mansard-roofed structure crowding the street. An eight foot fence enclosed the postage stamp sized yard in back. Though the first floor resi-dents were home, but the back yard was dark and quiet.

Sneaking through a neighbor's yard, Rance scaled a small tree and dropped into Schwartz's back yard. With the light that spilled from one of the first floor's rear windows he could see that there was a back door leading to a deck on the second floor. The bad news was that both Schwartz and his tenant shared a stairway. To access that upper back door, he would have to pass through the light of the first floor window.

As he crept up the outside stairs connecting the decks, Rance was washed with an overwhelming feeling of guilt. It was an annoying feature of his personality that cropped up irregularly since his childhood, since his days at Sacred Heart School, seven hours of secular education, one hour of religious instruction from the point of view of the Catholic Church.

Guilt. For the sins of an infant not old enough to realize that it was still an extended fetus. Guilt. For the sins committed by everyone that came before him. Guilt.

Even the last three weeks, weeks during which he had seen utter strangers as well as people he cared about murdered before him, even all that acerbic reality, that steeling experience, none of it could erase Rance's sense of right and wrong.

But countering that seminal resurgence of guilt was a much more powerful force, a tide of emotions that carried upon its crest the contents of his heart. Whether the future held anything for Rance and Jenny beyond what-if friendship, he still cared about her, still loved her.

So with his mind awash with distraction, Rance snuck under the light-flooded window, stole up the stairs, carefully stepping on the edge of each tread to minimize creaking, reaching the back door to Melvin Schwartz' residence.

The door was unlocked.

Anger was the first emotion he felt. Why in the hell would someone who lived in the city leave their back door open? He felt a cautionary wave sweep over him and he stepped back from the door. A trap? Maybe. He trusted Marty, but someone else was probably in on this as well.

Easing the door open, he stayed well hidden around the corner. He entered on his hands and knees and found himself gripping the cool tiles of the kitchen floor. He blinked several times, letting his pupils dilate.

The whole of the kitchen was actually off to his left. To the right was a small dining area with a round table and chairs. Enough light filtered into the house from the street lamps outside so that he could see reasonably well.

Another minute and he decided he would be able to stand. Moving through the breakfast room Rance entered what he guessed was some kind of parlor. Quickly leaving that room he went to the front of the house; television room, big couches, not in here. Upstairs.

Off the hallway he could see three bedrooms. A door that led to the bathroom was open. At the top of the top of the stairs he eased open the first door on the left. Bingo.

Schwartz, like most people, had a home office. Producing a penlight, he closed the door behind him and began searching. Schwartz only had a few things on thumb drives, easily copied. He then booted Schwartz's computer and found the communications application. Using the number that had been given to him by Marty, he connected to another computer deep inside the offices of the FBI's Boston office. Five minutes later he was finished.

Rance didn't breathe until his feet hit the pavement outside, and he went directly to the Hong Kong Chinese restaurant to celebrate his life as a burglar by drinking a scorpion bowl.

§

The President grunted and rolled over.

Rising in the dark and moving about the room with the familiarity of pulling on a pair of old jeans, Katarina dressed. Through the window she could see the first slivers of gray creasing the dawn.

Just one more day, she told herself. But how many times now had she heard that refrain? Too many. And too many times she had been so close, only to have...

Rance. What brought him in to all this? The fool, the only reason he wasn't dead now was because she was kind and Farrell had proved a buffoon. Though she was satisfied that Farrell would never give up their backup plan, she had decided that the father of her daughter had used up all of his...family privileges.

If they met again, she would kill him, instantly and without asking questions.

"Katarina," the President mumbled, reaching over and finding only a warm indentation where she had been.

She came to his side. "Shhh."

"What are you doing?"

"I have to tie up some business affairs. I'll be back soon."

He propped himself up on an elbow and looked at her in

the dark.

"Do you know what?" he said with the earnestness of a child. "I'm going to be the first president to get a divorce while in office. Then I'll marry you and you can be the First Lady."

"Don't be silly. You would lose the election."

"I'm a Republican, I can get away with it. We managed to rid ourselves of Armstrong, we can do anything. I can."

She covered his lips with a finger. For a moment she craved a laugh. He believed it. He really believed all that he said. So ironic, she thought.

"We'll talk about it later."

"Where are you going? Let me send some Secret Service with you."

She considered it. "Perhaps if you could spare Derek. He's been so...useful."

"Consider it done," said the President.

"I'll be back soon, darling."

And as she left the darkened room an empty, bloodless smile pulled itself across her lips.

§

He watched from the Tobin Bridge.

It was getting along toward dawn, only a few minutes before the black of the night started receding. Far below him, on the Chelsea side of the river, amidst the scores of warehouses, he saw the car come out slowly.

A long pier jutted out, rotting, into the Mystic River. Around it empty pilings jutted blankly and the water didn't move. The Mystic was close to dead.

Then there was a flash, and the car erupted in flames. Two figures were briefly illuminated by the pyre, running away, the blazing vehicle rolling slowly toward the end of the pier.

In another second the car was over, a floating inferno, drifting on the currentless river before finally.

It was the best five hundred bucks he ever spent.

§

The Four Seasons Hotel was across from the Public Gardens.

In Boston's center there were two parks: the Boston Common, huge, sprawling, randy, stomping grounds for Boston's rich immigrant heritage, a place for dogs to chase squirrels, for children to run wild, for bums to sleep on benches, former grazing grounds for the livestock that the residents of the city raised until the early nineteenth century; and there was the Public Gardens, home of the Swan Boats and the foot bridge, refined, richly floral, shaded, a Beacon Hill destination, quiet, small placards naming the various trees by both commonly and scientifically, keep off the grass.

It was about control. Charles Street divided the Boston Common from the Public Gardens, the gracious willows from the coarse oaks, the limpid pond from the fetid and empty concrete basin, the fine mown grass from the splotchy, dusty weeds. Charles was one of the busier streets in Boston, and to cross it without waiting for the light was to affix a cheap price to life. Traffic between the Common and the Public Gardens was thus limited.

Though Katarina had only been to Boston a few times, she

always stayed at the Four Seasons, and with a room which overlooked the Public Gardens and the Common she could plainly see the lines of demarcation which divided the city of Boston. This morning she could see the Shakespeare festival setting up. Very good. It was working just as she had envisioned it. Shakespeare always relaxed her, made her feel so vital. It would all work beautifully. For once.

True, on the surface it seemed unjust. But she knew what made the world work, now more than ever. There was no democracy; that was a fanciful notion fed to the masses in lieu of cake, an opiate for a godless society, and elixir that allowed the real power to function on a stage and at a level unimaginable to all but those involved. Historians would stagger through and try to interpret the effects they discovered, but being dreamers at heart, they would eventually cover the truth unintentionally and in such a way as to make the unreal seem normal and rational.

She sipped her coffee and smiled. Though the early shuttle from Washington was quick, she still hadn't allowed the jet lag to catch up to her. That would have to wait. By the end of today she planned on being in a plane bound for Tahiti. Once there, with the money safely wired to a variety of anonymous bank accounts in Switzerland, Luxembourg, the Cayman Islands and Argentina, she would send for her daughter.

There was a knock on her door.

"Come in."

A small, wiry man entered, the same man who had kidnapped Jenny Ryan, the same man who had identified himself to Rance as FBI Special Agent Muller.

"We've got the woman here," he said.

"Very good, Derek. I want to see her."

There was a pause, imbued by the lack of action on Derek's part.

"Is there a problem?" she asked.

Derek rubbed his chin anxiously. "It just makes me nervous, that's all. I'm thinking from your position on this. It's another complication. There's been too many of them so far. I just want things to go smoothly is all."

For Derek she had a sweet, small smile. So loyal, after all this time.

"We need her. Just until everything with Kaplan is completed. She is our insurance, Derek."

"What about Kaplan? What insurance to we have on him?"

Katarina smiled and held up a portable computer storage device the size of a pack of cigarettes. "He wants these-or, I should say, his employers want these. If Kaplan doesn't go back with these...well, let's say he'll wish he were never born. And believe me, a man as arrogant, as wildly successful as Kaplan does not wish that."

"You really think Vaughn will show up?"

"He is in Boston, Derek. He broke into Schwartz' house."

Derek allowed himself a smile. "He was too late."

"You're sure? I don't want Schwartz turning up."

"Absolutely. He had a little accident in his car, a fire, a crash into the drink. The only way he'll turn up is if crabs don't like barbecued shyster." He smiled sickly.

"The point is, Derek, that we can't take any chances. Should Rance-Mr. Vaughn-complicate things, this will allow us to control his actions."

"And when we're done here?"

Katarina smiled, a powerful, arrogant smirk.

"You'll think of something. Now bring her in."

§

"What do you mean, 'nothing'?"

Marty was looking good for a man minus a couple of pounds of flesh, and Rance wondered what drove a guy like that. A shark, he thought, a relentless eating machine.

"We've had guys up all night going through that stuff. But nothing on Katarina's case. Nice job, by the way." Marty smiled over his reading glasses.

"The door was open."

Marty's eyebrows went up. "Open? Why didn't you say so?"

Rance shrugged. "Does it matter?"

"What do you think, chowder balls? You think a guy like Schwartz is gonna leave his door open? In the middle of the city?"

"The People's Republic of Cambridge," Rance corrected.

"Don't be a smart ass." Marty removed his glasses.

Rance was feeling cramped. "Why don't you just get a court order and seize his office files."

"Believe me we're working on it. We have to find a conservative judge in Cambridge first, though."

"Good luck."

Marty looked at his watch and swore under his breath. "Every minute we waste is another minute we lose to them, another minute they gain on us. But there's something that really bother's me."

"What's that?"

"It doesn't add up. I mean, why come to Boston? Why would Katarina return to Boston as opposed to anywhere else? I mean, it's just a deal, it can go down in any hotel room in the world, right? Kaplan and her, they could have gotten together anywhere, so why here? Why Boston?"

Rance shook his head slowly. Marty's point was excellent, and only his concern about Jenny's safety inhibited his train of thought from considering it.

"What can you tell me about Katarina and Boston?" Marty asked quickly, his eyes sharp suddenly.

"Nothing, I'm afraid. We never came to Boston together, and she never asked me a lot about where I was from." He shrugged.

Marty snapped his fingers and pointed to Rance.

"What?"

"You."

"Me what?"

"You. You're the Boston boy. That and Schwartz. I have a feeling we're not going to find Mr. Schwartz again. That's why there was nothing at his place. Somebody beat us to it. So she came here to kill two birds with one stone-pardon the expression. But she already took care of Schwartz. He must have known something, something in that case, something that she never wants the world to know."

"And me?" asked Rance.

"Use your head. Jenny's missing. What do you think?"

A cloud darkened Rance's face. "She's going to use Jenny to get me."

"Bingo." Now Marty's grimmace deepened.

"Now what."

"That still leaves us with nothing. We don't know where, or how, she's going to make the exchange with Kaplan." He bit his lip and looked down, a tight-lipped frown pulling at his face. "There's gotta be something. There must be something concerning this SHAKESPEARE shit that would bring her and Kaplan specifically to Boston. Either that or that bastard Farrell lied to Colm."

Something clicked inside Rance. Between his ears he could feel his brain twisting into a knot, a mental dry heave, as if his mind were trying to cough up a bit of information that his subconscious was choking on. Jenny, he thought. There must be something to do with Jenny. But what?

It was in the paper.

Next to Marty's bed was a table cluttered with his reading glasses, empty glasses, a box of tissues, and the rumpled remains of that morning's edition of the Boston Globe. Ever the voracious reader, Marty had torn through every section, saving the Arts & Entertainment section for last. It had been folded open to an announcement for a huge spectacular to be held on the Boston Common beginning August first-today-a Shakespeare festival.

"You're doing fine if you want to catch flies," Marty said, remarking on Rance's open mouthed gape.

Picking up the paper, Rance read the story, then handed it to Marty.

"Shakespeare wasn't my thing," Marty said.

Then he double-took.

"Wait a minute. Shakespeare. Didn't you say that-"

"Yeah, Shakespeare. We were crazy about it."

"You think that's it?"

"You got anything else?"

"I'll call Robocop and have him meet you down there."

§

Jay Kaplan was exhausted.

Ireland, that fucking abortion, he thought. I'm never fucking going back to that place again. It was a stupid idea to begin with. What kind of fucking amateur do they think they're dealing with? Fuck them.

"Eddie!" Kaplan screamed. "Eddie! Get the fuck in here!"

A huge man squeezed through the small door of the aft cabin. He looked green. Kaplan knew that Eddie hated flying, even in Kaplan's own private Lear.

"When do we get to fucking Boston?"

"Jack just started his approach. We'll be on the ground in thirty minutes." Eddie took a deep breath. "Thank fucking God."

Thirty minutes wasn't soon enough for Kaplan, either. But not because he feared flying. The sooner down, the sooner done, the sooner the fuck out of here. What the fuck, he was a business man, too, right? He had customers waiting, waiting for the biggie, the biggest thing since the electric fucking light bulb, Kaplan had been telling him, and they had put up a lot of money, a lot of fucking money. And dealing with a cunt like this broad Katarina, shit. As far as Jay Kaplan was concerned, women were good for two things: fucking and fucking up.

"Send Alicia in," he ordered. Eddie scrunched back through the door and into the main cabin. A moment later a beautiful woman dressed professionally entered. Kaplan stood and unzipped his trousers.

"Come on, let's go, we only have a few minutes and I gotta blow off some fucking steam, right?"

§

Her wrists and ankles still hurt.

That was about all she could complain about, however, for her accommodations at whatever hotel she was in were opulent. The room was tastefully decorated, Monet prints on the wall, plush carpet underfoot, all traces of the hotel's identity carefully removed.

Jenny knew she was in Boston somewhere. Though the room's high windows denied her a view of everything but some nearby buildings and blue sky, the people talking in the hallway had Boston accents, thick Boston accents, the kind that need to be maintained daily. And the sliver of a skyscraper that looked a lot like the Hancock Tower.

That was about as far as she could orient herself. She could be anywhere from the Omni Parker House to the Ritz Carlton to the Four Seasons.

Trying to escape was useless, so she used the time to relax, eat the food that was sent to her and think. Think about what happened. Trouble was, she still didn't know what exactly happened that she should end up some kind of prisoner. Oh, the events and circumstances that caused it were evident to her: Katarina Favergé. But how it happened...

She remembered going to bed, that was it. When she woke up, she was stiff, red rings around her wrists and ankles, and it was, according to her watch, 36 hours after she had arrived home. Now for the why.

Rance and Marty had touched a nerve, and that could only be bad news. The only connection she had was through them–and the mysterious source who had fed her information. Schwartz, she had suspected all along. By turning the focus away from himself he was serving two masters. But could he have been responsible for her kidnapping? Was she too close? She hadn't even met her captors, dealing thus far with only what she assumed were the unidentified service staff of the hotel.

The door opened and a man walked in, a thin man with a wary look on his face and Jenny knew right away that he was the one. He wore a sports jacket big enough to conceal what she assumed was a handgun, and he walked with a clipped step, tense and coiled, darting eyes like probing radar.

"How are you feeling, Ms. Ryan?" he asked politely enough.

"Miss Ryan," she corrected. "Fine. Now do you want to tell me what this is all about? The partners at my law firm don't take kindly to unexplained absence, so their likely to have the National Guard out looking for me by now."

"We should all be so lucky." His smile was empty, almost menacing, and though she was taller than him he emanated with an energy that forced her think rationally. "Would you come with me?"

He waited for her to exit the room before him, motioning to the right, confident that she was smart enough not to try a foolish escape. Jenny had taken only a few steps before he ordered her to stop in front of the next door.

"Go in," he said.

§

Robocop, a.k.a. Ted Benson, met Rance at the Park St. MBTA station.

They were at the extreme southeast corner of the Boston common, the intersection of Park and Tremont. It was a busy place, blanketed with white-legged tourists staggering and pointing, vendors hawking everything from T-shirts to glow in the dark condoms, and the city's homeless population, out enjoying a fine, hot August first.

"Can I buy you a hot dog?" Rance asked, walking up to Ted.

Benson declined and Rance wasn't surprised. He imagined someone as Nordic and healthy as Benson slept in the gym, lifting weights and feasting on bean sprouts and dry tuna fish. To see if he could rankle him, Rance ordered an Italian sausage instead of a hot dog, the burning, greasy, fatty variety, buried with onions and green peppers and smothered in ketchup and mustard.

"If they sold beer," Rance said to Benson's horrific expression, "I'd drink two."

The Bailey Company's presentation of "A Midsummer Night's Shakespeare Festival: Boston Does Bill" was being staged at the other end of the common, where the trees opened to a huge grass field.

"I don't want to upset you, Ted," Rance said through a mouthful of scrumptious sausage, "but I hope you're heavily armed."

Benson rewarded him with a frown.

"I don't mean to be fatalistic," Rance continued, "but I've been shot at an awful lot during the last three weeks."

"That's what they train us for," Benson said evenly.

"I know it. And I'm glad you're here. My attempts at gun-slinging have been foolhardy and ineffectual. In fact, I'm much better at catching bullets than firing them. You want to see where I got shot a few weeks ago? Amazing, it's almost healed up."

"That's OK."

The Boston Common was literally jammed with humanity that evening: in-line skaters striking fear into the hearts of pedestrians; dogs chasing Frisbees; and the obsequious drifters, seated alone, picking through garbage cans, staring off into infinity remembering demons.

It was the homeless that disturbed Rance the most.

Like souls bedamned, the homeless walked the streets of the city endlessly, going nowhere, appearing as if from a fog. And every one with a story, Rance thought. Every one a blank slate. He shook them out of his head.

"Ted, if you don't mind me saying so, you look a little bound up. You know, like you haven't been getting enough fiber in your diet."

Finally Benson smiled.

"If you were this funny as a writer you'd still be on top of the best seller list."

"Ah, another Vaughn critic."

"I wouldn't say critic. But I did read both *Jungle Water* and *Snake Ranch*."

"Ted, do you remember in *Jungle Water* when Cassandra kills both her lover and her husband? Do you remember how coldly she committed the act? How detached she was? How she became 'a hard piece of Plexiglas, translucent and immovable'?"

"Cassandra was great. Strongest woman I've ever read about."

Rance was truly flattered, but he concentrated on his example. "I've only recently realized that Cassandra is Katarina Favergé. She's the modern incarnation of Iago. Funny how the mind works. I guess on some level I've always known they were all one in the same. But it took...it took a real shock for me to become conscious of what I've known all along."

Swallowing hard against the memory of Francoise, Rance gazed straight ahead.

"I have a feeling you're trying to reveal something to me."

"Like Iago and Cassandra, Katarina is strong. Not strong for a woman, just strong, and I don't mean physically. I mean that she's a mythical devil, capable of metamorphosing into what you want to believe she is, then cutting your throat. Like Cassandra she is beautiful, and she knows it. Like Iago she is bent on total chaos just so she can stand back and admire her handiwork. But there's one important difference between Iago and Cassandra on the one hand, and Katarina on the other."

They had reached the back of the large stage that would be used for the festival.

"What's that?"

"Katarina's real."

§

Katarina turned and faced Jenny.

Smiling, she walked over to where Jenny stood with Derek.

"Take the gag off," she ordered politely. "Care for something to drink, Miss Ryan?"

"I'm sure you don't have anything I want."

"Try me."

"Jameson."

"Derek." Katarina walked by Jenny and took a seat on one of the suite's couches. "Try to relax, Miss Ryan. With a little luck, this will all be over soon and we can all go home."

"You'll have to forgive my ignorance, but I don't see what I have to do with the 'this' you refer to."

"I'm afraid you have everything to do with today's circumstances. In a short time your Rance will try once again to do something foolish. That is why you are here. You see, Rance is full of foolishness these days, and I needed some insurance against his ruining...my plans."

Derek handed Jenny her drink, but Jenny shrugged and held up her cuffed hands.

"Let her go, Derek. There's no place for her to go in here."

"And what plans are those?" asked Jenny when she had been released.

"Now don't go and spoil everything, Miss Ryan. If you knew that, I would have to kill you. As it is, I'm going to have to kill Rance."

Jenny felt her face flush and judging by Katarina's reaction, her emotions had been evident. It angered her further to give this woman any kind of satisfaction whatsoever. But beyond that she felt a panic, a helplessness that enveloped her with a miasma that looked frighteningly like reality.

"I wouldn't bet on it," Jenny said softly.

"And I wouldn't make any stupid threats," Katarina snapped back, her anger quick. "I told you I would kill you, too."

Jenny took a step forward. "Then go ahead," she said, and threw her drink in Katarina's face.

Katarina didn't flinch. Instead a smile broke across her face and she held her gaze on Jenny.

"Putt the handcuffs back on her, Derek."

§

"I don't fucking believe this."

Jay Kaplan stood in the middle of his suite at the Ritz-Carlton reading the note that Eddie just handed him. On the couch in the background Alicia sat with another beautiful woman. They were watching MTV.

"What is this, some kind of fucking joke?" continued Kaplan, looking up at Eddie. Eddie had only one look in his repertoire: stupid. He made no attempt at changing it.

"What the fuck is *Othello*?" barked Kaplan. He turned and looked to the women. Alicia looked up.

"I think it's a play that Denzel Washington was in."

Kaplan crumpled the note with disgust and tossed it on the floor. He walked over to the bar and made himself a drink.

"I don't like it," he said finally. "This bitch is up to something and I don't fucking like it one fucking bit." He finished his drink with a flourish and returned to the crumpled piece of paper.

"All right, smart lady," he muttered, "if that's the way you want it, fine. *Othello* is gonna be your last fucking play."

§

As they neared the stage, Rance and Benson had to push through the crowds.

"I never thought a Shakespeare festival could attract such crowds," Rance said to Benson.

"College town," was Benson's reply, delivered with a wry grin.

"Say, you've got a pulse after all."

"And I hope you've got a plan."

"My plan is to meet Katarina. Right here."

"What makes you so sure she's here? And if she's here, how do you know she has Jenny?"

They had reached the stage entrance, and by flashing his FBI credentials, Benson got them full access. In the mayhem of the behind the scenes, he led Benson to the stage entrance. The company was just finishing a jolly rendition of *As You Like It* to the standing ovation from the crowd spread out on blankets and lawn chairs beyond the stage.

"Because," said Rance, "it's poetic. Katarina fancies herself a poet. It's what she thinks distinguishes her from the rest of the thugs. That and her treachery."

The cell phone in Benson's jacket pocket chirped. While he grunted into it, Rance scanned the crowd on the Boston Common, but saw only a sea of faceless strangers.

"Maybe you are right," said Benson, pocketing the phone. "Jay Kaplan's private plane landed just outside of Boston an hour ago. He's at the Ritz."

"I hope you didn't do anything stupid, like arrest him."

"Despite your misgivings for federal agencies, Mr. Vaughn, we do, from time to time, display a modicum of rationality. You get to play out your hunch–but only until–"

"Only until *Othello* hits the stage."

§

Jay Kaplan's white limo pulled up to the park entrance.

Across the street two FBI agents sat in an unmarked car observing him. Another agent, dressed as a Shakespearean character, tried to sell Kaplan a balloon and was rudely rebuked by Eddie. A fourth agent was selling tickets when Kaplan walked up to the window.

"My name's Jones," said Kaplan. "You got some tickets for me?"

"Jones, Jones, ah yes, backstage passes included, enjoy the show."

Kaplan grabbed the envelope from the agent and walked away. Once inside, he went directly backstage to the dressing rooms. Eddie knocked on #3, drew his gun and went inside. A second later he poked his head out.

"It's OK, boss. She's in here."

"She alone?"

"Yup."

Kaplan pushed Eddie out of the way and went in.

Katarina was waiting.

§

Benson had taken up a position on the opposite side of the stage.

Every few minutes he and Rance wandered out into the wings and scanned the crowd. On the stage, Iago was getting Michael Cassio drunk. Memories began to well up and pound Rance between the temples. He wandered backstage.

Too much pain, he thought, and none of it physical. His body was numb, his brain a jumble of images: Katarina in London, laughing; Francoise dying in his arms; and Jenny. Christ, I can't even remember my last words to her, Rance thought.

Stop thinking like that, he chided. It saps your energy and robs you of concentration. Jenny is alive and that's why you're here. That's all that matters.

He didn't want to admit it, but he was out of hunches. The Shakespeare festival had been just that-a hunch. If something didn't happen, he would be left with his pockets turned inside out looking for a ride.

And feeling the guilt.

But that's not going to happen, he reminded himself.

He was about to turn around when something funny caught his eye. There was a line of dressing room doors, and standing outside one of them was a huge man with a dopey little boy face. He wore an ill-fitting suit that did not conceal the bulge beneath his jacket that could only be caused by a large firearm. Rance stepped back just as the man turned his glance in his direction.

Fancy that, he thought.

Inside, he was throwing up.

§

Benson frowned.

Rance had slipped away. Shit. This is just what I need. If this guy Vaughn gets himself killed on my watch I'll be investigating moonshiners in Alabama until I'm sixty.

Having exhausted his search around the stage, Benson walked back to the dressing rooms. He was almost there when something stopped him.

Coming in a side entrance was a man and a woman. What made them stand out was the fact that the woman's hands were handcuffed behind her back–and that she matched the description of Jenny Ryan perfectly.

Benson faded back and drew his weapon, then fell in behind the couple. Years of training and experience told him that the man had some kind of weapon stuck into the woman's back. They were headed in the direction of the dressing rooms.

Benson didn't need a gut feeling to tell him what he had. He broke from behind a curtain and was almost on the couple when the man with the gun turned around.

Benson the athlete hit the small man with brutal force. As they went flying, Benson saw that Jenny too had absorbed some of his blow, and he made a mental note to apologize to her.

Grabbing him by the collar, Benson flung the man against a stanchion and tore the weapon, a gun, from his hand. Using his whole body he leaned onto the smaller man and jammed his gun in the man's face. Without turning away he called back to Jenny.

"Jenny Ryan?"

"Yes, who are you?"

"Special Agent Benson, FBI. Are you all right?"

"I'm fine."

"Do you know who this man is?"

"I was hoping you could tell me that."

Benson lowered his voice and and cocked the hammer back on his gun. "OK, pal, start talking."

§

Katarina was sitting in front of a mirror.

"What are you, the star of the show?" Jay Kaplan asked upon entering dressing room #3.

"That's what I love about you, Jay," Katarina said in that sultry accented voice. "Always so witty."

Kaplan mottled. "Yeah, well I got news for you. You're star is fading, sweetheart. That little fiasco you pulled in Ireland has got you on everybody's wish list, including mine. You won't live to see your next starring role."

Katarina stayed seated, her back turned to Kaplan.

"Such crassness is hardly the way to do business, Jay," she said.

"Business?" Kaplan said, his face breaking out into a macabre smile. "Business? Is this your way of doing fucking business? What are you, some kind of freak? Coming to some fucking play to do this?"

Katarina smiled and wrapped her fingers around the handle of her gun.

Iago's Fool

§

This is too much, thought Rance.

From his vantage point above the dressing rooms, he scanned the hallway to make sure nobody was around. Just that big goon directly below him. At Rance's feet was a huge sack of sand, the kind used to counterweight the stage curtain. It easily weighed a hundred pounds, and he thought about that goon being totally innocent.

If that's the case, then I'll have to apologize, he thought.

He tried to quietly lift the sack and swing it out over the edge, but a grunt escaped his lips. The goon looked up just as Rance let go of the sack.

§

Outside the dressing room door there was a muffled crash, followed by two soft grunts. Katarina Favergé and Jay Kaplan froze, their eyes fixed on the door. It opened, and Rance Vaughn walked in.

Kaplan's face decomposed into disgust, his shoulders slouching, his head slowly shaking. "Oh, no, not the fucking writer," he said as he reached into his jacket. "Can't anybody kill this fucking guy?" He drew out a pistol and pointed it at Rance's gut.

"A good question," said Katarina. She was standing now, facing Rance and Kaplan. Her right arm was extended and locked, her hand wrapped around the stock of a long barreled pistol of her own. At the end of the gun's barrel was a distended silencer, grotesque and incongruous, like a trash can on an opera stage. The gun pointed at both of them; it pointed at neither of them.

"Oh, I get it," said Kaplan. "You want to shoot the fucker yourself. Hey, fine by me. I'll pop him a couple of times when you're done."

"Put your gun down, Jay."

"What? Hey–"

She cocked the hammer back and stepped toward Kaplan.

"Put it down."

"Hey, hey, take it easy, sister. I know your all wrapped up. I'll just put it down, right here, okay? Nice and easy."

"For once, Rance, you've simplified things." As she spoke the corners of her lips curled slightly. Her smile confused Rance, but more confusing was the way the gun jumped suddenly, violently throwing her arm into the air, staggering her back a step.

Beside Rance there was a wet smack, followed by a surprised exhalation of air. Jay Kaplan staggered backwards, arms outstretched as if pleading, and crumpled to the floor. Katarina was still smiling.

"I'm afraid you've used up all your chances, Rance darling."

"If you think luck brought me this far, you're making a big mistake. It's over. And you're over."

"Isn't that just like you, to be so full of bravado. But this isn't fiction, and you can't write a happy ending. I swore that if you got in my way again, I'd kill you. Now it's time to make good on that promise."

Katarina leveled the gun at him and drew back the hammer.

"Is that what you promised our daughter? Did you promise Michelle you'd kill her father if you got the chance?"

Rance spoke fast as he played his final card. Time became liquid and he could feel the years melting between them. Static embraced his spine in a tornado of emotion, emotion that crackled so thickly he swore he could smell it.

And he knew she could feel it, too, for though she didn't flinch, didn't waver for a second, her eyelids betrayed her with a single flutter. Carpe diem, he thought. Here goes.

"You can tell Michelle right after you kill me. She's here in Boston. After your friend Farrell murdered your sister, I tracked Michelle down. In my spare time I've been donating blood and DNA samples to the French authorities. Francoise was able to pull some strings for me, and once I proved paternity the French government was more than happy to award me custody of Michelle–especially considering who her mother was. Sorry, Katarina, but the only way you'll ever see our daughter again is in your dreams."

Katarina hesitated. "You're bluffing."

"I'm afraid he isn't."

The voice came from the opposite end of the room, and before she could turn around, Benson stepped from the shadows, his gun trained on Katarina. To Rance's horror, Jenny was standing behind him.

Oh God, thought Rance. Jenny...

Somewhere inside him, in a non-specific place that had no apparent coordinates, a light flickered. In the space of a nanosecond it had mushroomed into burning feeling of joy, a sweeping feeling of love. He had played foolishly with Jenny before, and he never again wanted to lose her. In that instant

Rance realized how full and everlasting and complete his love for Jenny Ryan was. The only problem was all the guns in the room.

"Put down the gun, Ms. Favergé," said Benson.

Katarina's reply was to steady her aim at Rance, fixing her gaze along the barrel of the gun pointed at his chest.

"Go ahead," said Rance, launching his gambit. "It doesn't matter anyway, right? You've accomplished your true task already."

"I don't know what you're talking about."

"Come on, of course you do. Just like Iago, you need to have chaos. Total chaos, total misery. That was Iago's motivation, and that's your motivation. Have you forgotten your Shakespeare? After all, it was the bard himself who inspired this whole scheme in the first place."

"You're insane."

"I'm afraid the only crazy person here is you—and the President of the United States. You and he were the ones who hatched the whole idea in the first place. But back then he wasn't the President. Back then he was just a horny senator who happened to chair the Senate Arms Services Committee. That's when you walked into his life."

Rance edged closer to her, his eyes locked with hers, searching for a sign, an opening.

"You're mad," she whispered, but the conviction had left her words.

"Don't bother denying it, Katarina. The evidence is all in the sealed federal case against you. The only case Richard Armstrong ever tried. The case that the President himself had illegally sealed. The case that involved the misappropriation of millions of dollars for a company called Dynaware, which just happened to be the same company that was developing the nuclear defense systems that the United States would employ in the next century.

"What was your plan? After you sold off this technology to the cartel of terrorist who planned on destroying the world, what was your ultimate goal? Were you and Mr. President going to hold the world hostage? Did you plan on ruling over a nuclear wasteland from the bomb shelter deep beneath the White House?"

He took a deep breath and lowered his voice.

"Sorry, but it's not going to work out that way. You see, you thought you were Iago, but you're nothing more than a villainous whore."

"Stop it! Stop it!" She stepped back and spread her feet apart in an effort to steady herself.

"Well, you've got part of your wish, Katarina. Anarchy. Misery all around. And with that you're finished. You're nothing more than Iago's fool."

"No!" she screamed. "No!"

Perhaps the realization that all her plans were shattered, all that she had worked so delicately and diligently for was lost, was too much for her sanity to bear. Or perhaps it was the knowledge that she and Iago were one in the same, tragic villains. Whatever it was, the events of the room became hazy and surreal.

With his focus so intensely aimed at the gun in her hands, it took Rance several beats to realize that Katarina was running towards him. Though his instincts were screaming "Move! Move! Get out of the way!", his feet remained firmly planted on the floor, obeying the picture his eyes transmitted to his brain.

What he saw was the gun disappear, the gross silencer enfolding itself into her midsection by the will of her own hand. There was a muted *phhhtt!* as the gun went off, and then she crashed into his arms. The gun clattered metallically to the floor, a harmless piece of metal and gunpowder.

The force of her collision forced him back against the door, and her weight went limp in his arms. The memory of how she felt crashed back stormily to Rance, but he fought it back. Her eyes, huge dark ovals, turned up to his. Tears streaked her face and pain crimped her beautiful, full lips into a painful pout. She pulled his face to hers and kissed him and then, in a thin and breathless voice, she spoke:

"'I kissed thee ere I killed thee. No way but this: Killing myself, to die upon a kiss.'"

"Katarina," he whispered.

"Good-bye, Rance."

Part VI

Home

In front of the big, brown house, the beach shuddered with the pounding of the waves. Labor Day had come and gone, driving the tourists away for another year and leaving the beach once more to the locals to relish their crusty solitude.

From inside the house came the sounds of work: the banging of a hammer, the buzz of a power saw, the swearing that follows a crushed thumb.

"Are you all right?"

Jenny rushed over and looked at the wound.

"Try to be more careful," she said. "I'm hoping we can get enough done so that we can at least live here this winter."

Rance looked up at her and smiled.

"We'd be done in a week if you picked up a hammer, Mrs. Vaughn."

"Sorry. I was inside watching the President resign. I taped it for you."

"Not interested. He's getting off easy."

She brushed a clean spot on the sawdust covered floor and sat beside him. "Maybe he is getting off easy. But maybe going down in history as the most reviled world leader since Adolph Hitler is a terrible enough punishment. What could be worse for a politician, a man who has devoted his life to the winning of popularity contests?"

"Well rationalized, counselor."

Her gaze drifted out across the rock-dappled sands of Green Harbor beach.

"Do you think people will come?" she said after a long silence.

"Are you kidding? They'll come in February for that view."

Far out to sea, the remnants of a powerful hurricane that had wreaked havoc with the American coastline swirled angrily, pushing a strong surge of frothing waves against the beach. The storm, the eleventh to be named this season, had been called Katarina by the hurricane gurus.

"It's too bizarre," Jenny said, "that it should be named...that. After all that's happened..."

"I think it's rather just. I mean, look at it now: just another unorganized bag of clouds and winds and rain waiting for the jet stream to tear it up over Europe. Just like she was torn up once we got that case transcript opened."

"I never did ask you how you managed that."

"It was Marty. He dug up some Dutch uncle who had been a federal judge in Boston. Marty un-retired him long enough to get the case reopened and faxed to every major newspaper in the free world."

"What would we do without the fourth estate?"

"'Fair is foul, and foul is fair. Hover through the fog and filthy air.'"

"Very poetic, Mr. Vaughn. But that's *Macbeth*, not *Othello*. And speaking of poetry, how's the book coming?"

"I sent the manuscript to my agent this morning." Rance's gaze was far away.

"What did you call it?"

He came back. "I didn't. I told Mel to think of something. I did the hard part. I put everything into it, everything, even the part about Katarina running into my arms as she shot herself. For ten percent of everything, Mel can come up with a clever title."

"Do you think Michelle will ever come?" asked Jenny after a few minutes.

"I don't know. She's living with her Godmother and she's understandably upset. Isabelle was the only mother she had ever known. But when I talked to her on the phone, she sounded very grown up. Maybe she'll come visit next summer."

They sat like that for a while, just the ocean and the wind and the old shack waiting to become an inn by the sea.

"I thought there'd be some kind of closure, some kind of weight lifted from me," he said softly. "But it still hurts."

Jenny took his hand and squeezed it. "It's supposed to hurt. This isn't the movies and sometimes endings aren't happy."

She stood up.

"Have you thought about a name for our inn?" she asked,

changing the subject and brightening by degrees.

Rance was silent for a minute, dividing his gaze between his beautiful wife and the ocean.

"How about Michael's Inn by the Sea?"

"I like it."

He stood and hugged her, covering her slender neck with kisses.

"The question is," he said between light busses, "can you give up tax law?"

Jenny laughed and pulled his head around until his lips met hers. "The question is, Mr. Vaughn, can you give up lobstering?"

For a moment more he just looked into her eyes and let the drunk feeling overspread him.

"Lobstering I can live without. But not you."

"Well then, would you join me out on the deck for a drink?"

"We don't have a deck yet."

"How about a beer on the seawall?"

A mighty cacophony of waves shuddered the beach, and Rance sensed the storm passing.

"Make mine a Jameson's."

The End

Montreal, February 1996

www.ingramcontent.com/pod-product-compliance
Lightning Source LLC
Chambersburg PA
CBHW070208260626
47160CB00002B/485